Tempted by the Wolf

Tempted by the Wolf

Highland Shifters
Book 5

Caroline S. Hilliard

Copyright © 2022 by Cathrine T. Sletta (aka Caroline S. Hilliard)

All rights reserved.

This publication is the sole property of the author, and may not be reproduced, as a whole or in portions, without the express written permission of the author. This publication may not be stored in a retrieval system or uploaded for distribution to others. Thank you for respecting the amount of work that has gone into creating this book.

Produced in Norway.

This book is a work of fiction and the product of the author's imagination. Names, characters, organizations, locations, and events are either the product of the author's imagination or used fictitiously. Any resemblance to actual persons, living or dead, organizations, events or locations is purely coincidental.

ISBN: 979-8-3587-0896-9

Copy edited by Lia Fairchild

Cover design by Munch + Nano
Thank you for creating such a beautiful cover for my story.

CONTENTS

About this book	i
Chapter 1	1
Chapter 2	11
Chapter 3	26
Chapter 4	34
Chapter 5	43
Chapter 6	53
Chapter 7	63
Chapter 8	75
Chapter 9	86
Chapter 10	97
Chapter 11	108
Chapter 12	119
Chapter 13	128
Chapter 14	140
Chapter 15	149
Chapter 16	160

Chapter 17	173
Chapter 18	187
Chapter 19	194
Chapter 20	208
Chapter 21	221
Chapter 22	235
Chapter 23	246
Chapter 24	253
Chapter 25	263
Epilogue	271
Books by Caroline S. Hilliard	279
About the author	281

ABOUT THIS BOOK

True mates. How can something so right be so wrong?

Vamika doesn't want a mate. Not a shifter mate anyway. Shifter males are all the same. Smooth and attentive until you're trapped for life. Then you're reduced to property, expected to do your mate's bidding.

Vamika has seen it happen plenty of times, but it will never happen to her. Not even meeting her true mate changes her mind. She'll resist his warm brown eyes and caring personality if it kills her.

Callum never expected to find his true mate. And then to have her reject him outright. Why? Is it due to his limp?

Callum knows he's not good enough in the eyes of most shifters, and he has learned to live with that. But to not be good enough in the eyes of the one person who matters, almost rips his heart out.

But he won't give up. He has fought his whole life to be accepted for who he is. And if his mate doesn't want him, he'll learn to live without her or die trying.

This work is intended for mature audiences. It contains explicit sexual situations and violence that some readers may find disturbing.

CHAPTER 1

It had been two days since Vamika met her true mate. Two days and counting. She was exhausted from running herself into a stupor every night, but she was still happily unmated. Or happy might be pushing it, but she considered each day she remained unmated a victory.

Callum followed her every minute of every day. Not literally, of course, but in her mind. It didn't matter that he hadn't tried to contact her since they'd met two days ago; he was still with her all the time, like a shadow blocking out the sun from her life and reinstating the fear she thought was a thing of her past.

A knock on her door threw her out of her own head, and she blinked her eyes a couple of times to focus on where she was. Familiar walls surrounded her, and she took a deep breath to settle her racing heart.

"Vamika?" Henry's voice sounded through the door to her room. "I need to talk to you."

She sighed and rose from her bed. "Just a minute." Taking another deep breath, she let her eyes travel down her body. Her long braid was messy, but at least she was decently dressed.

Vamika's fists clenched at her sides, and her jaw tensed. She didn't want to talk to Henry at the moment, but he was her alpha and refusing him felt wrong.

She walked over to the door and opened it. Henry was much taller than her five foot three stature, and she had to tip her head back to meet his gaze.

"Can you join me in my office, please?" His face was neutral, and she narrowed her eyes at him in suspicion. He wanted something, but it was impossible to tell what it was.

"Okay," she said reluctantly. Frowning, she stepped out of her room and pulled the door shut behind her. "Has something happened?" Concern of another kind pushed her thoughts of Callum a little to the side. Perhaps this was about Ambrosia, the evil witch who was trying to hurt shifters to get revenge for her daughter's death. Two days ago, the woman had killed Freddie, her daughter's mate, and she'd almost killed Sabrina, a good witch trying to stand up to her. Ambrosia had made it clear that she wanted all shifters dead, and there was no doubt she was serious.

Henry glanced at her but didn't say anything, just turned and headed down the stairs toward his office. And she had no choice but to follow if she wanted to know what was going on.

He indicated for her to enter the room ahead of him, and as soon as they had both entered, he closed the door behind them. There was no one else in the large room, and she headed over to take a seat on the couch without looking at him.

"I want you to join in the search for Ambrosia."

Vamika's gaze snapped to Henry's. He was still standing. "What?" Her eyes widened, and her heart rate sped up. If he meant what she thought he did, she wasn't going to do it.

Henry's stern stare pinned her in place. "You heard me. I want you to join in the search. Leith and his friends need all the help they can get, and you know what the bitch looks like."

The blood drained from her face. Helping Leith would mean coming face to face with Callum again, and the thought filled her with both heat and dread. A strange combination but understandable, at least to her. "But I can't. I—"

"Yes, you can." Henry narrowed his eyes and crossed his arms over his chest. "And you will."

"No!" She was up and moving toward him before she could stop herself. "I don't want to see him again. Ever!" Coming to a stop two feet in front of Henry, she forced herself to maintain their eye contact, even though his alpha power was demanding that she avert her eyes and submit.

"It's nonnegotiable, Vamika. You will pack and leave within the hour, and I will call Leith and tell him you're on your way to help."

Power slammed into her, making her knees wobbly. Her body shook with the need to sink to the floor and give in to her alpha's command, but she locked her knees to stop them from betraying her. "Please." Her voice was thin and weak, making her wince at the sound of it. "Don't make me."

Henry's stare didn't waver. "You will do as I command, and there are two reasons I won't relent. One, Leith really does need the help. And two, your true mate needs you and you need him. You deserve someone who will respect you, and he's that someone."

Vamika's knees gave, and she landed on the floor in front of Henry with a thud. Her gaze lowered to his feet. She had lost the power struggle, but she still had a question that she pushed out with a shaky voice. "How do you know he will respect me?"

"Has he contacted you since he left here?"

Shaking her head, she frowned. "No."

"If Callum didn't respect you and your decision to reject him, he would've been back by now, making sure to be in your face constantly until you accepted him."

She wanted to object, but instead she clamped her mouth shut. Tears pricked her eyes, and she swallowed thickly. A part of her wanted to believe Henry was right, but it was more likely that Callum was just biding his time to strike when she least expected it. Perhaps waiting until her body was driving her insane with need, and she was less likely to refuse him again. And now she would make his job easier by showing up on his, or at least Leith's, doorstep.

Henry breathed out a sigh, and his power eased. "You will thank me one day, Vamika. When you get to know your true mate and realize he's perfect for you."

Shaking her head, she chuckled bitterly, before she tipped her head back and met Henry's gaze. "I don't understand how you can be so sure about him. You only met him two days ago like I did, and you speak like you've known him most of your life."

Henry nodded. "True. But I spoke to Duncan, and he swears Callum is a man of integrity. And I trust Duncan's opinion. Like you said, you only met your true mate two days ago, and the two of you didn't spend much time in each other's presence. Give the man a chance to show you who he is. Let him tell you about himself. You might be surprised how well suited you are."

Shaking her head slowly, Vamika wanted to tell Henry to fuck off and leave her to make her own decisions. But she didn't. He'd already ordered her to go to Leith's, and she couldn't refuse. Or she could, but in effect it would be the same as leaving the pack. And she didn't want to leave. This was the only pack in which she had ever felt like her opinion mattered, even though she was a woman, and it was all Henry's doing.

She also knew why Henry was doing this to her. He had an unshakable belief in the concept of true mates and dreamed of finding his own one day. And she hoped he did find his mate, and that she happened to be as perfect for him as he expected her to be. Henry was probably the only man Vamika truly respected in the world, and he deserved someone special in his life.

Vamika lowered her gaze and stared at Henry's feet again. "I will go and do everything I can to help search for Ambrosia, but don't expect me to come home with a mate. I can't promise you that."

"Whether you end up mating or not is your choice, Vamika. But I expect you to spend time with Callum and get to know him before you make that decision. He deserves that much at least. The things you have been through are not his fault, so don't blame him for your past."

Nodding slowly, she fisted her hands to prevent herself from shuddering. "Okay."

Just the thought of spending time with a shifter who wanted to become her mate had her fear spiking. But she would do it. She would spend time with Callum, but only with other people present.

∞∞∞∞

Callum rose from where he had been sitting on the bed and moved slowly toward the door of his room, which was located next to the master bedroom on the bottom level of Leith's house. It was time he joined the happy couples again and resumed his search for Ambrosia. Finding her was more important than his struggle to come to terms with the fact that his true mate didn't want him.

Her brutal rejection had replayed a million times in his head the last couple of days, and he had no idea how many more times he would have to relive that scene before it would leave him be. His eyes were scratchy from the sleepless nights, and his mind was struggling to focus on anything for more than a minute at a time when he managed to drag it out of the endless replay.

Exiting his room, Callum pulled his shoulders back and raised his chin. He was going to act like he was fine if it killed him. And acting like it would eventually make it happen. Hopefully. Breaking wasn't an option. It never had been before, and it was no less true now.

He ascended the stairs two steps at a time, putting

more energy into his movements than was strictly necessary. It made him feel better to prove that his disability didn't stop him. He could accomplish anything if he put his mind to it. Obstacles were only there to teach you a lesson and make you stronger when you conquered them, and he had conquered a lot of obstacles in his life. His true mate rejecting him wasn't anything different, and he would overcome that as well.

When he reached the hallway on the top level of Leith's terraced house, a noise from outside drew his attention. A car door had just slammed.

Something drew him toward the front door, like whoever was out there had attached a line to his chest and was reeling him in. He closed the distance to the door in a few long strides before yanking it open and stepping out onto the porch.

His eyes met the dark-brown orbs from two days before, and his jaw dropped in utter amazement. She had come for him. Vamika had realized her mistake in rejecting him and had come for him. Heat filled her eyes, and the sight suffused him with a joy so intense it threatened to burst his chest open to reveal his frantically beating heart. His true mate wanted him like he wanted her.

He let his gaze caress her body from the top of her head to her toes. She was even more beautiful than he remembered. Dark skin the color of rich sepia was begging for his touch, and her ruby-red lips were making him salivate in anticipation of their first kiss.

"Stop!" Her voice was high-pitched and trembling, and his eyes snapped to hers. They were wide and filled with fear and much closer than they had been a few seconds ago; without even realizing what he was doing, he had closed the distance between them, and she was suddenly within touching distance.

Quickly taking a step back, he frowned. "I'm sorry, I didn't mean to scare you. I'm just so happy to see you."

Her eyes narrowed, and the dark-brown orbs darkened to almost black. "Don't be. I'm not here for you."

She might as well have reached into his chest and squeezed his heart in her fist because that was how it felt. His lungs seized, and he wheezed as he stumbled a couple of steps back away from her. Nothing had changed. She still didn't want him.

Anger suddenly surged through him and forced his lungs to start working again. "Then why the fuck are you here?" He straightened to his full height and took a step toward her. "To rub it in my face?"

"Callum." Duncan spoke his name softly at the same time as his hand landed on Callum's shoulder. "Let's go inside. Vamika is here to help us in our search for Ambrosia."

"Why?" Callum couldn't tear his gaze away from the woman in front of him. She had backed up a couple of steps and crossed her arms over her chest, her eyes a bit wider than usual. "What can she do that we're not already doing?"

Duncan sighed beside him. "Callum. I believe you're scaring her. Let's go inside."

"Fuck this!" He spun and stormed into the house before hurrying down the stairs, almost stumbling in his haste to get away from her. After reaching the bottom level of the house, he yanked opened the external door and ran toward the beach.

His sense of obligation was warring with his need to leave and go home to his house in Fearolc. If Vamika was going to stay at Leith's house with them, he didn't want to be there. It had been agony enough being surrounded by happy couples all the time, but with his true mate in the house, it would be unbearable.

As soon as he reached the beach, he kicked his shoes off. He then grabbed the collar of his T-shirt and ripped it clean down the middle before discarding the torn garment on the sand.

Callum ran into the water until it reached his thighs before diving into the loch. His shorts weren't made for swimming, but he didn't care. He let his body glide beneath the water for hundreds of yards until his lungs burned, forcing him to the surface. Treading water, he sucked in huge gulps of air until his breathing evened out.

He couldn't leave. It didn't matter that his mate would be in his face, making his life a misery. The others needed him to locate Ambrosia. There had been no sign of her since she almost killed Sabrina two days earlier, and that just increased the urgency of him finding some clue as to where she was. Who knew what she had been up to in the last forty-eight hours, but it couldn't be anything good. When he first heard of Ambrosia, he had been of the opinion that she might not be as bad as everyone claimed, but he had been proven irrevocably wrong. The witch was evil. There was no doubt about that.

Kicking his legs, he started swimming toward the opposite shore of the loch. His mind and body were still reeling from the surprise encounter with Vamika, and he needed to regain some semblance of control before he returned to the house. And the only way he could think of to do that was to tire himself out. Hopefully, none of the humans in the area were paying too much attention to him swimming, because he was moving through the water much faster than was humanly possible.

CHAPTER 2

Vamika trudged down the path toward the small beach. It was half an hour since Callum had left in a fit of rage, and although she felt awkward seeking him out after his reaction to her arrival, she couldn't stay in the kitchen with the happy couples another minute. It was sickening how caught up they were in each other, and being stuck in the middle of them was getting on her nerves.

She hadn't expected the pure happiness on Callum's face when he first saw her. His brown eyes had been shining with warmth and joy, and she had been too shocked to shut him down immediately. He clearly hadn't been informed of why she was there.

Then his happiness had turned to anger when she hit him with her harsh words. And she understood why. For some reason Henry hadn't been clear why she was there, or perhaps Leith hadn't conveyed the message correctly. At least there was no doubt that Callum hadn't expected to see her, and when he did, he assumed she was there for him. To accept him.

Sand filtered between her naked toes, and she stopped close to the water's edge. Scanning the rippling surface of the loch, she caught sight of him a few hundred yards out, heading toward the beach. He was swimming like he had a great white shark snapping at his feet, powerful strokes carrying him toward her with amazing speed.

Callum stopped swimming just a few yards from the beach, and when he rose, the water barely covered his knees. The image of him naked from two days ago had burned itself onto her retinas, but that was nothing compared to the stunning man wading toward her now. Water droplets covered his lightly bronzed torso and sparkled in the sun as they made their way across his perfect skin, showing off his sculpted chest, powerful shoulders, and defined abs on their way south. Her eyes were drawn to the V of muscles disappearing into his low-riding shorts, and she suddenly wished the garment would slide down his thighs and reveal his impressive package.

She shook her head at her own stupid wish just as he noticed her and came to an abrupt stop. His hands fisted at his sides, and his eyes narrowed in a glare.

"I'm sorry, Callum." It wasn't what she had intended to say, but she might as well tell him what she was thinking. "I had no intention of giving you false hope. I thought you had already been informed why I was here. Henry told me he'd call Leith when he ordered me to help you."

Callum shook his head slowly, his lips curling into a sneer. "Is that so." It wasn't spoken like a question. "I guess no one thought to tell me that."

Vamika didn't know what to say, and she tore her gaze away from him to stare out over the loch. "I promised to spend time with you while I'm here." Her eyes widened, and she clamped her mouth shut. *Why the fuck did I say that?* Somehow her mouth seemed to have lost touch with her brain.

Callum closed the distance between them. He towered over her, and she felt small and vulnerable as his power wrapped around her and caressed along her spine. Her eyes snapped to his and widened even more when a strange mixture of fear and heat spiked through her and sent her heart galloping. She wanted to take a step back to put more space between them, but she locked her knees to stand her ground. Letting this man scare her was a mistake she couldn't allow herself to make again. It would only come back to bite her in the ass later. In her experience a man knew how to use a woman's fear to his advantage.

Keeping her gaze captured, he bent his head slowly toward her, and she suddenly realized what he intended. Her eyes automatically dipped to his lips, and her already galloping heart jumped a couple of hurdles in shock. She needed to back away from him before their lips met, but her whole body was frozen in place as she anticipated his kiss.

His lips were less than an inch away from hers when he spoke. "I'll pass, thank you." He abruptly stepped to the side and strode away from her.

Vamika was left standing there with her heart almost beating out of her chest and struggling to breath. She had been convinced he would kiss her, but as it turned out that hadn't been his plan at all. And apparently he didn't want to spend time with her while she was there either.

Her stomach twisted into a knot, and her eyes pricked like she was going to tear up. She shouldn't be surprised that Callum resented her after how she had treated him, but for some stupid reason, she was hurt instead of relieved at his reaction. It didn't make any sense, but then this whole true mate thing didn't make any sense to her. Why couldn't shifters be allowed to choose whom they wanted, or didn't want, to mate? Her own body was betraying her, and she didn't know how to fight it. Fighting your own body wasn't the same as fighting a person, unfortunately, because she knew how to fight someone if she had to.

Vamika took a deep breath before letting it out slowly. Narrowing her eyes, she bit her lip hard enough to taste blood in order to force herself to regain her composure. What had just happened was good. In fact, it was perfect. She didn't have to worry about Callum pursuing her while she was staying at Leith's house, and she didn't have to pretend she wanted to spend time with him to honor her promise to Henry.

Staring out over the loch, she allowed her heart time to settle. There was only one solution to the forced proximity to her true mate, and that was to find and destroy Ambrosia as fast as possible. Preferably within the next twenty-four hours. Then there would be no more reason for her to stay, and she could return to her pack without having disobeyed Henry's direct orders.

So, all she had to do was to come up with the perfect plan for finding and neutralizing Ambrosia quickly. *Easy-peasy.* She chuckled but it was a decidedly bitter sound.

∞∞∞∞

Duncan and Julianne were the only people in the kitchen when Callum walked in. They were sitting on the couch by the big windows facing the loch. Duncan's arm was wrapped around Julianne's shoulders while they were both watching something on Duncan's phone.

On hearing Callum entering the kitchen, they raised their heads to look at him, and a smile spread across Duncan's face. "You should see this. It's—"

Callum couldn't stop his irritated growl. "Why didn't you tell me Vamika was coming? Or didn't you know either?"

Duncan's grin disappeared, and he sighed. "Leith told me about an hour before she showed up. I was going to tell you as soon as you rejoined us, but you said you needed a minute, so I didn't want to bother you. I didn't realize she was going to show up so soon, or I would've made sure to find you and tell you earlier. I'm sorry, Callum."

Callum clamped his mouth shut and gave Duncan a short nod of acknowledgement. It wasn't Duncan's fault, and making him feel bad wasn't right. But Callum couldn't trust his own words at the moment. He wanted to yell at someone for getting his hopes up only to have his heart ripped from his chest again.

"Perhaps it's a good thing, though. Her staying here." Duncan gave him a small smile. "Being around you, she's going to have a hard time resisting the mating bond."

Callum gritted his teeth and shook his head. "I don't think so. She doesn't like me, and I don't think that's going to change. Being forced to see me might even make her hate me more. If that's even possible."

The front door banged open, and Trevor and Jennie stormed into the kitchen. Trevor's eyes were narrow with anger, and his alpha power radiated from him like he was struggling for control. "Have you seen the news?"

Callum shook his head. The news hadn't been high on his to-do list for a while. He'd been too busy searching for Ambrosia and having his heart torn to shreds to care about the humans' constant squabbles.

"A couple has been found murdered at a remote location up north." Trevor's face was contorted into a grimace like he had a sour taste in his mouth. "According to the man who found them, the couple looked to have been killed during or right after sex, and the woman had a nasty bitemark on her shoulder."

Duncan rose from the couch and approached them. "When did they die? Did it say?"

Trevor nodded. "Three or four days ago. And they both have burn marks on their heads. Cause of death hasn't been established yet."

Callum recalled the nasty burns on Freddie's head after Ambrosia had killed him. "But you're thinking this is Ambrosia's work."

"Fuck!" Duncan sighed and grabbed Julianne's hand tightly in his when she came to stand beside him, making her visibly wince. "The evil witch probably tricked them into mating and killed them just after it happened. That answers our question of whether Ambrosia would hurt the shifters she was enticing with a promise of increased power."

"Yes, I agree." Trevor put an arm around Jennie and pulled her close. "The question now is whether she managed to increase her own power by stealing theirs, and I fear the answer is yes."

Callum nodded slowly. "If it happened three or four days ago that would mean Ambrosia had already killed them by the time we met her at McFarquhar's Bed two days ago. Is that why she was almost successful in killing Sabrina? I was too far away to feel Ambrosia's power, and since I never met her before that day, I wouldn't have been able to tell if anything had changed, anyway."

"That goes for me too. I've only seen her from a distance before." Duncan turned to look at his mate. "Julianne's the only one who had met her before that day. Michael and Steph might've been able to tell if her power level had changed, but they didn't arrive until after Ambrosia was gone."

Julianne chuckled but there was no amusement in her eyes. "And I'm not going to be much help. I can feel Duncan's power at times." A blush rose in her face and made her cheeks glow. "But that's probably because he's my mate. I'm human. I don't know the first thing about establishing someone's power level."

"That's okay." A wicked grin spread across Duncan's face. "I like the way you respond to my power."

"Duncan!" Julianne's blush intensified, and she tried to pull her hand out of his grasp, but he didn't let her go.

Duncan's grin widened and amusement suffused his face. He opened his mouth to say something, but

Callum got there before him. Listening to the flirting between the mates was getting on his nerves.

"I'm sure I can find out more about the murder and the victims." Callum turned to Trevor. "Maybe the rest of you can call the alphas in the area to find out if they are missing anyone."

Trevor nodded. "We'll get on it. Assuming we're right and the couple was indeed mating at the time they were killed, we know the male was a shifter. It's impossible to know whether the woman was as well, at least at this stage, but considering Ambrosia's advice to Jack to find a human to mate, the woman might well have been human."

"I'll see what I can find out." Callum sighed. "But it might be days until their identity is established, unless the police have found some IDs, or one or both of the victims have been reported missing." What he didn't say was that he might be able to access information online that would help him ID the victims himself. It was better for everyone if they didn't know the extent of his hacking skills. If someone was to go down for breaking into the police network, he wanted to reserve that particular experience for himself.

Vamika chose that moment to enter the kitchen, and Callum couldn't help the way his eyes roved over her enticing form. He had been an inch away from kissing her down at the beach, and with the way she had been staring at his lips, she might even have let him if he'd tried. But she had already told him she didn't want him, and he wasn't into taking liberties. A no was a no, and until she gave him a clear indication that she wanted him, he wouldn't touch her. But he had no hope that she would change her mind about him. Her words had been harsh and clear. There had been no uncertainty as to what she'd meant.

There was a frown on her face when she stopped two steps inside the room, probably wondering why they were all standing in the middle of the room instead of sitting down at the kitchen table or on the couches by the windows. Callum had no intention of explaining it to her, though. He would leave that to someone else while he went downstairs to work on his laptop in the living room.

Passing by her to get out of the kitchen, he avoided looking at her. But he wasn't able to avoid her delicious scent, which hit him straight in the nose. Salty caramel with a hint of chili. He shuddered as her scent triggered his constantly simmering need for her, making it pulse through him with renewed intensity. It was enough to make him stumble, and he had to grab the door frame to stay on his feet. Embarrassment made him tense, but he managed to keep moving without further incidents.

Cursing his weak leg, he made his way down the stairs to the living room. No wonder Vamika didn't want him. It was a wonder anyone did with how clumsy he was. But for some reason, it didn't seem to matter that much to human women. They fawned over his looks and his muscular body, and that seemed to be enough to overshadow his limp. Or perhaps that and the fact that he listened and made sure to show that he appreciated them.

The same thing didn't work with shifter women, though. They expected perfection, and a physical disability was completely unacceptable, to the point of making them turn away in disgust when they noticed his limp. Physical strength and power level were more important than intelligence to them, and personality didn't seem to factor in at all. At least that was his experience.

Sitting down on the couch, Callum opened his laptop. It was time to focus on Ambrosia. The threat she presented to shifters was more important than his struggles. It was likely she was behind the deaths of the mating couple, and he'd seen firsthand how she had used her power to throw Sabrina several yards through the air like she was nothing but a rag doll.

Ambrosia wasn't going to stop until she had eradicated all shifters. He had no doubt about that. And it didn't matter that her reason for doing so was her daughter's death. It was tragic, sure, but it didn't warrant killing all shifters.

Which left them with only one option. Find her and kill her. There was no redemption for someone like her. If she was alive, she would keep killing, and if she was able to siphon power from shifters during mating, time was of the essence. They had to destroy her before she became too powerful for them to do so.

Killing people increased her power, which in turn gave her more power over people's minds and allowed her to kill more people with less effort. It was an escalating scenario that would quickly spiral out of hand, and he, for one, was going to do everything in his power to stop that from happening.

Blocking everything else from his mind as best he could, Callum dived into his search for information about the murders. Getting into the police network was easy. The tricky part was making sure he didn't alert anyone to him being there.

There were a lot of pictures of the victims and information about the location, as well as the presumed identity of the man based on a driver's license found at the scene. Presumed due to the state of the man's face preventing them from making a positive identification based on facial features alone. Burns to the victims' heads, reported by the man who discovered them, turned out to be an understatement. Both the victims' faces were horribly disfigured, almost like their features had partially melted before the dehydration and decomposition had begun.

The police were still working on confirming the male victim's identity. No dental records had been found so far, which was no surprise since the man was a shifter. Tooth decay and other dental issues weren't a problem for shifters, so there would be no records to retrieve.

Fingerprints had been taken, but no match had been found. Again, not surprising. No shifter in their right mind would allow their prints to be recorded, or if they were, the shifter would have someone remove them without a trace. Unless the prints served a purpose for a while by being in the system.

No next of kin had been found for the man based on his presumed identity, and no information linking him to any other people at all, which was strange but not unheard of among shifters. A long lifespan meant that a lot of the shifters currently alive were born more than a century ago, and keeping records showing their real age wasn't a smart thing to do and wouldn't be trusted anyway. The fact that there was nothing linking him to any friends was unusual, but a few shifters cut themselves off from the outside world and preferred to live a solitary life, and the male victim might have been one of those.

The female victim's identity was still a mystery, as well, and the police didn't have any promising leads. They were still working through dental records and missing persons' profiles so something might turn up. And Callum hoped that it would. It was a slim chance that the woman's identity would reveal something useful about Ambrosia, but at this point he was ready to work every lead he could find.

Samples for DNA testing had been taken from both victims, and the results were expected back from the lab in a few days. The DNA from the male wouldn't reveal anything that would help them in their search for Ambrosia, and the sample would probably be reported as contaminated since it would show some unusual results. The results from the female victim's DNA test, on the other hand, would be more interesting, and it would hopefully reveal her identity if that hadn't already been established by then.

Callum sighed. If this was Ambrosia's doing, and he was quite certain it was, he wondered if it was just the first couple to be discovered. For all they knew, she had killed other couples as well. Their bodies just hadn't been found yet.

A quick search didn't reveal any similar killings, and hopefully that meant that there weren't any, but only time would tell.

Movement on the stairs drew his attention, and he raised his gaze to see Leith and Sabrina ascending from the lower level of the house.

Leith nodded at Callum, with the corner of his mouth lifted in a semblance of a smile. "Hard at work again, I see. Any news about Ambrosia?"

Sabrina smiled at Callum before her eyes traveled to look fondly up at her new mate. Leith and Sabrina were the latest addition to the mated couples, who included most of Callum's friends.

Frowning, Callum met Leith's gaze. "Nothing on her present location, but there's been a development that we think is her doing." He relayed the news Trevor had shared and the information Callum had been able to retrieve from the police network.

Leith's eyes narrowed, and he clasped Sabrina's hand in his like he wanted to make sure she was safe. He probably remembered all too vividly how Ambrosia had almost taken his mate away from him.

Sabrina's eyes widened, and her mouth opened in a look of horror and disbelief, before she blinked and found her voice. "Three or four days ago. So, before we caught up with her at McFarquhar's Bed. I remember her being very powerful, even though I can't recall everything clearly from that day. It's probably due to the head injury."

A low growl drew Callum's gaze to Leith. The man looked like a thundercloud, and Callum had no trouble understanding why. If there was anyone who had been personally affected by Ambrosia's malice, it was certainly Leith and Sabrina.

Callum couldn't even imagine what Leith had gone through seeing his mate die. Just the thought of something like that happening to Vamika had his veins freezing to ice and his heart squeezing painfully in his chest. His true mate might not want anything to do with him, and that fact was threatening to break him, but watching her die would kill him outright.

Keeping his gaze on Sabrina, Callum spoke. "I'm assuming Ambrosia attempted to absorb some of the power from the couple as they mated, but is there any way to find out whether the bitch has become more powerful than before?"

Sabrina's brows pushed together as she considered his question. "None of us have felt Ambrosia's power both before and after she killed that couple. I felt how powerful she was two days ago, but that was the first time I met her, so I don't know what her power felt like before. Steph and Michael haven't met the evil bitch since she disappeared during Jack's failed mating ceremony. So no, as far as I know, there's no way to verify that she's more powerful now and by how much. At least not until we meet her again. Steph and Michael might be able to tell if her power level has changed since the last time they met her."

Callum nodded, and his eyes dipped to the screen still showing the results of his last search. "That's what I thought. At least I haven't been able to find any evidence that she has killed other couples than the one all over the news today. That's something I guess, but I think it's only a matter of time before she kills again. Particularly if she felt a noticeable increase in power as a result."

Sabrina nodded. "I agree. She'll kill again if she hasn't already." Turning to Leith, she stared up into his eyes. "I need to try to locate her again, but this time I want Steph to help me. Together we might be able to pinpoint Ambrosia's location, despite the fact that I wasn't able to get even a rough idea yesterday."

"Okay." Leith's gaze was full of concern when he studied his mate's face. "But I want to be close in case something happens. Steph doesn't have the control you have."

Sabrina shook her head. "That's not true. She has far more control than she thinks. She just didn't know she could use her power for more than healing. I'm the one who has been struggling with control, but that seems to be a thing of the past now that I've become who I was supposed to be all along."

"My mate." A loving smile stretched across Leith's face, and he turned his body toward Sabrina before bending his head.

Callum quickly lowered his gaze to his laptop. People kissing in front of him had never bothered him before, but since his true mate rejected him, any display of affection between the mated couples staying at Leith's house was like taking a hard punch to the gut. It hurt and made him feel nauseous.

"Leith." Sabrina chuckled. "We've just... I need to speak to Steph if she's available."

Footsteps across the floor made Callum look up from his laptop to see Sabrina walk toward the stairs. He breathed a silent sigh of relief at not having to witness a full-on make-out session between the couple.

CHAPTER 3

Vamika felt awkward sitting on the couch in the kitchen with Trevor, Jennie, Duncan, and Julianne surrounding her. They were pleasant people and tried to include her in their conversation, but they were still Callum's friends, and even if they didn't say anything, she felt like they resented her for rejecting him. And no wonder. They wanted what was best for their friend, and there was no doubt as to what they considered best seeing as they were all newly mated and practically glowing with love and happiness.

She couldn't help wondering, though, how long it would take for the men to start bossing their mates around like they were servants indebted to their masters. The men acted like they were in love with their mates for the time being, but how long would it last before they dropped the act and gave in to their true natures? Actually, she was a bit surprised that they hadn't already.

Perhaps the men were keeping up the charade in

order to trick her into believing they were different and that she didn't risk anything by mating their friend. Although that didn't seem plausible. Based on what she could gather from their conversation, Trevor and Jennie had already been mated for over a week by the time Vamika and Callum first met. So, the fact that Trevor still treated Jennie like she was the love of his life wasn't likely to have anything to do with persuading Vamika to accept Callum.

Sabrina entered the kitchen, and her gaze swept over them, where they were sitting by the large windows, before stopping on Julianne. "Have any of you seen Steph and Michael?"

Julianne shook her head. "Not for a while." A wicked grin stretched her lips, and her eyes sparkled with amusement. "Have you tried knocking on their door? I'm sure they won't mind being interrupted if they're in their room."

"Very funny." Sabrina lifted an eyebrow at the other woman with a small smile curving her lips. "Sounds like you're speaking from experience. Mated life getting boring already, is it?"

Trevor and Jennie burst out laughing, and Julianne's jaw dropped open like she hadn't expected the jab.

"Hey." Duncan's eyes widened, before he narrowed them on Sabrina. "My mate doesn't have time to be bored when I use my tongue to—"

Julianne's hand covered Duncan's mouth as her face quickly took on a deep shade of red. "Okay, that's enough. You have nothing to prove. Nothing at all. I'm not bored, and you don't have to go into details about why, okay?"

Duncan's eyes filled with amusement as his gaze

lingered on his flustered mate's face.

Vamika's shoulders tensed as she observed the interaction between the couple. But Duncan made no move to remove his mate's hand from his mouth, allowing her to silence him while his eyes shone with amusement and love.

It was so unusual that Vamika felt herself bracing in anticipation of him suddenly exploding and punishing his mate for her behavior. The men she had grown up with were always in charge, and any act that threatened their superiority was unacceptable. She had been witness to punishment for what was deemed inappropriate behavior several times. Public humiliation was the usual form of punishment, but some men preferred more violent methods of correcting bad behavior.

Vamika flinched when Duncan suddenly moved, snapping his head to the side to dislodge Julianne's hand covering his mouth at the same time as he threw his arms around her and pulled her close. But instead of biting her shoulder to control her like Vamika had expected, he kissed his mate until she moaned into his mouth.

Averting her eyes, Vamika felt her heart racing. Her hands were fisted so tightly in her lap that her nails were biting into her palms while she waited for the inevitable cry of pain signaling that Duncan had put his mate in her place. Because she doubted that any of these men were as courteous to women as Henry.

Vamika had met Henry several times in her youth since her father had a friend in the pack where Henry grew up. Henry had always been different. Powerful, yet not showing off or using his power to control others. He had always been respectful to people, men as well as women. Even knowing that, it had taken her several months to fully trust him after she joined his pack.

But she didn't believe there were a lot of shifter males like Henry out there. In her experience they were extremely rare, and to believe that all the men staying in Leith's house at the moment were like Henry would be insane. The probability of that was so low that it could be deemed insignificant. The women in the house had no idea what they were in for when their mates decided they'd had enough of the farce they were currently living.

Julianne's happy laughter made Vamika frown and lift her gaze. Duncan was grinning at his mate when he let her go. It seemed the men were still biding their time and letting their mates believe they were more valuable than servants.

"Well, I'm going to risk Michael and Steph's displeasure and go knock on their door." Sabrina sighed.

Duncan laughed. "Displeasure. That sounds about right." His amusement died and he frowned. "But why the rush? Has something else happened? I take it you've heard about the murdered couple."

"I've heard." Sabrina nodded. "And I want to try locating Ambrosia again. I had no luck yesterday with Leith's help, but if Steph and I work together we might get somewhere. Even a rough location would be better than nothing. At least then we can alert any shifters in that area and make sure they know to be careful."

"Anything we can do to help?" Trevor's expression was serious when he stared at Sabrina. "If you can draw on all of our combined power, it should make the spell more potent, shouldn't it?"

Sabrina pursed her lips in thought before shaking her head. "Perhaps, but also a lot more unstable. And if we can't control all that power, it can blow up in our faces. Literally. I won't risk it. Particularly not the first time Steph and I try to work together. We need to get used to combining our powers before we can add any more fuel to the mix."

Leith walked into the kitchen, immediately followed by Callum, and Vamika's gaze was drawn to the second man. His blond hair was messy, like he had run his hand through it repeatedly, but somehow it made him look even more attractive not less. Callum's lips thinned when his gaze met hers for a second, before he yanked it away to look at the other people in the room.

Vamika's hands itched to bury themselves in his hair. She wondered if it would feel as soft as it looked, and how it would be to grab fistfuls of it while his mouth was busy pleasuring her. A small moan escaped her throat at the thought.

Her heart rate sped up as she held her breath in mortification and let her eyes dart around the people in the room. Thankfully, nobody seemed to have noticed her unchecked reaction to seeing Callum, including the man himself, who was currently staring out the window.

"I take it Steph and Michael are not available at the moment?" Leith stopped next to Sabrina and looked down at her as he put an arm around her waist.

"No." Sabrina raised her gaze to Leith's. "And I'm not relishing the fact that I have to go knock on their bedroom door. But it can't wait. People's lives are at stake."

Leith nodded. "I am sure they will understand, my angel. I can go get them if you like."

Sabrina's expression softened into a smile before she shook her head. "Thank you, Leith. But I can handle it myself."

The corner of Leith's mouth curved upward in a small smile. "I know you can. But I am happy to help any way I can."

Instead of saying anything, Sabrina rose to her toes and kissed the corner of Leith's mouth before she disappeared out of the kitchen.

Vamika couldn't help being fascinated by the way the couples talked and behaved toward each other. It was so unlike the couples she knew. The male shifters in the house were making a show of being attentive and caring, and the women were all acting like it was perfectly normal. Like this was how it was going to be forever. It was so convincing that Vamika was almost inclined to believe it herself. But her common sense and experience told her it wouldn't last.

Her gaze was drawn back to Callum. He was staring defiantly out of the window with a scowl on his face, clearly fighting the urge to look at her. Because there was no doubt the urge was there just like it was for her.

Her heart fluttered in her chest with how much she wanted to go to him, smooth that scowl off his face and tell him she wanted him too. Tell him he was the most gorgeous man she had ever seen and that his limp didn't matter to her.

Duncan had said Callum had been through a lot,

and she had no trouble believing it. Disabilities were rare among shifters, made even more so because those who were born with one were seldom allowed to live. It was a brutal custom but justified by the argument that a weak member was a liability and put the rest of the pack at risk.

The fact that Callum had survived to adulthood spoke to his own strength but also to the strength of the people around him. And to her that was impressive as well as a sign to be cautious. These people had to be more ruthless than they seemed if they could deal with the potential threats that would follow a shifter with a disability.

"Okay."

Vamika turned her head to see Sabrina entering the kitchen.

"I'm meeting Steph down at the beach to try the locating spell." Sabrina glanced around the room. "There aren't usually any people around there except for the people in this house, so the risk to the general public should be minimal. But just to be on the safe side, I don't want any of you down there with us either."

While she was talking, Leith had closed the distance to his mate. He narrowed his eyes at her. "I cannot agree to that. If something happens, I need to be there."

Sabrina's eyes softened as she raised her gaze to his. "You can be there as long as you give us a little room, okay?"

He gave her a short nod. "Agreed."

Sabrina smiled. "And you can keep a lookout for anyone approaching."

"I can." Leith nodded again.

Sabrina let her gaze swing around the room. "The rest of you can watch from the terrace if you want, but there won't be much to see. It will look like we're meditating that's all."

"So no fireworks?" Julianne grinned. "That's kind of disappointing."

Smiling, Sabrina shook her head. "Magic in real life isn't the same as in the movies. Fireworks usually means that something went wrong, and someone got hurt. So, unless that's the goal, there are no visible clues as to what we are doing."

CHAPTER 4

Callum snuck a peek at Vamika where she was sitting on the couch. She looked decidedly uncomfortable among his friends. Her back was ramrod straight, and she was sitting on the edge of her seat with her hands fisted in her lap. Wide eyes stared at Sabrina, and her lips were clamped together like she was struggling to stay still.

Perhaps she was trying to stop herself from getting up and leaving. She'd been ordered by her alpha to help them for some reason. Callum didn't understand why. Henry knew Vamika had rejected him, so why did the alpha feel the need to push them together in the same house?

It didn't matter, though. Callum would stay away from her as much as possible and only talk to her if it was strictly necessary.

They all moved out onto the terrace to observe Sabrina and Steph on the beach, even though Sabrina had said there wouldn't be anything to see. Trevor,

Jennie, Duncan, and Julianne moved over to the railing while Vamika moved to the corner of the terrace by the kitchen windows, where she could watch the women on the beach while keeping a distance to the couples by the railing.

Callum stopped right outside the door, still not sure whether he should stay to watch or go back downstairs to the living room to work. But he couldn't seem to make himself move. Not when Vamika was standing with her back to him, which left him free to rest his eyes on her beautiful form unobserved.

Her long braid was hanging down her back, brushing her ass, and he wanted to go over to her and remove the hair tie to let her hair flow freely. Just the thought of running his fingers through the long soft strands had his need for her roaring to life. His cock was rock hard in an instant, and he put his hands in his pockets to try to curb his urge to go play with her hair.

Like she knew what he was thinking, she suddenly grabbed her braid and pulled it over her shoulder to hide it from him, and he almost groaned in disappointment. Long hair had always been his weakness, and he was almost ashamed to admit that he had never considered being with a woman with short hair. He just couldn't imagine having sex without having at least one of his hands fisted in the woman's long hair.

Twenty minutes went by in virtual silence on the terrace while they watched the two witches sitting silently on the sand, holding hands. It looked peaceful, but from what he had been told, it was intense and exhausting to use your magical power like that.

Everyone straightened when Sabrina and Steph

suddenly rose, but to everybody's frustration, the women didn't move toward the house. Facing each other, they were discussing something, and every one of them standing on the terrace watching leaned forward like it would enable them to hear what the women were saying.

Julianne breathed a sigh of relief when Sabrina finally left the beach and started walking up the path to the house. "I really hope they've found Ambrosia. We need a break right about now."

Duncan leaned in and kissed his mate's cheek before he spoke. "I'm sure they have. Sabrina looks quite determined."

As if on cue the blond woman raised her gaze to the terrace and swept it over them standing there. But her eyes didn't stop on Julianne as Callum had expected. Instead they came to rest on Vamika.

Callum tensed at the assessing expression on Sabrina's face. He didn't know what blondie was thinking, but it had something to do with his mate, and whatever it was, he didn't like it.

Sabrina disappeared from sight, heading toward the lower entrance, and Callum swung his gaze to Vamika just as she turned her head toward him and frowned. He was much closer to his mate than he had been just a few seconds earlier, having obviously shortened the distance between them without even realizing it.

He didn't move back, but he turned to face the door to the terrace where Sabrina would no doubt appear any minute to explain what she wanted with Vamika.

Sabrina appeared as expected half a minute later, but before she could say anything, Julianne beat her to it. "Did you find her?"

The blond woman shook her head. "No. It feels like we're being blocked, but we both feel like we're close to breaking through the barrier or whatever it is that's preventing us from locating her. And we think Vamika might be able to help us with that."

"How exactly?" Callum narrowed his eyes as he took a step toward Sabrina. The thought of Vamika in the middle of all that magic that could get out of control had his spine stiffening. He didn't want her anywhere near the beach with the two witches. Not if he could help it.

Sabrina narrowed her eyes right back at him. "By giving us a little of her power. She has been subjected to Ambrosia's manipulation just like Michael has, and we believe having them both supporting us with their power might help direct the spell toward the bitch. We need to find her, Callum. Immediately, before she kills again."

"Not by risking Vamika." He crossed his arms over his chest and stared down into Sabrina's eyes. "I won't allow it."

"I'm right here, you know, and I can speak for myself."

Callum turned his head to glare down at Vamika, who had come to stand beside him without him even noticing. He had been too busy focusing on Sabrina and her plan to put his mate in the middle of what amounted to a potential magical bomb.

Vamika scowled up at him with her arms crossed and her back straight like she was trying to look taller than her five foot hardly anything. "You don't own me and you sure as hell don't have any say in what I do or don't do. That's up to me and me alone." Her eyes were practically shining with defiance and fury.

His skin itched like his fur was trying to break through. Every instinct he had was telling him to protect his mate, and his muscles tensed in preparation to do just that. "No! You don't get to put yourself in danger like that. I won't—"

"Too bad." Vamika chuckled, but there was a bitterness to the sound. "And people are wondering why I don't want a shifter mate. You're all the same. I'm not a child, and I have the right to make my own decisions, and I'll never let you or anyone else take that right away from me."

Callum turned his body toward her as fury shot through him, making his heart race and heat build in his chest. No doubt his face was red with anger, and a vein was pulsing at his temple. "So, you're going to risk your own life just to spite me, is that it?" Leaning over her, he made no secret of how fucking pissed off that made him. And if he had to scare her to make her back down, he would.

"No." She didn't back up like he had expected her to. In fact she surprised him by turning toward him and taking half a step forward to close the distance between them. Tipping her head back, she locked her stare on him with fury making her eyes glow like molten black lava. "I'm going to help you find Ambrosia like I was sent here to do."

Those eyes. They were practically shooting lightning at him with her rage. He'd never seen anything more wildly stunning. His lust, which had been temporarily squelched by the thought of Vamika putting herself in danger, roared back to life with unsurpassed intensity, and left him speechless as his mind was overrun with need. All he could do was stare at her while he was trying to remember what was going on.

Callum's gaze dropped to her lips. He wanted to kiss her. Needed to kiss her. His lips were tingling with how much he wanted to press them against hers and taste her sweet mouth. Those ruby-red lips would be so soft against his as he devoured her.

"Stop! What are you doing?"

Hands on his chest pushed him away, and he blinked a couple of times to regain his focus.

Vamika had taken a couple of steps away from him, her eyes wide and her lips parted as she slowly shook her head. "Were you trying to kiss me? What's wrong with you? I just told you I don't want you."

Callum winced as pain lashed through his chest, and he swallowed to try to make his throat work. She was right. He had been trying to kiss her. What was wrong with him? The only explanation he could come up with was that he was losing it.

"I'm sorry. I..." He stopped and dropped his gaze to the floor, not knowing what to say. All he wanted was her, for her to accept him, and his body seemed to be overriding his good sense to make it happen.

"Yes, well. Don't try that again." Vamika's voice was hard like granite. "The next time you do something like that, I'll knee you in the balls to make sure you get the message."

He just nodded without looking at her. "Okay." There wasn't much else he could say. Trying to explain what had just happened would only sound like a lame excuse, so he was better off saying nothing.

"Let's go. I'm ready."

Vamika's words caught his attention, and he lifted his chin to see her leading the way toward the terrace door with Sabrina following.

Swearing at his own inability to ensure his mate's safety, he followed the two women into the house and down the stairs.

They had just exited the door on the lower level when Vamika turned around and narrowed her eyes at him. "What are you doing?"

He crossed his arms over his chest and met her gaze with what he hoped was a blank expression on his face. "What does it look like I'm doing?"

She sighed and rolled her eyes like she was dealing with an insolent child. "You're supposed to watch from the terrace like everyone else."

Chuckling, he gave her a small amused smile. If she thought he'd let her stay that far away from him when she chose to put her life at risk, she had another thing coming. He might have been wrong in trying to kiss her when she had told him she didn't want him, but he wasn't wrong in wanting to protect her. "No, I'm not. Not when my mate's in danger. Why do you think Leith and Michael are at the beach with their women? To sunbath?"

Vamika threw her hands in the air in exasperation, before she turned away and continued down toward the beach.

Callum followed his mate and Sabrina down the path, all the while trying to come up with a good reason that would dissuade Vamika from participating in Sabrina and Steph's experiment. But none of the arguments he could think of would hold against her stubborn assertion that he had no say over her.

Leith nodded at him when they arrived at the small beach, and Callum went to stand beside the other man. He had no idea how the man, who had almost lost his mate to another witch's attack, could calmly stand back and watch this without objecting.

"Aren't you worried Sabrina could get hurt?" Callum turned his head to look at Leith. The man's pose was relaxed, like what they were witnessing was perfectly normal and completely safe.

Leith gave a short nod, but his calm expression didn't change. "Yes, but what do you think would happen if I tried to say no?"

Callum sighed. "You have tried saying no before then."

Leith gave another short nod and turned to look at him. "I have. And if anything, it made it worse. Sabrina is a headstrong woman, and I love that about her, but I am still trying to adjust to the consequences. I am not used to being overruled, and it can be infuriating when she willingly puts herself in danger to save other people."

"Yes." Callum frowned and turned to look at the women and Michael sitting down on the sand. "So, there's nothing I can do to prevent Vamika from exposing herself to magic without making her angry and having her accuse me of controlling her?"

"No." Leith didn't make any effort to soften his short and concise answer.

Sabrina and Steph linked hands and instructed Vamika and Michael to put one hand on each of the two women's shoulders to ensure that both witches had access to both Vamika and Michael's power.

Callum had to lock his knees not to stomp over there and yank Vamika away from them. But it would only make Vamika loathe him even more, and since he couldn't exactly tie her up, his interference would only cause a short delay instead of stopping her. In the end she would still put herself at risk, but he would be worse off for trying to stop her. So, all he could do was stay close to make sure he would be there for her if something happened.

The four people on the ground closed their eyes, and being this close, Callum could feel the magic like a potent power start to emanate from the two witches. It made the hairs at the back of his neck stand up, and he took a step forward before he could stop himself.

A hand closed lightly around his upper arm, and he turned to glance at Leith, who shook his head at him. "You can cause them all to get hurt if you interfere now. Stand back and let them complete what they have started. It will be over soon."

Callum nodded and took a step back, but his heart was racing in his chest, and he was practically vibrating with the effort to stop himself from storming over there.

CHAPTER 5

Vamika's anger over Callum's controlling behavior was immediately pushed to the side when magic started swirling around her like a virtual whirlwind. She wanted to yank her hands away from the two women, but instead she took a deep breath to try to soothe the cloying fear that was crawling through her like a million ants. The magic felt familiar yet not, like she had felt something similar before but couldn't quite remember it. And she probably had felt something similar when Ambrosia had gotten into her mind, making her black out for a couple of minutes.

"Now start feeding us your power gently." Sabrina's smooth voice broke through Vamika's fear.

She took another deep breath and let it out slowly as she focused her mind on what she had to do. They were going to find Ambrosia, and contrary to what Vamika had thought when she arrived, she might be able to help with that, after all. Her bad experience with the evil witch's magic might not be for nothing.

Letting her power flow through her palms into the two women was a strange sensation. She had only ever used her power passively to make people keep their distance. Human men who didn't take no for an answer could be persuaded to stay away by making them physically uncomfortable when they got too close. Being nauseous wasn't usually conducive to being horny.

Pain suddenly stabbed into the side of her head about an inch behind her left temple, and her whole body jerked in response. Crying out, she ripped her hands away from the two witches and cradled her head in her hands. Squeezing her eyes shut, she tried to breathe through the pain as a memory assailed her of cold pale-green eyes staring into hers, and a low mesmerizing voice telling her to stay where she was and be calm. Then the agony intensified, growing until it felt like the left side of her head was on fire.

Strong arms came around her, and she was brought against a hard chest. Someone started whispering words of comfort in her ear in a soothing deep voice, and she breathed a sigh of relief when the words seemed to wrap around the pain and strangle the roaring, agonizing fire until there was nothing left but weakly glowing embers.

Her mind was foggy, but clinging to the strong arms holding her and listening to the murmured words helped her relax. The fear she had felt earlier disappeared, and her mind calmed as she rested against the hard chest of the man holding her. Hopefully, he wouldn't let her go just yet. It felt so good being in his arms with the sound of his whispers eradicating her fear and pain.

Her mind cleared slowly, and Vamika frowned when she remembered where she was and why. The pain had come out of nowhere, but it had unlocked a memory of Ambrosia. The witch had told her to be calm and stay where she was, but it was the memory of power Vamika had felt penetrating her mind when the witch spoke that had Vamika's heart rate speeding up again.

"Rest now. Don't worry. You're safe. Everything will be okay."

Callum speaking in a low voice next to her ear made her jerk in shock, and she almost opened her eyes as she realized who was holding her. But she managed to stop herself just in time. Opening her eyes would reveal that she was awake and aware of what was going on, and she wanted another couple of minutes to relax in his strong arms before she made it known that she was conscious. As soon as he knew she was awake, she would have to push him away, and she couldn't bear to do that just yet. Not when being in his arms felt so amazing.

"I've got you, baby girl. Just relax. I've got you."

His strong arms were wrapped around her from behind, and she was leaning back against his chest with her hands holding onto his forearms with a death grip. His skin was warm under her palms, and she wanted to smooth her hands up his muscular forearms to his thick biceps. But that would alert him to the fact that she was lucid, so she tamped down on that urge.

Relaxing her grip on his forearms, she let herself slump against him, pretending that she had fallen asleep. Perhaps if she was convincing enough, he would carry her back to the house and put her in his bed and...*nothing*. She couldn't allow that no matter how sweetly he was taking care of her at the moment. Only minutes had passed since he tried to make decisions for her, just like a shifter man always did, and she'd do well to remember that.

Vamika opened her eyes and tried to sit up, but Callum's tight hold on her prevented her from moving.

"Vamika, are you all right?" Callum spoke next to her ear. His breath brushed the sensitive shell of her ear, and she squirmed against him as the sensation ignited her need for his touch. Everywhere.

She swallowed hard to make sure her voice would come out normal, and she wouldn't sound like she was going to turn around and plaster herself against his hard body before kissing him like she wanted to devour him. "Yes. Now please let me go." Her voice was a little throaty, but that could be attributed to the fact that she had just been screaming in pain.

"Okay." Callum nodded against the side of her head before unwrapping his arms from around her to let her sit up. "What happened? Is the pain gone?"

"Yes." She nodded and met Sabrina's gaze. The blond woman's brows were furrowed as she stared at Vamika with concern. "I think the magic unlocked what happened when Ambrosia took over my mind. I suddenly remembered her eyes staring into mine, and her telling me to stay where I was and be calm."

Sabrina nodded. "Anything else you can remember?"

Vamika shook her head. "No. Everything is blank after that, until I woke up from the spell, or whatever it was, she cast over me."

Sabrina gave her a small smile. "Yeah, that fits with my theory that your mind was sort of put on hold for a while."

A growl next to Vamika's ear startled her, and she automatically leaned forward to put more distance between herself and the shifter male still sitting directly behind her with his legs on either side of her.

"Is no one concerned about the pain she just suffered? All caused by the magic she shouldn't have been subjected to in the first place." Callum's voice was rough and deep with his fury, and it almost made her smile that he was so angry on her behalf. Until she realized why he was angry and any urge to smile died. He might have felt a shadow of her pain through the mating bond. She wasn't sure whether that was possible for true mates before they mated but even if he had felt just a fraction of the pain she had experienced, it would have been uncomfortable. It was impossible to say whether he was more pissed off about her pain or his own discomfort. But she suspected the latter played a part.

Sabrina's gaze swung to Callum. "I don't like that this turned out to be a painful experience for Vamika, and I didn't expect it to be if that's what you believe."

"Well, that's the last time she'll be close to any of you while you're using your powers. I won't—"

"Allow it. Yes, you keep saying that." Vamika sighed and rose to her feet before she turned to face Callum, who had gotten to his feet as well. "The thing is, Callum, I don't need a keeper or a bodyguard, and most assuredly not a jailer. I'm my own person with a right to decide for myself what I will and won't do."

Callum's whole body looked tense as he scowled

down at her from his superior height. He was a tall Adonis of a man, and she couldn't help wishing he wasn't a shifter. He might have been just as protective and stubborn as a human, but he wouldn't have had the power to enforce his will. As a shifter, though, he was stronger than her, and if he chose to physically restrain her, she wouldn't be able to fight him and win.

"But you got hurt." Callum's face was red with anger and a vein was pulsing at his temple. "I don't want to see you in pain."

Vamika shrugged. "Then you should stay away from me, and you won't have to see it. It's simple really." But she couldn't help being thankful that he had been there and taken care of her. She even had a feeling that being in his arms had made the pain disappear faster than it would have otherwise. That was probably a result of the mating bond, though, and had nothing specifically to do with Callum as a person.

"Fuck!" He spun away from her and stomped down to the water's edge, where he stopped with his back to her. The tension in his body made his muscles more defined, and she let herself admire his thick shoulders and his tight ass. The men usually posing on the front of fitness magazines had nothing on Callum. He was perfection, and the way he had held her and whispered to her while she was in pain had been so sweet. If not for his tendency to want to control her, she might have actually followed Henry's advice and tried to get to know him better.

Ripping her gaze away from the gorgeous and maddening man, she turned away to face the others. "Did you manage to find Ambrosia?"

Steph sighed and shook her head slowly, and

Michael put an arm around his mate and pulled her close.

"But we know she's still in Scotland, and most likely somewhere north of here." Sabrina's brows pushed together. "It's not a lot to go on, but at least we know that she hasn't gone far. Yet. I'm more concerned with how she's able to block us from finding her. I've never heard of anyone being able to do that."

Vamika frowned. "So, you can find anyone you want to no matter where they are?" It was a bit disturbing that something like that was even possible, and it had some implications for her personally that she didn't want to dwell on.

"No." Sabrina shook her head as she rose to her feet. "Only people I have met before, and the more time I've spent with them the easier it is for me to find them. Their location doesn't matter much. They could be next-door or in China, and it wouldn't make much difference."

"Okay." Vamika felt herself relax a little. "Is that true for every witch?"

"Well." The blond woman shrugged and glanced at Steph before swinging her gaze back to Vamika. "I'm coming to realize that what I know of witches and their powers is less than I thought. A month ago I would've said yes, because that's what I've been taught, but I'm not so sure anymore. Perhaps some witches can locate a person based only on an image or a video of that person, or by including a friend or family member of the person in the spell."

Vamika tensed. This wasn't what she wanted to hear. She didn't want to be found, at least not while she was outside pack grounds. Staying with the pack, she was protected. They would fight for her because she was one of them, and any threat to her was considered a threat to all of them. But outside pack grounds, she was vulnerable simply because her pack was too far away to get to her in time to help her.

"I wouldn't worry about it, though." There was a look of understanding in Sabrina's eyes that made Vamika frown. "The number of witches able to pull something like that off would be few, or I'm sure the witches in my family would know about it."

Vamika nodded slowly. "Good to know. Are there any other spells we can try to locate her?"

"No!" Callum was behind her in an instant, so close she could feel his breath caressing her neck. She felt herself bristling but before she could snap at him to back off, he continued in a low voice. "Please, Vamika. At least not yet. You've just recovered from whatever damage the unlocking of that memory caused to your brain. Please take some time to make sure you are fully healed before you let anymore magic touch you."

Her eyes widened at his begging. It was most likely just a change of tactic to get her to do what he wanted, but she preferred it to him telling her no.

She slowly turned around to look up into his eyes. As he stared down at her, a muscle was ticking an inch below his ear with how tightly he had clamped his jaw. And power was emanating from him like he was struggling to hold himself back.

His power wrapped around her and caressed along her spine, before it attacked all her sensitive parts at once. Her lips started tingling, and her nipples tightened to hard peaks. But what made her gasp was his power vibrating against her clit before plunging inside her to caress her aching channel. His power wasn't a physical thing, of course, but the sensations it created was real.

A knowing grin spread across Callum's face as he studied her expression that was no doubt reflecting her rapidly increasing need for him. She tried to relax her face into a neutral expression but based on his widening grin, she wasn't successful.

He wasn't playing fair, and he knew it. But if he thought that crap was going to work on her, he needed to be taught a lesson. And who better to do that than her.

Without giving any indication of what she intended, she jumped and wrapped her legs around his waist. Astonishment registered on his face as she threw her arms around his neck, and he stumbled back a couple of steps before he regained his balance.

Vamika plastered her lips to his before plunging her tongue into his mouth. It took him a second to respond, but—*holy hell*—when he did, she almost forgot her plan. The man knew how to kiss, and her mind was quickly turning syrupy with the raw need he created in her.

His lips moved enticingly against hers when he took control of the kiss, his tongue exploring every part of her mouth while playing with her tongue. And all she wanted was to stay in his arms and kiss him until they fell down from exhaustion or lack of air.

But she had a plan, and a scorching kiss wasn't going to stop her no matter how much her body was screaming at her to mate him already.

After pulling a little back, she bit down on his lower

lip until she tasted blood. Callum jerked and loosened his grip on her, and she used the opportunity to unwrap her legs from around his waist and jump away from him. Keeping her eyes on his face to assess his reaction, she backed slowly away from him. With his strength he could easily overpower her, unless she correctly judged his attack and managed to counteract his movements. She knew a thing or two about neutralizing an attack, seeing as she was small, and it was the only means she had to protect herself against a stronger opponent.

But the fury she had expected to see on his face never showed up. Callum's brows pulled together, and his eyes widened as he lifted his hand to touch his bleeding lip. He met her gaze, and on seeing her expression, his whole body seemed to deflate. "Why?"

She tensed at the pain in his voice. The pain she had just inflicted. His question wasn't about the physical pain in his lip but the emotional pain of rejection. Vamika had expected him to get angry and prove her reason for refusing to mate him, but instead she had hurt him again.

It was for the best, though, since she knew what would happen after they mated, but seeing the stark pain in his eyes was affecting her more than she wanted to admit. She didn't want to feel anything for him, but seeing him like this had her throat clogging, preventing her from answering him. Not that she would have known what to say, anyway. It would have been so much easier if he had just gotten angry like she had expected.

CHAPTER 6

Callum stared at the beautiful woman in front of him, whom he had thought was finally accepting him. His lip was throbbing painfully, but it was nothing compared to the pain in his chest. She had just ripped his heart out again, and he didn't even understand why. Why would she kiss him like that, a scorching kiss that almost brought him to his knees, only to yank his heart out and stomp on it?

Her eyes were wide as she kept her gaze on him, but he struggled to interpret the expression on her face. It looked like a mix of fear, determination, and pain, or perhaps he just wasn't able to understand what he was seeing.

She swallowed hard but made no attempt to answer his question. But there was no doubt she still didn't want him, no matter if her kiss had convinced him otherwise for a glorious little while.

Vamika suddenly spun and hurried up the path toward the house, leaving him alone on the beach. The others had left while they were busy kissing, probably in order to give them some privacy.

Callum sighed and turned around to stare out over the loch. Not for the first time he wanted to leave and go back to his house in Fearolc. At least there he would be able to grieve in peace and try to come to terms with his situation without being forced to interact with the reason for his misery.

What had he done to deserve this? Or perhaps that wasn't the question at all. He had assumed at first that Vamika not wanting him was mainly due to his disability, but now he wasn't so sure. She had never seemed to pay any special attention to his leg at all, and he would have noticed since he was used to shifters staring at it with shock and disgust clearly visible on their faces. But he'd never caught her doing that even once. On the contrary he had seen heat in her eyes several times when she was looking at him, and even though that might be the mating bond's doing, he didn't think she would be able to hide her disgust so easily when she couldn't hide her lust.

The one thing she had repeated several times was that she didn't want to be owned. And she had reacted badly whenever he had tried to protect her, as in telling her that she wasn't allowed to put herself at risk.

Closing his eyes, he groaned at his own stupidity. Allowed. He had actually used that word. Like she was a child. Or worse, a woman not allowed to make her own decisions. He had even asked Leith about it, and yet Callum had repeated his controlling behavior again when Vamika had asked if there were any other spells they could try.

He had no desire to control his mate, but he had a

strong need to protect her. And she might not recognize the difference since they barely knew each other.

"Fuck!" Callum let his chin drop to his chest. Telling her what she wasn't allowed to do wasn't the only thing he had done to control her. He had used his power on her. Unintentionally at first due to his anger, but when he noticed the heat in her eyes, he had failed to stop. He had continued even though it was clearly turning her on. And that was right before she launched herself at him and started kissing him.

No wonder she bit him and made a show of rejecting him again. He had been a manipulative asshole. He who prided himself on being respectful to women. And she had pointed out that he was out of line by hurting him like he deserved.

While walking slowly back to the house, he tried to come up with a sincere and convincing apology. Vamika wasn't a trusting person, which probably meant she'd had her trust betrayed more than once. And all he had done since meeting her was try to make decisions for her and show her that he didn't trust her to take care of herself.

But that was going to change. He was going to apologize for his behavior and promise her that he would never tell her what to do or not to do again. Perhaps if he was lucky, she would allow him to prove to her he respected her and only wanted what was best for her.

∞∞∞∞

It was after dinner by the time Callum managed to

convince Vamika to speak to him alone for a minute. She was clearly reluctant to be alone with him, but she still followed him down to the living room where they could talk privately without being too far away from the rest of the extended household who were gathered in the kitchen.

He walked over to the couch and sat down before looking at her. She was so short compared to him, and he wanted to make sure he seemed as nonthreatening as possible.

Frowning, she approached him slowly with her arms crossed. "Whatever you want to tell me, please get it over with. I want to be back in the kitchen with the others in less than five minutes."

"Okay." Callum nodded and tried to swallow the lump in his throat. His heart was racing, and his hands were clammy. He felt like his whole life depended on his next words, and he didn't think he'd ever been this scared in his life.

Sliding off the couch, he dropped to his knees on the floor in front of his mate while keeping his eyes on hers. She quirked a brow at him in question but didn't say anything.

"I'm so sorry, Vamika. All I want to do is make you happy, but all I've managed to do since we met is make you angry."

She narrowed her eyes at him and took a step back away from him. "I'm not interested in hearing this, Callum. I don't need anyone to make me happy."

"Please hear me out." He took a deep breath. "I'm sorry I tried to stop you from helping Sabrina and Steph. I just didn't want you to get hurt. And look what happened? You were in serious pain."

Vamika sighed and rolled her eyes, before she turned her back on him and started for the stairs.

Callum fisted his hands to stop himself from yelling and running after her to stop her. He'd lost his chance to explain by turning his apology into an accusation and an *I told you so*.

A few more seconds and she would disappear up the stairs, but there was one more thing he wanted to say before she was out of earshot.

"I never meant to use my power on you." He stared at her back as she reached the stairs. "I'm sorry for not stopping when I saw the effect it had on you. That's inexcusable and it won't happen again."

His mate disappeared up the stairs without a glance in his direction or any acknowledgement that she had heard his last words. But what had he expected? She had been clear from the start that she didn't want him. His only hope was that she had heard his last words and realized he meant them. Not that it would help him much. He was fucked, and not in the literal sense he wanted.

There was one more thing he was going to do before he went to sleep. It wouldn't sway her opinion of him or persuade her he was worth taking a chance on, but he wanted to do it anyway. She was his mate, and it was the least he could do to make sure she was comfortable while staying in the house.

∞∞∞∞

Vamika nodded and forced a smile at Sabrina. The woman was friendly; they all were, even knowing that Callum was hurting because of her. They made an effort to include her in their conversation, and she tried to make a polite comment here and there, even though she was naturally quiet, and talking to people wasn't something she excelled at.

Henry had been giving her some advice on how to come across as more open and friendly, but considering she wasn't the open and friendly type, trying to come across as such felt like a betrayal. She valued honesty in other people, even to the point of crassness. It was so much better than people glossing over everything that wasn't perfect in their lives and pretending to live their dreams, even when they clearly weren't. She'd had more than enough people in her life who had done that and knew how much pain it usually concealed.

Callum hadn't shown up in the kitchen after apologizing to her for his behavior, and she kept pushing her gaze to the doorway, hoping he would show up. For her sanity it was better not seeing him, because every time she did, he stole a little more of her determination to stay away from him.

His apology had been less than eloquent, or quite frankly, horrible, but the sincerity in his eyes had been real. She'd had to clamp her mouth shut not to admit to him she believed him before turning away and fleeing from those beautiful eyes that were almost enough to make her swoon. And she never swooned. It was a concept that belonged in romance novels and not in the real world.

Leith approached the couch where she was sitting beside Sabrina, and she expected him to sit down next to his mate. But instead he stopped and faced her. "Callum wanted you to have the room he has been staying in while he has been here. He has opted to sleep on the sofa in the living room so you can have a proper bed and some privacy while you sleep."

Her eyes widened in surprise as she stared up at Leith. "He did? But I... That's not necessary. I can stay on the couch."

One corner of Leith's mouth curved a little in something resembling a smile. "You will have to speak to him about that. He has already packed his things and installed himself in the living room. And he has cleaned and prepared the room to make sure you would feel welcome."

Vamika's jaw dropped open. Male shifters didn't clean. That was a woman's job. That and cooking and taking care of the kids, and practically everything else that needed doing around the house. Except for Henry, of course, and perhaps the men in this house. Leith seemed to be fond of cooking, and she'd noticed the other men were happy to help out in the kitchen. But cleaning?

"I can take you down there now." Sabrina smiled when Vamika turned to look at her. "It's a beautiful room. I stayed there when I first arrived here."

Vamika could only nod. Her mind was struggling to come to terms with the fact that Callum had done something like that just to make sure she was comfortable. And after she had just walked away from him in the middle of his apology.

"Come on then." Sabrina rose and headed for the door, and Vamika quickly followed. She grabbed her things where she had left them in the hallway outside the kitchen before following Sabrina down the stairs to the living room.

Her eyes automatically sought out the couch as soon as it came into view. The room was dark, and Callum had turned the couch around so the back of the large piece of furniture was shielding his sleeping form from view of anyone passing through the room. Or at least she assumed he was sleeping. There was no movement as far she could detect, but she wasn't going to go over to him to find out no matter how much she wanted to.

They continued down the stairs to the bottom level of the house, and she followed Sabrina when the blond woman opened a door and entered a small bedroom. It was a beautiful room and smelled fresh and clean.

"And this is the bathroom." Sabrina opened a door to the right and turned on the light. "I think I'll leave you to it so you can get settled." The blond woman smiled at her before heading out the door.

"Thank you, Sabrina." Vamika smiled as the other woman glanced at her over her shoulder.

"You're welcome."

Sabrina closed the door behind her, and Vamika was left standing there staring at it. She couldn't remember the last time she had genuinely smiled. It was probably years ago. She'd been a happy child until she started to understand what was going on around her and what her life would be like as a grown woman.

Shaking her head, she quelled the intruding memories before they could take over. She had managed to escape that life, and she was never letting anyone take her back to it. Ever.

Glancing around the room, she took in the beautiful wall paintings before her gaze landed on the perfectly made bed with a deep-red rose nestled on the pillow.

Her heart rate sped up as she stared at the perfect specimen of a flower before slowly making her way over to the bed and picking it up. It was stunning and probably the most flawless rose she had ever seen, making it obvious that it had been selected with care.

The rose became blurry as her eyes filled with tears, and a sob escaped her throat just as the tears overflowed down her cheeks.

Callum had prepared the room for her, and he had been the one to choose the flower. She'd never received flowers before, not like this. The flowers she had received had always been delivered with an expectation of public praise and gratitude. Callum's gift wasn't like that. He wasn't there to receive any praise or gratitude, and the flower was given without announcing it to anyone. It was all for her. And it was the sweetest thing anyone had ever done for her.

Swallowing down her sobs, she put the rose on the bedside table before wiping away her tears with the back of her hands. Both her mind and body were screaming at her to go to him, but she couldn't. The probability was too high that he would change after they mated, and that would be devastating. Even more devastating since she was starting to see the relationship that might have been possible between them if he didn't change into an asshole.

"Stop it, Vamika. You know how this will end if you give in." A last sob tore out of her throat before she sucked in a deep breath and forced the stupid fairy-tale fantasy ending playing with her mind down deep. It was better buried in memories she hated and kept locked away in her mind. That was where it belonged, her dream of a happily ever after.

CHAPTER 7

Vamika woke with a small cry and sat up abruptly. She was panting like she had been running flat out for miles, and her clit was throbbing insistently between her legs, demanding she do something about the need that was running rampant in her body.

The dream that had left her in this condition was still vivid in her mind, and she fisted her hands in her T-shirt and squirmed as an image of Callum looking up from between her legs assailed her. His eyes were sparkling with amusement as he vibrated the tip of his tongue against her clit, and the image alone was enough to push her closer to release.

Before she realized what she was doing, she jumped out of bed and stormed out of the room. And once she was on the move, she couldn't stop. Her legs were carrying her toward the man who had been the hero of her dream, and all she managed to do was slow down enough to avoid waking the whole household.

The living room was dark and quiet when she

reached the top of the stairs, but like any shifter she didn't have a problem seeing in the dark. Holding her breath, she carefully tiptoed across the room to the couch before rounding the end of it to lay her eyes on Callum.

He was lying on his back with a thin blanket covering him from his waist down. His eyes were closed, and his breathing was calm and even in sleep. And he was gorgeous.

His blond hair was sticking up in all directions, a sign that he had been tossing and turning for a while before falling asleep. Or perhaps in his sleep. But sleep had smoothed all the concern and hurt from his face, making her realize he was younger than the other men in the house, perhaps no more than thirty.

Vamika wanted to reach out and touch his cheek just to feel his smooth warm skin against her palm. But she didn't. She stayed perfectly still and just watched him breath calmly in sleep, drinking in the sight of him while she could do so undisturbed and without consequences.

Her gaze dipped to his hard chest and rippling abs, and she barely contained a moan of yearning to touch him. The couch was too narrow to comfortably contain his muscular form, resulting in one arm hanging outside the seat of the couch with his hand trailing on the floor. The other arm was curled up with his hand tucked behind his head, showing off his thick bicep and the muscles along his ribs.

Taking deep, controlled breaths to try to temper her desire, she let her gaze travel down his torso to where his lower body was hidden by the blanket. She had seen his cock before, and she had been dreaming of his thick length pushing into her channel ever since. If only she could find a way to lower the blanket without waking him, she would be able to verify whether her memory was serving her correctly, or if the image had somehow grown in her mind.

Holding her breath, she reached out with both hands and pinched a fold of the blanket at his waist carefully between her thumbs and forefingers. Watching his face for any sign of him waking, she lifted the blanket slowly before folding it down over his thighs.

Vamika kept her eyes on his face for a few more seconds, but there was no change to indicate he was waking up or had noticed what she was doing.

She let her gaze travel from his face and down his strong body, forcing herself to go slowly while her whole body tensed with desire as her anticipation grew. Her channel clenched, and a small moan escaped her lips when her eyes finally landed on his cock resting against his lower belly.

It wasn't erect but based on its current size, she didn't think her memories had deceived her. Callum had a large cock, and the image of it and its owner had been the source of some of the best orgasms of her life in the last couple of days.

Her channel clenched again, and she squeezed her thighs together, making her aware of how wet she was. Her panties were practically drenched with her need.

After shooting another gaze at Callum's face to verify he was still sleeping, she let her hand dip into her panties. Her clit was throbbing, and she shuddered with pleasure as soon as her finger came into contact with the swollen nub.

This wouldn't take long if she could manage to stay quiet and avoid waking the gorgeous naked man on the couch. Letting her eyes rest on his cock, she rubbed her clit firmly for a few seconds until she suddenly realized that Callum's shaft was swelling.

Her gaze snapped to his face, and she held her breath while scrutinizing his features and chest. But there was nothing to indicate that he was waking up. Whatever the reason for his erection it was happening in his sleeping mind. Or perhaps it was a subconscious reaction to her close proximity or scent.

Which was fine by her, because the sight of his fully erect member was turning her on even more. Staring at it, she clamped her mouth shut to prevent herself from moaning and let her middle finger slide inside her aching pussy.

"Would you allow me to help you with that? My fingers are longer and thicker than yours."

She let out a startled cry as her gaze snapped to his. His eyes were practically glowing with desire when he met her gaze.

Her face flamed with heat from being caught playing with herself while staring at his cock, but she couldn't pull her gaze from his. Those eyes. She wanted to see what they looked like when he came. But that would mean giving in to her desire to fuck him, and she couldn't do that.

"I would love to make you come, Vamika." Callum's voice was deeper and rougher than usual, and the sound made her shudder with need. "And I don't expect anything in return. All I want is to give you pleasure and watch you come apart. Will you let me do that?"

"I…" She swallowed as her heart was threatening to beat its way out of her chest. Her pussy clenched in hopeful anticipation around her finger, making her realize how small and inadequate it was compared to his.

Her gaze dropped to his hand still trailing on the floor. He hadn't moved since he woke up, not even a tiny bit, and it made her wonder how long he had been awake. Had he even been asleep when she walked into the room? It was impossible to know.

His hand, though, with long thick fingers. She desperately wanted one of those fingers inside her instead of her own.

A shiver ran through her, and she lifted her gaze to his before letting it roam his face and particularly his lips. She'd already tasted his lips, and she wanted to again, but if she let him kiss her, she didn't think she would be able to stop until they were mated.

Letting him use his fingers to make her come was different. It wouldn't be as intimate, or at least that was what she was counting on. "Yes." Her voice was husky and didn't sound like her at all.

One of his brows rose in question. "Yes, as in I can touch you?" The heat in his eyes intensified and made his brown eyes even more beautiful.

Nodding, she pulled her finger out of her pussy before pushing her panties down her legs, exposing herself to him.

His eyes zoomed in on her naked lady parts, and he let out a long groan as he slowly sat up and turned to face her, putting his face inches from her naked pussy.

She sucked in a breath as need assaulted her, making everything tighten. Heat pulsed in her lower belly, and she put her hands on either side of his head, fisting his hair, and tried to guide him to where she wanted him.

He chuckled, and his eyes rose to hers, his hands covering her fists before gently peeling them away from his head. "Easy there, baby girl. I've got you. Just give me a few seconds."

His large, warm hands grabbed her hips and moved her back a step. Then he slid off the couch and sat down on his knees before pulling her closer. "Spread your legs a bit more for me. I need access to all those fun parts of yours."

Moaning, she did as he said, which put her throbbing clit an inch from his hot mouth. She wanted to plaster herself against him and beg him to devour her, but she held herself in check to let him take charge, breathing through the burning desire that was threatening to incinerate her.

One of his hands smoothed back from her hip until it grabbed hold of one of her ass cheeks. The next second she was pushed forward to land clit first against his mouth, forcing a startled cry from her lips when he sucked hard on her swollen nub.

A finger breached her entrance before pushing into her. She panted as her channel stretched to accommodate the thick intrusion, making her realize that he wasn't using one finger to fuck her but two. And they felt so good rubbing against her sensitive internal walls.

"Fuck!" He growled the word against her clit. "You're so fucking wet."

"Please, Callum." She bucked her hips against him, needing him to fuck her with those long thick fingers of his. "I need to come."

"Oh, you will, baby girl, you will."

His mouth attacked her clit with licking and sucking at the same time as his fingers started pumping into her core. She gasped and mewled as the heat pulsing in her lower belly quickly developed into a raging inferno.

Her orgasm abruptly exploded through her with a force that almost blew her mind. Her knees gave, but Callum held her firmly with an arm wrapped around her thighs while he kept up his attack on her cheering lady parts.

The unprecedented pleasure finally faded, and she sagged against him as he lowered her gently to sit on his lap with her forehead resting against his shoulder.

"Thank you," she whispered. "That was amazing."

He chuckled, and his shoulder shook with the sound. "I'm glad you think so. I can repeat that anytime you want me to."

Vamika sighed. She could definitely get used to that, but it would mean… *No!* She wasn't going to think about that. At the moment all she wanted was to revel in what he had just done for her and how it had made her feel.

She lifted her head from his shoulder and met his burning gaze. Callum had just given her the most glorious pleasure of her life, but she hadn't done anything for him. He had said that she didn't have to, but after what he had just done, she wanted to give him something in return.

But before she could decide what to do, he lifted his hand and put his two wet fingers in his mouth. She froze when he let out a deep groan as he started licking them clean of her juices, and his eyes flamed with desire.

His shoulder moving made her look down to see his other hand close around his straining cock. The thing was even bigger than before, and her jaw dropped open when he gave it a firm stroke, and precum leaked out to cover the skin stretched tightly over the thick head.

His hand quickly picked up pace, while he stared at her and slowly licked his fingers clean. His chest was vibrating with a deep growl that was getting more intense by the second.

Callum pleasuring himself while obviously enjoying the taste of her was easily the hottest show she had ever watched. Her recent orgasm was soon forgotten, and her body was begging her for another release.

Putting a hand on Callum's shoulder to hold on, Vamika reached between her legs. She gasped when her fingers came into contact with her sensitive clit, and Callum's gaze snapped to what she was doing. His eyes on her playing with herself only served as fuel to her fire, and watching her seemed to have the same effect on him.

His strokes became more erratic as she rubbed herself and squirmed on his lap, until he suddenly jerked and hot jets of his cum hit her chest while he snarled.

The next instant pleasure exploded through her, and she mewled like a cat while waves of ecstasy spread through her body. It wasn't as intense as the orgasm Callum had given her, but it was better than the ones she usually achieved by herself.

As her heart rate slowed, she lifted her head from where it was resting against his shoulder. Callum's eyes were hooded, and there was a small smile on his lips. God the man was too beautiful for his own good. She could stare at him for hours, and she still wouldn't have looked her fill.

"Fuck, baby girl. You're so hot, hell is jealous." His eyes dipped to her lips, and he visibly swallowed before he slowly leaned toward her.

She licked her lips in anticipation of his kiss and leaned forward a little to meet him halfway when she suddenly jerked with realization at what she was doing. He was her mate, but she couldn't mate him. It would ruin everything.

Snapping her head back, she scrambled to her feet and ran. As she stormed down the stairs, she heard him calling her name, but she didn't stop until she was safely inside her room with the door looked behind her.

A sob tore from her throat, and tears ran down her face as she leaned back against the door. Every cell of her body wanted her to mate him, but how could she when watching him turn into a cold manipulative asshole would tear her heart out. It wasn't worth it, and it never would be.

After peeling herself away from the door, she stumbled into the bathroom and turned on the shower. She didn't bother to undress before she got under the spray.

The water landing on her face from the shower seemed to break a dam within her, and she let her tears run freely as wrenching sobs almost choked her with their intensity.

Why couldn't she have met a human man like Callum? She would have been able to mate him without him turning into her warden. But that wasn't possible anymore. Her body and mind wanted only one man, a man who could make her body sing for him with mind-blowing pleasure. A man whose face and body were at the top of her new scale of gorgeousness, and nobody else would ever measure up, even if she had been able to consider someone else. Which she couldn't. Not after meeting her true mate.

∞∞∞

Callum stared at the ceiling without seeing it. A simmering pain had settled in his chest after Vamika suddenly ran off, but he was trying to talk himself into being optimistic about what had happened and treat it as a step on the way to winning his true mate. Because there was no doubt about it, he needed Vamika to become his mate. He couldn't live without her.

Her fire was magnificent and addictive, and he definitely wanted to explore that side of her, but it was only one aspect of the person she was beneath the fear and anger. She had an enormous capacity for love if she would just let her guard down a little. He had seen it in her eyes. But something held her back. Something she had experienced in the past had shut her off and made her pull away from other people. And he wanted to know what had happened to her to make her react like that. It wasn't something trivial, and he hated the fact that someone had hurt her.

Perhaps he should ask Henry about it. Her alpha might know her background, or enough of her background to be able to point him in the right direction. But before he talked to Henry, he wanted to try to get some answers from Vamika herself. It felt more honest to talk to her directly instead of asking her alpha about her.

Callum sighed and turned to look out the window. Dawn was approaching, and he didn't think he'd be able to get any more sleep. Not with his mind and body in turmoil. His dick was like granite, still wanting to continue where they had stopped when Vamika ran. And his mind was a mess of elation, doubt, hope, and anger. And awe of the amazing woman who was his true mate.

Sitting up, he looked down his body. He'd never had anyone admire him the way Vamika had. If the heat radiating from her eyes had been any hotter, he would have burst into flames within seconds. Talk about devouring someone with your eyes. She had done that to him, and not for a second had his weak leg made her flinch or caused the fire in her eyes to cool.

Of course he had been lying down or sitting on his heels the whole time, but still. Shifter women didn't forget his disability. Once they had seen how one leg was less muscular than the other, they couldn't unsee it.

Which was just further evidence that it wasn't his leg that was the reason why Vamika didn't accept him as her mate. And he didn't think it had anything to do with sex. If that had been the case, she wouldn't have let him touch her. No, it was something else, and it had something to do with her not wanting to be owned, whatever that meant to her.

He'd have to get her to talk to find out what had

happened to her that was so bad she had rejected him before she had even talked to him. But he wasn't sure how to persuade her to talk to him. He needed a plan, and it had to be a good one.

CHAPTER 8

They were all gathered around the large kitchen table for breakfast. Callum's eyes kept going back to Vamika, who was seated directly across from him at one end of the table. Leith and Sabrina had set the table and told everyone where to sit, so it seemed he had at least a couple of allies in his quest to win his mate.

Because that was what it had turned into for him. At one point he had been resigned to give up his true mate altogether, but that was before their encounter during the night. He had to win her because he wasn't ready for that to be the end of it. He needed more, preferably a lifetime's worth.

She hadn't said a word to him so far this morning, only given him a small nod of acknowledgement when he said good morning. But her eyes had widened before she quickly looked away, and he had taken that as a good sign. What they had done was obviously still vivid in her mind, and it was affecting her just like it was him.

"Bryson called this morning." Leith's voice sounded from the other end of the table, and Callum turned his head to look at him. "The man killed during mating was a panther, an alpha panther living in a cottage close to where the couple was found. There is still no confirmed ID for the woman as far as Bryson has been able to find out."

Callum nodded slowly. "I can check the system after breakfast to see if there's any new information about the woman, but finding out who she was is unlikely to help us find Ambrosia. If this is anything like what happened to Steph, the shifter is probably the one responsible for tricking the woman into mating him. Although there was no evidence at the scene to indicate that she was forced, so there's reason to believe that she agreed to the mating. Unless Ambrosia mind-fucked her, but I really hope that wasn't the case."

Several of the people around the table flinched at his harsh words, and he had no trouble understanding why. But Ambrosia had turned out to be much worse than he first believed, and there was nothing he would put past her at this point in her mission to kill shifters.

"Mate." Sabrina's eyes widened before her head snapped around to look at Leith. "I just remembered something Ambrosia said after killing Freddie."

Leith's whole body tensed, clearly remembering what Ambrosia did to Sabrina after Freddie was killed.

Sabrina grabbed Leith's hand and squeezed it as she gave him a small smile. "She said something about beasts, as in shifters, using the excuse that you're their mate. And then she went on to say that when you finally think your daughter is safe, they come for her as well. Do you see?"

Leith's eyes widened in understanding. "Ambrosia has a mate. She is or has been mated to a shifter."

"Holy fuck!" Duncan's exclamation made the rest of them nod in agreement. "There's some poor fucker out there mated to that bitch. Talk about choosing the wrong woman to mate, because there's no way they can be true mates with her acting like this."

"I agree." Leith nodded. "And it makes me wonder where her mate is. Based on her words and her attitude, she hates him, and that might be one of the reasons for her hiding her identity and her whereabouts. She is hiding from him."

"Or." Jennie cocked her head. "She's keeping him locked up or incapacitated somewhere. Would her power work on her mate?" Jennie looked at Steph before swinging her gaze to Sabrina.

The blond witch bit her bottom lip, and her eyes widened in shock or surprise, or perhaps embarrassment judging by the heightened color to her cheeks.

Leith's head tipped forward like he wanted to hide his expression, but not before Callum saw the way his lips twitched like he was trying to stop himself from bursting out laughing.

"Sure." Sabrina's voice was a bit high-pitched, and she cleared her throat before continuing. "It would, but usually a witch's power over someone will lose its effect if the distance between them increases beyond a couple of hundred yards. The distance depends on the witch, but the point is she wouldn't be able to travel around and keep him under some kind of spell at the same time. She'd have to tie him up or keep him stationary using other means than her power."

"So he's her prisoner." Trevor frowned. "And it doesn't sound like finding him will help us. He's already been overpowered by her. I don't know how much help he would be, unless he knows something about her that will enable us to stop her."

"He doesn't deserve to be kept prisoner like that, though." Julianne's brows pulled together in thought. "Or perhaps he does. We don't know anything about him. Maybe he's part of the reason Ambrosia wants to build her power and kill all shifters. That might be what she meant when she spoke about using an excuse that you're their mate. He might be a cruel and manipulative asshole, and she's better off without him."

"I wouldn't be surprised." Vamika's muttered words made Callum frown as he turned to look at her, but her head was tipped forward, and she didn't meet his gaze. He wanted to know what she'd meant, but it would have to wait until after breakfast. None of the others seemed to have noticed she made a comment. It might not even have been her intention to say it out loud.

"We need a picture of Ambrosia to show to the shifters we've been talking to." Duncan turned to him. "Do you think you can try again to find a photo of her?"

Callum turned to Duncan, who was sitting next to him, and nodded. "I'll try, or we could get someone to make a drawing of her based on a description. There are people who are really good at that. I can't draw for shit, though, so it won't be me."

"Marna." Jennie's voice sounded excited. "My friend Marna is amazing at drawing people, faces in particular, and she's seen Ambrosia, even if it was at a distance. I'm sure she'd be happy to do it."

"Perfect." Callum smiled at the blond American woman, who had turned out to be Trevor's true mate. "Call her. The sooner the better."

Jennie nodded. "I will. But they're back in America now, and she's one of those people who refuses to keep her phone on at night because she hates to be disturbed when she's asleep. Unless it's Carlos disturbing her. I think she's all right with that. I know I am when my mate needs me." She turned to Trevor, and the wicked grin he gave his mate was enough to make Callum turn away.

What people were saying about new mates was true. They seemed to be glued to each other's side and disappeared for hours at a time obviously fucking like bunnies in heat. The last few days he'd been living in the middle of it, and although it hadn't bothered him in the beginning, it had been driving him crazy since Vamika rejected him, and he thought he'd never experience the same. But Callum had changed his mind about his future. He would convince Vamika to be his somehow, but first he needed to find out what was preventing her from accepting him.

Callum studied the black-haired beauty sitting across from him. "Vamika, would you mind helping me after breakfast?"

Her eyes were wide when they snapped to his. "Um, I..." She visibly swallowed, before sitting up straighter. "How can I help you? I don't know anything—"

"You can help me check some footage I've gathered to see if we can find a picture of Ambrosia." He smiled at her. Good thing he'd brought another laptop. Leith probably had a computer they could borrow, but Callum had a feeling his own was better.

Frowning, Vamika swung her gaze around to look at the others sitting at the table. "Wouldn't it be better if someone else who's better with computers helps you?"

Julianne shook her head firmly. "Nope. We're all busy. But we need a photo of her. I hope you can find one."

Callum did a mental fist pump and made a mental note of thanking Julianne later. His friends were obviously trying to help him, and it served to remind him how special these people really were.

"Okay." Vamika's frown deepened as she stared at Julianne before turning to meet Callum's gaze. "I guess I'll be helping you then."

***

Callum grinned at her like he'd just won the lottery, and Vamika wanted to yell at him for tricking her into spending time with him like that. She couldn't refuse to help him, and he knew it. It was true they needed a photo of Ambrosia, and Vamika would be able to recognize the woman after meeting her twice.

And she wasn't as bad with computers as she'd let on. It was one of the ways she'd been able to connect with people and discover the world while she was still living with her parents' pack. She'd been restricted in her physical movements, but online she could do whatever she wanted because she was good at hiding what she did.

After clearing off the table and putting the breakfast dishes in the dishwasher, she followed Callum down to the living room. They would probably have been more comfortable sitting at the kitchen table, seeing as Leith didn't have an office, but Callum insisted the others needed the space and that there would be less people to disturb them in the living room.

She didn't buy it, but the others seemed all too eager to back up his arguments. There was no doubt they were all determined to see Callum happily mated, but she wasn't going to let them destroy the rest of her life by trapping her in a mating from hell. Even though she had trouble seeing Callum as an abusive person who didn't care about other people's feelings. But that was how most women were lured into mating, wasn't it? By letting themselves be convinced the man wooing them actually cared about them.

Callum went over to his bag and pulled out a second laptop. After placing it on the coffee table next to the one he was using, he lifted his gaze to hers. "How much do you know about computers? I assume you've used one before."

She nodded. There was no point lying to him. He'd realize soon enough that she had some experience. But it might be a good idea to downplay what she could do. "I know the basics, I suppose."

"Great." His lips stretched into a smile, and she looked down at the computer to avoid drowning in it.

"Does it have a password?"

He nodded. "Yes. I'll log in. Then I can show you some of the camera footage I collected from Inverness and the surrounding area based on the location of

Ambrosia's phone. I've looked through some of it, but I haven't had time to go through all of it yet. And it didn't seem worth spending time on considering everything else that happened. The footage I reviewed didn't give us any relevant information as to where she is staying or what her plans are apart from what we already know, and there was no clear view of her face."

She glanced at him before looking back down at the laptop. "Okay. So, all you want me to do is to find a decent image of her, is that it? Or is there anything else you want me to keep an eye out for?"

"Well, anything you notice that can help us find her is, of course, valuable, like people she talks to or places that seem to be of relevance to her. If you're in any doubt whether it might be relevant or not just ask me and we can have a look at it together."

Vamika nodded but didn't lift her gaze to look at him. Every look was tearing at her determination to keep him at a distance. His voice had the same effect on her, but that was more difficult to avoid. She couldn't exactly tell him to shut up.

He logged onto the laptop before moving over to let her take her place in front of it. "It's downloading the video files from my file server at home at the moment. It'll probably take a few minutes." He leaned toward her and pointed at the screen, and she flinched as his delicious scent hit her directly in the nose. Her channel clenched, and heat started simmering low in her belly. The mating bond was getting more insistent. Sitting next to her mate was going to be torture if he didn't keep more of a distance.

"Callum!" His name came out more forcefully than she had intended, and his head snapped around to face her, putting his lips no more than two inches away from hers. And those eyes. His beautiful brown eyes were staring into hers, making her want to mate him just to make sure she would be able to stare into those eyes every day for the rest of her life.

"Vamika." Her name was spoken in a deeper voice than before. "Are you all right?"

It took everything she had to turn away from him, and she did it so abruptly that her braid whipped around.

A groan made her freeze until she felt him tugging on her braid, and he whispered something under his breath that she didn't catch.

"What did you say?" She slowly turned her head back to look at him.

"I love your hair." The words were barely understandable his voice was so rough, and his eyes burned with a heat that rivaled what she'd seen in them the night before when he was well on his way to an orgasm.

She could only stare at him with wide eyes while he wrapped her braid slowly around his hand until his fingers brushed her neck. He then tugged a little and cocked his head as he speared her with glowing eyes. "I want to kiss you."

Vamika wasn't sure what it was about the situation that turned her on the most. The molten heat in his eyes, the moderate pain he was inflicting, or the control he had over her by keeping her locked in place.

Pulling in a shuddering breath, she shook her head with the tiny movements allowed by his grip on her hair. "No." The word came out weak.

"Please." His gaze dropped to her lips. "Just one

kiss."

She fisted her hands in her lap and pulled in another deep breath as need pulsed through her. "No." Her voice was firmer this time. "Let go of my hair."

He squeezed his eyes closed, and his jaw tensed like he was fighting serious pain. It was an expression that didn't belong on his beautiful face, and she winced when her heart squeezed painfully in her chest.

Vamika was just opening her mouth to tell him she was sorry, when he let go of her hair and rose from the couch. Without another word, he walked away from her and disappeared down the stairs.

"Oh, Callum," she whispered, and her chin dropped to her chest as she closed her eyes against the pain in her chest. She wanted to run after him and throw herself into his arms. Promise him forever and watch as joy and heat lit up his eyes. Her desire to soothe his pain and make him happy was almost enough to make her ignore the consequences.

But some sense remained in her tortured mind. *Thank God.* It was hard to picture Callum as anything other than caring and protective, but she'd seen it happen before. Andrew had seemed decent and attentive, even patient, for several months. But when she turned away from him because she didn't have any romantic feelings for him, he started to change. Gone was the decent and patient man he had been, and he started acting like their mating was inevitable.

And that was when she found out her father had promised her to him. To Andrew. Like some piece of meat, her father had gifted her to Andrew, the son of a successful businessman in another pack her father felt would be beneficial to have a family tie to. It was the day she fled and never looked back, and the day she promised herself never to mate a shifter.

Pulling in a deep breath, she lifted her chin. There was no point sinking into destructive memories. It only brought her down, but it was also a good reminder of why she couldn't mate Callum. No matter the pain of staying away from him, the pain after mating him and watching him change would be worse. She needed to keep that at the front of her mind.

Her gaze found the computer screen and the list of video files that was waiting for her. And she dived into the work, eager to focus on something else than Callum and the pain that had been so clearly marked on his face.

CHAPTER 9

Callum walked along the beach as he cursed his own stupidity. He knew Vamika was still trying to keep her distance from him, even though she had lost that battle for a little while during the night.

His intention with getting her to help him checking the camera footage was to spend time with her alone to get to know her a little better. They hadn't really talked to each other at all so far. The interaction between them had mainly consisted of arguing or touching without many words spoken.

But it hadn't taken more than the feel of her hair against his arm, and he had lost it. Her hair was beautiful and an absolute turn-on, but instead of clamping down on his urge to touch her hair, he had let it make him forget his main goal. Begging her to kiss him had been a mistake, and a mistake he undoubtedly would be paying for by her pushing even further away from him.

"Fuck!" Callum kicked off his shoes as he

approached the water. His shirt landed on the sand just as he reached the water's edge. Hopefully, a swim would calm him down and take care of his throbbing erection, which was threatening to poke a hole in his shorts. Wrapping her hair around his hand had filled his cock so fast he was surprised there hadn't been a sound effect to accompany the change. But he needed his desire to cool so he could go back and resume his plan to get to know Vamika, in a friendly and non-sexual way.

The cold water was refreshing but not as calming as he'd hoped. He was still sporting a semi when he walked back to the house with his shirt draped strategically over his forearm to hide his condition from anyone who happened to look his way.

Ascending the stairs, he prayed Vamika was still there. It was no more than twenty minutes since he'd left, but that was plenty of time for her to leave and find something else to do. And that would make it harder for him to find another good excuse to convince her to spend time with him alone again. The others had proven helpful in that respect earlier, but there were only so many chances he would get before his excuses would wear thin.

To his delight and relief Vamika was still in the living room. She was staring at the screen of the laptop without so much as a twitch to her lips to show that she'd noticed him walking into the room.

He opened his mouth to say something, only to close it again when he thought better of it. There were other ways to draw her attention, even if it went against his intention to get to know her in a way that wasn't based on sexual need.

After stopping just three feet from the coffee table across from where Vamika was sitting, he undid the tie at the waist of his shorts before pulling the wet garment slowly down his thighs. He didn't look at her directly but made sure to keep her face in his peripheral vision.

Callum wanted to cheer when her eyes snapped to his groin and widened as his cock sprang free. It was no longer just semihard, and under his mate's gaze, it soon turned harder than granite. It would be uncomfortable sitting down to work with his throbbing cock demanding attention, but it was worth it for the heat in his mate's eyes.

His balls pulled up tightly to his body, screaming at him to do something to release some of the pressure, but they would just have to deal. He wasn't going to touch himself in front of her. All he wanted was for her to know how turned on he was, because if she was anything like him, and from what he'd observed the night before he believed she was, knowing that he was horny as hell made her hot for him as well. And he wanted her hot for him. He was hoping she'd give in and make the first move, because if she did, he'd be there for it. But until then he was going to work alongside her as planned.

He stepped out of his shorts before strolling over to his bag. After finding another pair of shorts, he took his time pulling them on. There was no hiding his hard cock straining the fabric, but then that wasn't his intention either.

He didn't bother with a shirt. Vamika liked his body, not just his dick. She hadn't been able to hide that fact with the way she had been ogling him. And he was going to take advantage of that. It would give him less means to hide his erection if someone else paid them a visit, but he'd make do with the laptop. It was big enough to hide his tenting shorts, at least if they didn't come too close.

Sitting down on the couch next to Vamika, he made sure to leave a decent gap between them. He didn't want to provoke her into leaving, seeing as she hadn't run away yet. She had reacted to him leaning toward her earlier, even though he'd had no other intention than to point out the files being downloaded. So, he would be careful not to do that again.

Callum turned his head to look at her with what he hoped was a neutral expression. "How are getting on? Have you found any good footage of her we can use to pick out a still?"

She visibly swallowed before answering him. "Not yet."

"That's fine. I'm sure we'll find something soon." He gave her a pleasant smile, even though she didn't look his way. A smile could often be heard in a person's voice, and he wanted to come across as happy and relaxed. He wasn't relaxed in any sense of the word, but he'd pretend to the best of his abilities.

"Which videos have you watched so far?" Callum looked at the files listed on his screen, the same ones he had downloaded onto the laptop Vamika was using.

She changed her position a little, and he couldn't help noticing the way she squeezed her thighs together. Either she needed to pee, or her girly parts were giving her hell, and he was betting on the latter being the case.

"I started at the top and am on the fourth one

now." Her voice was a little breathy, and he had to look the other way to hide his grin.

Taking a deep breath, he managed to force his face back to normal. "Okay, I'll start at the bottom of the list then."

They worked in silence for ten minutes until Vamika turned to look at him. "Um, Callum, what do you make of this?"

He looked up just in time to see her eyes dip to his lap for a second before they rose to meet his gaze a little wider than before. "What are you looking at?" Swinging his gaze to her screen, he had to clamp his jaw shut not to grin at her reaction to seeing his shaft still standing proud.

She squirmed in her seat, and he bit the inside of his cheek to stop himself from laughing with glee. He wanted her to ache for him, and she clearly was. He just hoped it wouldn't take too long before she acted on it. And hopefully before she got pissed off and left. But that might be too late already.

"Why are you doing this to me?" Her voice was a low snarl.

His eyes widened as they snapped to hers. "I—" His voice choked off as she suddenly leaned into him, and a hand crawled up inside his shorts along his inner thigh. The thigh that wasn't as muscular as the other one.

"You're making this impossible." Her eyes were narrow with fury, but there was no mistaking the desire in them. "But perhaps you enjoy being hard all the time."

Her hand was an inch from reaching his balls. Putting the laptop on the seat beside him, he slid a little down in his seat and widened his legs to give her better access. He couldn't for the life of him find his voice, but he kept his gaze on her blazingly beautiful brown orbs.

Callum was aware that he was putting himself at risk exposing his balls to her like this, but he didn't think she wanted to hurt him. That wasn't why she had refused to become his mate.

Vamika's hand closed around his balls, and his whole body jerked at the sensation. Her soft hand caressed them gently, making his cock throb with anticipation of release. He was so turned on he might actually come from having his balls fondled. That would be a first.

His chest started vibrating with a low growl as he was getting desperate for her to touch his massive erection. He needed to come more than his next breath, and if Vamika didn't touch his straining shaft soon, he would have to do it himself.

Without warning she let go of him and pulled her hand out of his shorts, and he couldn't help the little whine of disappointment that escaped his lips. He was so close he could practically taste his release. One firm stroke and he'd go off like a rocket.

"I think we should get back to work. You like working under pressure, don't you?"

Vamika's angry voice made him freeze with his hand in the air two inches from his swollen shaft. He'd been about to take care of his own desperate need, but her words stopped him and made him groan with regret.

"I'm sorry." He only had himself to thank for his condition. His mission to drive Vamika crazy with desire had backfired, and she was right to put him in his place. "I'm a dick for using the need we both feel to try to make you give in to me."

Her eyes widened in surprise for a second before her expression changed to one of determination. She grabbed his hand and stood. "Come with me."

"What?" Callum looked up at her with a shocked expression. He had no idea why she wanted him to follow her. "I can't go anywhere looking like this." Gesturing to his groin, he winced at the tightness in his balls.

"No one's going to see you." She tugged on his hand as she took a step back. "Please come."

He groaned at her choice of words. *Oh, I'd love to.* After easing himself up off the couch without poking a hole in his stomach, he let Vamika lead him down the stairs and to the bedroom she was staying in.

He felt his eyes widen and his heart rate speed up at what her bringing him to her room might mean. "Vamika, what—"

"Sssh." She turned to him and shook her head after closing the door behind them.

"But—"

"No." She shook her head again before putting her hands on his chest and pushing him against the wall. "Don't say anything."

Her hands gripped the waistband of his shorts and pushed it down his legs to expose his engorged shaft. It was still throbbing like it had its very own heart, and it wouldn't take many strokes of her hand before he lost it.

He shuddered and groaned when her delicate hand closed around him; well, closed was stretching the truth a bit. Her hand wasn't big enough to reach around his girth.

Vamika bit her bottom lip as she slid her hand slowly up his length to the head. Using her thumb, she caught a drop of precum that had leaked out and smeared it around the rim.

A shiver raced through him at the feeling, and she tipped her head back and stared up at him with a small smile on her full ruby-red lips and tenderness in her dark-brown eyes.

His jaw dropped open as he took in the extraordinary beauty of his mate. She was a dark goddess, and nobody would ever be able to compete with her when it came to beauty.

"I love you." The words were out of his mouth before he could stop them. It was too early for him to tell her that, but they were already out there, and he couldn't take them back.

Her eyes widened in shock, but before he had a chance to explain she bent and wrapped her lips around the head of his cock.

All coherent thoughts seized as he stared at the back of her head as she took as much as she could of his length into her hot wet mouth. Her hand squeezed the base of his cock before she flattened her tongue against him and lifted her head until only the head of his shaft was still inside her mouth.

It was too much. Just knowing that his cock was in her mouth was too much. Her other hand closed around his balls just as she tightened her lips around him, and that was it for him.

His orgasm tore through him, and he roared as wave after wave of pleasure rolled through him as his shaft pumped his seed into his mate's hot mouth. His knees buckled, and he would have landed on his face on the floor if Vamika hadn't supported his weight.

By the time his orgasm faded, he was wheezing to pull air into his starving lungs, and he was slumped against the wall with his arms around Vamika.

His amazing mate was in his arms. He was the luckiest man on earth. His chest practically sang with joy, and his grin was a mile wide. She'd finally accepted him, and he would do everything in his power to make her happy.

Transferring more of his weight onto his own shaky legs, he straightened a little to take his weight off Vamika. He'd never come that hard in his life, and he couldn't wait to experience it again. But that would be after he had given his mate all the pleasure she could possibly take.

Callum tightened his arms around her and bent his head to whisper into her ear. "Now it's your turn, baby girl."

Her hands pushed into his chest, and he loosened his hold on her and lifted his head to smile down at her.

She was frowning up at him, and he was just opening his mouth to ask what was wrong when she spoke. "Please leave, Callum."

His jaw dropped open, and he jerked like she had just hit him, pain cutting through his body. *Had she just said... No.* "What?"

Closing her eyes, she sighed. "Please leave. I would like some time alone."

"But." He stared down at her tight expression. "Aren't you... I mean, don't you want me to—"

"No." Her eyes snapped open, and she stared straight into his eyes. "I don't." She shrugged out of his arms and took a couple of steps back away from him.

All he could do was stare at her. He didn't know what to say. His heart lurched painfully in his chest, and he winced as his chest tightened in response and made it hard to breath.

She crossed her arms over her chest and nodded at the door. "I told you to leave."

He wasn't sure what happened next until he found himself kneeling on the floor just a few steps outside her bedroom door. Somehow he'd managed to pull up his shorts and walk out the door, but he hadn't gotten far before he had collapsed. His breathing was still labored, and the pain in his chest had intensified into a regular sharp stab with every beat of his heart.

Vamika still didn't want him, and she probably never would. He had failed on all counts, and instead of pulling her closer, he'd pushed her away. She didn't even want him to pleasure her, even though she had let him and enjoyed it the night before. He wasn't sure exactly what had changed since then, but something clearly had, or she wouldn't have told him to leave.

He struggled to his feet, his whole body feeling numb except for the pain in his chest. There was no possible way he could stay in this house anymore. It was enough of a torture to remember how she had looked when she told him to leave. Her expression had been rigid, not giving away any emotions, but it was clear enough that she had made up her mind.

It wouldn't serve any purpose to go back and try to plead with her. She didn't want him, simple as that. He didn't know why, and he never would. And what did it matter anyway? He wasn't going to see her again. He would make sure of it. If he survived this, he would leave Scotland and never return. He had some good friends there, but he would be better off alone without the constant fear of running into her.

CHAPTER 10

Vamika stood staring at the door through which Callum had disappeared a few minutes earlier. It felt like she was frozen in place, unable to move one finger or she'd crumple to the floor.

She had just torn his heart out. And it wasn't the first time, but this time was the worst. Because she was starting to think that she was wrong about him and all the shifter males in this house.

Callum wasn't like her father or other shifter males who treated their mates like servants. He was an amazing man who wanted to protect her and care for her.

The night before he had asked to pleasure her, and he had. By God, he had. But he had never asked for anything in return. He could have, and it would have been a reasonable request, but he hadn't. He had asked to kiss her, and he'd asked to pleasure her, but he'd never asked for her to pleasure him. Callum wasn't a greedy man who focused on what he wanted for himself. No, he was quite the opposite. A man who wanted to protect her and give her what she needed and wanted.

They didn't know each other well yet, mainly because she had kept him at a distance. She had been scared of talking to him, particularly after starting to suspect that he was a good man. Getting to know him would develop their attachment beyond the mating bond, and that was a risk she hadn't wanted to take. She was terrified of him turning into an asshole if they ever ended up mated, and she would be better equipped to handle that change if she didn't fall in love with him first.

Vamika's knees wobbled, and she stumbled back a few steps until her legs hit the bed. Tears blurred her vision, and she dropped to the floor by the foot of the bed as they started to overflow down her cheeks. Fear had an icy grip around her spine, and it was trying to tell her that she'd done the right thing by telling Callum to leave, and that she would be better off without a mate to control her and force her into a life of servitude and sacrifice. Like her mother, and like several other women in her pack. To watch her mate turn into a cold and controlling man wasn't something she would be able to live with.

Callum had told her he loved her. The words had shocked her to her core, and she had immediately concluded that he was only saying that to trick her into accepting him, but the way his eyes had been shining with the emotion and backing up his claim had confused her.

So she'd done the only thing she could think of to give herself time to process his words and decide on what to do. She'd taken his cock into her mouth. Which had turned out to be the completely wrong thing to do. The taste of him had made everything inside her tighten and purr for him, and it had almost caused her to give in to the temptation to accept him. Because what could be better than a life in his arms with his love surrounding her. Right?

Wrong. Her weakening resistance to him had terrified her. She had to get out of his presence to be able to come to her senses, because she was quickly losing her battle against her own desire to mate him. So she'd told him to leave. Cruelly and without explanation, she had ripped his heart out and sent him away to deal with his pain alone.

"Fuck, you're a bitch, Vamika!" The words rang in her ears, and she nodded at the truth in them. She didn't deserve a man like Callum. He was too good for her. She was a cold and broken woman who should never have been presented with an amazing true mate like him. But for him she needed to change that. Because he had only one chance at love and happiness and as fate wanted it, that was her.

Standing, she pulled in a deep breath and invited the rage that was always simmering deep inside her to come forward and take over. She was done being afraid. For so many years, she had used her fear as a shield to fend off everyone who might hurt her. Her fear had been a filter that had removed the goodness and decency in the people she met from her vision and left her seeing only their flaws. And everybody had flaws. It was part of being a person. But people were more than their mistakes and weaknesses, and some people didn't have any significant weaknesses to speak of at all. But she had made all flaws into a possible threat, fueling her fear, which in turn made everyone's flaws seem even greater.

But no more. For some reason Henry had managed to escape her fear filter almost entirely. She had no idea how. But she trusted her alpha. He was a great person, and she was coming to realize that the people in this house were just like him. Including Callum.

Swiping at her face to remove the tears, she ripped open the door and stormed up the steps to the living room. Callum wasn't there, but his laptops and his phone were still there, so he couldn't be far away.

Vamika spun and rushed back down the stairs. After yanking open the external door, she ran toward the beach. Callum wasn't on the beach, and her eyes scanned the surface of the loch as she ran. He'd gone for a swim right after she arrived the day before. Right after she had spit in his face that she wasn't there to see him. But either he had gone for a really long swim this time that put him out of sight, or he hadn't gone swimming at all.

Vamika turned and stared back at the house. Most of the current residents in the house were probably in the kitchen, unless they had gone out for some reason or were having sex. They were all newly mated couples and seemed to sneak away a lot to fuck each other's brains out. But she had never met a more harmonious group of people in her life. It was one of the things that had kept her on her toes since she'd arrived, just waiting for one of the men to blow up or act like an asshole and confirm her preconception of shifter males. But it hadn't happened, and she didn't think it would. These men were different, and there were probably others like them out there that she just hadn't met yet or that she had misjudged based on some minor flaw.

Breathing out on a deep sigh, she started walking back to the house. Callum had probably joined the others in the kitchen, but she didn't have the stomach to meet everybody at the moment. They would already know that she had hurt him again and were probably pissed off at her. And with good reason. She wouldn't be surprised if they told her to leave.

Her steps were heavy when she ascended the stairs to the living room. Callum was still not there. She was desperate to talk to him and explain, but she couldn't face everyone else. And she wanted to talk to him alone. It would be better to just wait for him in the living room. He would probably be down soon anyway to continue their search for Ambrosia, and she would talk to him then.

Vamika went over to the couch and sat down. Both the laptops' screens were locked, and she didn't have the password to unlock any of them. She couldn't continue reviewing the videos until Callum got back, but she might not have been able to concentrate on that, anyway. The pain and disbelief in his eyes when she'd told him to leave kept popping up in her mind, and she couldn't push it away. She wasn't even sure she wanted to. The pain she was feeling as a result of hurting him was nothing more than she deserved.

Close to an hour must have gone by when she heard someone coming down the stairs. The footfalls were too light to be Callum's, though, which turned out to be a correct conclusion when Sabrina became visible as she walked down the last few steps.

Vamika's heartbeat sped up in anticipation of Sabrina's anger and disappointment. It was bound to come, and she would just have to take it, as long as they didn't tell her to leave. She wouldn't go until she'd had a chance to apologize and explain to Callum. Even though it would probably sound like a lame-ass excuse for putting him through hell.

"Oh, you're here alone." Sabrina frowned. "Are you finished? Did you find a picture of Ambrosia we can use?"

Shaking her head slowly, Vamika stared at the beautiful blond woman for a few seconds while her heart started racing in apprehension. "What do you mean by, 'oh, you're here alone'? Isn't Callum upstairs in the kitchen?"

Sabrina cocked her head, and her eyes widened slightly. "No, I haven't seen him since breakfast, since you both headed down here. Did he just go upstairs? Because in that case he must've gone outside."

Vamika's heart squeezed painfully in her chest, and she jumped to her feet. Something wasn't right. She just knew it. Without looking at Sabrina, she stormed past her and took the steps upstairs two at a time.

Leith, Duncan, and Julianne were sitting on the couches by the window in the kitchen. But Callum wasn't there.

They all stared at her, and Duncan rose to his feet with his eyes narrowed accusingly like he knew what she had done to his friend. "What's wrong?"

"Callum." Her voice broke, and she had to swallow to regain her ability to speak.

"What's wrong with him?" Duncan walked toward her slowly with anger simmering in his eyes. "What did you do?"

"I…" She bit down on her explanation. She would tell them what she'd done, but first they needed to find him. "He's gone. I can't find him anywhere. We need to find him."

"Gone?" Duncan's eyes widened, and his body stiffened. "Where?"

"I don't know." Anger spiked through her and made her take a step toward the big man. "I just said I've looked everywhere. He's not downstairs, or at the beach. I thought he'd gone up here, but then Sabrina said she hasn't seen him since breakfast. We need to find him."

Leith and Julianne had come to stand beside Duncan, both looking worried.

"Fuck! When did he leave?" Duncan's eyes were narrow when he stared at her. There was no doubt as to whom he blamed for Callum's disappearance, and he was right.

"About an hour ago."

"An hour." He spit the words out. "Why didn't you tell us earlier? Have you tried calling him?"

Throwing her hands up in exasperation, she glared at him. "I just told you. I thought he was here. In the kitchen. With you. And no, I haven't tried calling him." Her shoulders sagged as her anger turned into worry. "His phone is on the table in the living room. All his stuff is there as far as I can tell."

Without saying anything, Duncan suddenly stormed past her out of the kitchen. It took her a second to react before she spun and ran after him.

He was standing on the porch right outside the door, and she stopped behind him, trying to look around him to see what he was staring at.

Duncan sighed before he turned around to face her. "He's taken my car. The keys were on the small table over there." He nodded to the hallway behind her. "It was parked behind his, so he couldn't get out. He probably just needed some time alone." His eyes narrowed on her. "What did you say to him?"

There was a chance the big man was right, and Callum just needed some space, but her gut was telling her something was wrong.

Shaking her head slowly, she stared up into Duncan's eyes, hoping he would see her concern and sincerity. "Something is wrong. I can feel it. Please help me find him."

Duncan opened his mouth to say something but was interrupted by Leith's voice sounding from behind her. "Sabrina might be able to help with that."

Vamika spun just as the woman in question spoke from where she was standing at the top of the stairs. "I'll find him. I'm sure he's fine." She smiled, and her eyes were soft with compassion.

"Thank you." Vamika breathed a sigh of relief. Sabrina would find him. Apparently she was good at finding people. Apart from Ambrosia, who was able to block Sabrina's efforts to locate her. "Can I help?"

"No." Sabrina shook her head. "I'll see if Steph is available to help. We could do with some more practice working together. Otherwise Leith can help. He knows the drill."

"Okay." Nodding, Vamika prayed it would work and that Callum was okay. Just out for a drive as Duncan had said.

Pain. All he could feel was pain.

Callum tried to pull air into his starving lungs, but all he could manage was a shallow breath. His lungs seemed unable to expand like they should.

He tried to open his eyes, but his lids wouldn't move, and he couldn't turn his head. Something was biting into his temple, but the pain of it was lost in the pain everywhere else.

His mind was sluggish like it was trying to move through thick mud. What had happened? He had obviously blacked out, but he couldn't remember why or where he was when he lost consciousness.

Focusing all his energy on his right hand, he tried to move it. But there was no response. He couldn't even feel his right hand. Was it even there anymore?

Fear seized him in a tight grip, and he would have screamed if he'd been able to. He already had a weak leg, and it had made his life a living hell at times. He couldn't lose a hand as well. They would all look at him with disgust, think he was useless. Even his mate. She didn't want him for some reason, but she'd never looked at him with disgust. But she would. Like everyone else.

The small shallow breaths he managed couldn't sustain his increased heart rate, and darkness crept into his mind, threatening to pull him under again. His sensible self was telling him to calm down, but fear was choking him unlike anything he'd felt since he was a kid.

"You've made a right mess of yourself, haven't you?"

The voice cut through his fear, somehow stopping the full-blown panic attack he was entering into. It sounded familiar, but not like someone he knew well. But he was unable to look or ask to find out who was talking to him.

"I'll get you out of there. Perhaps your corpse can be of some use to me."

If he hadn't been unable to move already, he would have frozen in place when he suddenly realized who was there.

Ambrosia. The voice belonged to none other than Ambrosia. Was she the one responsible for his mangled body?

"A shame with your car. It was a beautiful machine."

Car.

And just like that it all came flooding back. Vamika telling him to leave. Getting into Duncan's car. Putting his foot down to get as far away as possible. A deer in the road. Swerving before shooting off the road at high speed. Rolling. Blackness.

Fuck, he'd totaled Duncan's car. Callum would buy him a new one, of course, but that wasn't the point. He hadn't asked to borrow it.

"This wreck filled with your blood might be a suitable present for your mate, I think. An appropriate payback for ruining the perfect mating I had planned for her."

No! His lungs seized. How did Ambrosia know Vamika was his mate, and what did she mean she'd had a mating planned for Vamika?

Unless...Ambrosia thought he was someone else. She thought he was Duncan. Wow, he must look bad if she couldn't even tell them apart. Although she might not have paid enough attention to remember what Duncan looked like. But she clearly knew who owned the car.

Metal screeched, and something moved against his leg. There was no pain, just a sense of movement, which could be a good thing or a bad thing. There was no doubt he was severely injured. It was more a question of what kind of injuries he had sustained. He could heal from almost anything within a relatively short time, but he couldn't regrow lost limbs.

A hand curled around his neck, and he would have flinched if he could. The thought of Ambrosia touching him was unnerving to say the least.

"Hmm, you're still alive. I guess you can thank your shifter physiology for that. I've never seen breathing raw meat before. Make that canned raw meat." She chuckled, making his stomach lurch and threaten to empty itself. Or perhaps that was just a delayed reaction to the accident.

The woman was creepy, and apparently she liked talking to herself. Because he didn't think she realized he could hear her. That there was a consciousness within the raw meat, as she so eloquently put it.

"Well, this is going to hurt."

It was all the warning he got before the structure pinning him in place was ripped apart, and with it what felt like pieces of his body. The pain that had been intense before tore through him before dumping him into blackness.

CHAPTER 11

Vamika stared at Sabrina and Steph where the two witches were sitting on the floor facing each other. Their eyes were closed, and their faces were tense with concentration. They had been sitting like that for almost ten minutes, and Vamika was getting restless. Her hands were clammy, and her heart was racing, and it was all because her gut was telling her that something was wrong with Callum.

Her mate wasn't simply out driving. Something had happened to him. Something bad. She could almost taste his pain, even though she couldn't feel it directly. He was hurt and needed help.

"What's taking so long?" She spoke the words under her breath.

Leith was sitting beside her, and on hearing her talking to herself, he leaned a little closer and spoke in a low voice. "It usually takes a few minutes to connect, after which they need to zoom in to the exact location. If he is on the move, it can take a little longer."

Vamika took a deep breath before she nodded and turned to look at Leith. "Thank you. I'm just worried."

She wasn't just worried. She was about to have a full-on panic attack if she didn't get any answers soon. Callum needed her. He needed all of them.

This was all her fault. He wouldn't have left if she'd accepted him and treated him like the amazing man he was. But no, she had been too caught up in her fears to see he was different. That he was perfect for her, just like Henry had said he would be.

Sabrina breathed out a deep sigh and let go of Steph's hands, and Vamika was halfway over to her before Leith stopped her by gripping her upper arms from behind.

"Slow down, Vamika. Let them catch their breaths."

She wanted to shout at him to let her go, but instead she stood still and tried to breathe through the anxious tension in her body. These people were doing all they could to help. And not just for her sake. Callum was their friend. They cared about him. Some of them had been Callum's friend for years.

Sabrina turned her head, and her gaze was unreadable when their eyes met. Whatever the witch had discovered wasn't good.

"No." Vamika breathed the word before her voice broke on a sob. This couldn't be happening. She'd just found him. She couldn't lose him already. "Please tell me you found him."

Frowning, Sabrina visibly swallowed. "We have an approximate location, and he seems to be stationary."

"But?" Vamika wanted to run over to the blond woman and shake the answers out of her, but she held herself in check. "There's a but."

Sabrina nodded. "His power signature is weak like he's seriously injured."

"I knew it." Tears welled in Vamika's eyes. "We have to leave immediately." She spun and was on her way to the entrance when Sabrina spoke in a firm voice behind her that stopped her in her tracks.

"Or someone is blocking our access to him. A combination of the two is also possible."

Vamika swallowed hard as her veins filled with ice. Then she slowly turned until she could meet Sabrina's steady gaze. "Ambrosia?"

Sabrina gave a short nod. "Most likely."

Fear so icy it made her gasp for breath gripped her body. Callum was suffering at the hands of Ambrosia, and knowing what she was capable of...

Her knees hit the floor when her legs buckled. She was cold and shaking uncontrollably, her life suddenly meaningless if Callum wasn't in it. But worse than that was the pain he was suffering at the hands of the witch until she finally decided to end his life.

There was only one thing Vamika could do. Callum had endured enough in his life, and he wasn't going to suffer any more if she had anything to say about it.

Fisting her hands at her side, she got to her feet as she stared at Sabrina. "Tell me where I should start looking for him."

Sabrina gave her a short nod. "I'll show you on a map."

After bringing out her phone, Sabrina brought up the map and pointed at Loch Lochy, located between Leith's house and Fort William. "Somewhere in this area on the eastern side of the loch. Perhaps as far north as the middle of the loch or as far south as Spean Bridge. It's a large area to search, I know, but it's all I've got. We can try again in half an hour to see if we can get a more exact location." Sabrina glanced at Steph, who nodded in agreement. "We'll stay here and call you with an update regularly."

Vamika nodded at the blond witch. "Thank you." But inside she was screaming in hopelessness. The area was too big. They wouldn't get to him in time. Asking individuals in the area was a bit tricky since it made people aware that they were looking for someone, and that kind of attention wasn't welcome. But she would do it. If someone discovered something they shouldn't, she didn't care as long as she found Callum.

"Let's go." Duncan headed toward the door, and she quickly followed.

They ended up driving two cars. Trevor and Michael were in Trevor's car, and she joined Duncan in Leith's car. Leith decided to stay with the women at the house just in case Ambrosia showed up. It was possible considering she had picked up Julianne not far from his house, and for all they knew the evil bitch could locate people using her power just like Sabrina could.

An uncomfortable silence reigned in the car. Duncan wasn't exactly impressed with the way she had treated Callum, and he was right to resent her for it. Callum was his friend, a friend who had experienced a lot of ridicule and rejection due to his disability, but her rejection as his true mate was even worse.

Vamika sighed and glanced at Duncan, who was driving before she turned back to look at the road. "We need to come up with a plan. I don't know how to find him. He could be anywhere within that large area, and we don't have time to search everywhere and talk to everyone."

Duncan glanced at her. "If he's been taken by Ambrosia, she's probably brought him to a house. Somewhere shielded from nearby houses and the road, since she wouldn't want anyone to see what she was doing. Unless she doesn't care, since she can make people forget. But as far as we know, she can only make one person forget at a time, so she'd probably want to stay under the radar as much as possible."

Vamika frowned and tried to focus on how to find her mate while pushing back any thoughts of what Ambrosia might be doing to Callum. "What about your car? He was driving your car. There must be some way we can locate it, or at least we will recognize it if we see it. Well, you will anyway. I'm not sure what it looks like. Cars don't mean much to me."

"I will keep an eye out for my car. But Ambrosia might've had the foresight to hide it. At least that's what I'd have done. Or she has left it somewhere for us to find, and she has taken him somewhere else. That would be a good way to confuse us and throw us off their scent."

Vamika squeezed her eyes shut as she tried to contain her worry. "I'm scared, Duncan. He needs us. He's hurt. I can feel it. Not the pain exactly but there's something inside me telling me that he's suffering."

Duncan nodded slowly. "It's the mating bond. Even if you haven't mated yet, the mating bond is still there. It's tying you together, and it's the reason you can feel a shadow of what's happening to him, and he can probably feel the same from you. Those feelings will only get stronger when you mate."

Vamika turned to look at Duncan. "I know some mates develop the ability to discern their mate's feelings, or at least some of them. A shadow as you call it. But I didn't expect to feel it so acutely. What I'm feeling is more than a shadow, and we're not even mated yet."

Duncan chuckled, but there was no amusement in the sound. "You're true mates, Vamika, and the rules are different for true mates. The bond between ordinary mated couples is strong, but the bond between true mates is much stronger."

Vamika nodded. It made sense, but it was still a bit scary. She had never even considered the possibility of finding her true mate. It was rare and most shifters never did. That was why shifters didn't wait around to see if their true mate would show up some day. They mated when they connected with someone, or they were forced into it like she would have been if she hadn't run. Yet she was currently staying in a house with several true-mated couples. It was unprecedented, and she wondered how it was even possible.

Fisting her hands in her lap, she scanned the road and the scenery flying by. If only they could find Callum and rescue him from Ambrosia's clutches, they might be the next mated couple. If he still wanted her after everything she had put him through since they'd met.

∞∞∞∞

Pain was everywhere. Callum couldn't remember ever being in this much pain. But then he had just been in a car accident, and Ambrosia hadn't exactly been gentle when she extracted him from the wreck.

"Ah, you're awake. About time." Ambrosia's voice was coming from somewhere to his left.

He had obviously done something to alert her to the fact that he was conscious. Or conscious might be pushing it. He was aware but his brain was foggy. And he couldn't seem to open his eyes.

"You should be happy your mate can't see you at the moment. You look a bit...damaged." She chuckled, and the sound made him shudder.

Callum gasped as his pain spiked. Apparently shuddering wasn't a good idea with his broken body.

Ambrosia didn't seem to notice. "But with the way the car looked I'm not surprised. It's a wonder you're still alive at all. I mean even shifters can't survive having their heads cut off, right? And there wasn't much keeping it attached to your body when I got there. To my knowledge surviving something like that is an impossibility. Just like it is an impossibility for a shifter to survive severe brain damage. But what do I know? I wasn't mated for very long. Well, I'm still mated. My mate just isn't around much, or should I say, I don't keep him around much. Too bad I can't kill him until I find a way to survive comfortably without him. But I will. You can trust me on that."

Callum wasn't sure why she was sharing this with him. Perhaps because she was going to kill him? But why then did she save him from the wreck at all? If what she said was true, and his head was barely attached to his body when she found him, it wouldn't have been difficult for her to separate his head from his body completely. And everyone would have thought it was a result of the crash, so there would be no need for her to find a way to dispose of his body. If she even cared about that. She hadn't at McFarquhar's Bed. They'd had to remove and bury Freddie's body not to attract attention to themselves.

Ambrosia had mentioned something about Callum being of use to her, though, and that was probably why he was still around. But what exactly she'd meant by that he didn't know. He wasn't going to help her, that was for sure. So if that was what she was expecting she would be disappointed.

Pain of another kind tore through his heart. The reason he had been out driving like a maniac in the first place. His mate had rejected him again, just when he had thought she was finally coming to accept him and perhaps even care about him.

Vamika had told him to leave, and he had lost hope that she would ever accept him. She seemed to enjoy his body but not him. And it had been fantastic to be wanted for his body, but it wasn't the main thing he wanted from his mate. He wanted her love and acceptance for whom he was. But something was holding her back, and not even the insistence of the mating bond was enough to persuade her they were meant for each other.

Callum pushed the thoughts of his mate to the back of his mind. He needed to concentrate on what to do about Ambrosia, and thoughts of his mate would only destroy his focus.

If the witch was hoping to use him against his friends, she had another thing coming. He wouldn't allow that to happen no matter how much the evil bitch threatened him. There was nothing she could do to him that would be worse than what he was already going through.

Physical pain. Check. His body was already broken.

Emotional pain. Definitely. All the pain of rejection and ridicule he had suffered throughout his life was nothing compared to being rejected by his true mate.

The only scenario he could think of that would be worse was if Ambrosia somehow managed to capture Vamika. But his friends wouldn't let that happen. They would keep his mate safe even if he was no longer around to do it himself. And there was no reason for Vamika to be sought out by Ambrosia. The witch didn't know they were mates since she thought he was Duncan, so there was no reason for her to try to use Vamika to convince him to do her bidding.

He already knew he wouldn't be able to live without his mate, but he suspected that Vamika would be able to go on without him. Otherwise she wouldn't have been able to keep pushing him away like she had.

Perhaps he could use his situation for the greater good of shifters? But it depended on him being able to find a way to take Ambrosia down. He didn't have a clear idea how to do that yet, and his brain wasn't working at an optimal level to come up with a cunning plan. But if he could stall for time until his mind could rid itself of the fogginess, he was hoping he would be able to think of a way to destroy the witch before she could hurt any more people. It might cost him his life, but perhaps he was counting on that.

Callum drew in a deep breath, noticing his lungs seemed to be working much better. That was a relief. Tightening his muscles in his right arm, he wiggled his fingers slowly. They moved, but it required a lot more concentration and energy than it should have. He had no idea how long he'd been unconscious, but he needed a lot more healing before he could hope to overpower or outsmart Ambrosia.

He sucked in another breath before trying to open his eyes again. One eye responded and opened slightly, allowing him a narrow slit to see through. It was enough to see that he was inside a structure of some kind. Light was streaming in from one window, but that seemed to be the only source of illumination in the room that he could see. He was lying on a flat surface, but he didn't think it was a bed. Judging from the hard surface he was resting on and the elevation with respect to the window, he concluded that he was lying on a table or workbench.

Turning his head had pain shooting down his spine and down his legs all the way to his toes. And he wasn't able to rotate his head more than about forty-five degrees to the side. But it allowed him to see a little more of the room he was in. It looked more like a shed than a cottage. Tools were hanging on one wall, and the walls themselves were made of rough wood. This didn't look like a place that housed people. It was a place for storage.

Ambrosia suddenly stepped into his field of vision, and he flinched at the sight of her.

"Oh, I think you recognize me." She grinned down at him, and he wanted to look away, but he didn't. "You know who I am. But I think I might've been mistaken about who you are."

She reached out and grabbed a handful of his hair and tugged. "You're not Julianne's mate, are you? But you are one of the people who found me at

McFarquhar's Bed. How is the long-haired asshole doing after suffering the loss of his mate? Is he dead yet? I certainly hope so. You're all assholes, you know. Shifters." She spat the word as she wrinkled her nose. "I will rid the earth of your kind, but you won't be around to see that now, will you? I'm going to do you a service by killing you first, but don't bother thanking me."

Callum just stared at her as she went on talking. She obviously didn't expect him to say anything, and he wasn't going to. And even if he had decided to try, he wasn't sure he had a voice to use yet.

Tuning out her rambling, he contemplated his options. He wasn't in any physical shape to fight her. So he'd have to come up with another solution. And fast. It seemed he was almost out of time.

CHAPTER 12

They had just rounded a bend when Duncan slowed the car. Vamika glanced at him, noticing he was frowning heavily.

Mirroring his frown, she turned her head to look back. "What is it? Did you see something?"

After pulling into a small gravel road, he stopped the car. "There were skid marks on the road, and one of the trees on the side of the road had some broken branches on one side. I want to take a closer look. It might be nothing, but I don't want to dismiss it before I know for sure."

"I'll come with you." Vamika opened the door and stepped out of the car. She was trying to act calmly, but her heart was racing, and her palms were clammy in apprehension of what they might discover.

They had to walk a couple of hundred yards back along the road before they reached the skid marks. Duncan was right. There were trees lining the side of the road, and one of them was missing quite a few branches on one side of the trunk. They looked like they had been snapped clean off.

The terrain on that side of the road was declining, but it wasn't steep. It was covered in trees and shrubs, but something seemed to have carved a rough path downward through the greenery recently. But whatever it had been, if it was still there, it wasn't visible from the road.

Duncan started making his way down through the shrubs, and Vamika followed a bit behind. It was slow-going through the uneven terrain and vegetation, but she could have kept pace with Duncan if she wanted to. The truth was she was weary of what they would find down there, and she preferred to hang back and let Duncan see whatever it was first.

Her eyes widened in trepidation when she heard him swear. Whatever he had found, he wasn't happy about it. And his swearing didn't sound like he was angry. It was a sound of shock or sadness, or even disbelief. And after pushing away some of the shrubs between her and Duncan, she came face to face with the reason for his swearing.

Vamika gasped, and her heart squeezed painfully in her chest when she saw the mangled wreckage of Duncan's car. Not long ago Callum had been driving that vehicle and turned it into a tangled mess of metal. His speed must have been extremely high for the car to end up in this condition and at such a distance from the road.

Duncan turned to look at her with a worried expression on his face. "He's not here. But wherever he is, he's hurt. I don't think you should come over here. It's not a pretty sight."

Vamika ignored him and made her way over to the metal cadaver that was once a vehicle. She gasped when she saw the amount of blood that was pooled in the driver's seat and smeared all over the rest of the car. Could anyone live through loosing that amount of blood? Even a shifter would be in trouble suffering that kind of blood loss. But she didn't think he was dead. She would have felt it.

Duncan was examining the damaged frame on the driver's side. "Someone used a lot of power to rip this side of the car open. And I am betting that it was Ambrosia. Callum was alive when she took him. Otherwise, why would she bother? She would have no use for a dead shifter."

Vamika sucked in a breath at Duncan's harsh words. But they were true. "He's still alive. I can feel it. But it's a miracle."

Duncan studied her face like he was trying to assess how she was really feeling. "True. Either she witnessed him fly off the road, or she saw the signs of a possible accident like I did. Whatever the reason, she decided to come down here and take a look. How she even managed to get him out of the car by herself I have no idea. She has obviously used her power, but ripping open a vehicle like this would challenge even my strength as an alpha. Trevor or Leith would be able to do it without breaking a sweat, I'm sure, but they are both exceptionally strong. And apparently so is Ambrosia."

Vamika took a deep breath to try to focus through her fear for Callum's life. They were going to get him back. They had to. But in order to do so, she had to be able to think. "I don't think Ambrosia would bring him back up to the road even if she had a car parked up there. It's a busy road and it would draw attention. I think she carried him in another direction, and with the amount of blood that's in the car, there should be a visible blood trail for us to follow."

Duncan nodded. "Good thinking. Let's find the blood and follow it. I'll call Trevor and let him know where we are and what we've found."

∞∞∞

Callum didn't attempt to move while he watched Ambrosia walk around and move in and out of his field of vision. She was talking constantly like it was a way for her to help her think, and she seemed to be happy not to have anyone question or comment on what she was saying.

But he needed to make his move soon. Her restlessness made him think she was getting ready to kill him and get out of there. She hadn't mentioned what she was planning to do next, but he wouldn't be surprised if whatever it was would hurt someone. And he was in a position to change that. At least he hoped so.

"I can help you." The words rasped through his dry throat and were barely recognizable, but at least he could speak and make himself understood and that was all he required.

Ambrosia spun and walked right up to him. "Really. And how can you do that? In case you haven't noticed, you can't even move. So how do you think you can help me?"

Callum stared straight at her without blinking. "If

you heal me, I can give you information that will help you kill all shifters."

Throwing her head back, she laughed. "Oh, that's priceless. You're going to betray your friends to help me." Her laughter cut off abruptly, and her eyes hardened as they pierced his. "I don't believe that for a second. You're way too loyal. You all are to your own kind. Not so much to humans, though. You take what you want from us without any consideration for our wishes or wellbeing. We don't matter to you because you consider us lesser beings."

She chuckled with a sneer curling her lips in disgust. "But no more. I will end that. There will be no more manipulation and taking what you want without asking first. You will all die."

He barely contained a shudder at the hatred in her eyes. At least she was consistent in what she wanted. Hopefully, he could use that against her. "I know some powerful people, and they're onto you and your plan to kill all shifters. But if you kill them first, there will be no one to warn the rest about you. I'm assuming that taking on several powerful shifters at the same time is too much even for you. But if I serve them up to you one at a time, you'll be able to kill them or use them depending on how you want to play this. I think that is a fair deal for healing me."

Cocking her head, she narrowed her eyes on him like she was considering his proposition. "I don't trust you."

Keeping his expression blank, he held her gaze. "I know. But what have you got to lose? I'm not a shifter with any significant power. You can kill me at any time, and you know it. Even if I'm healed and at my full power, I wouldn't be any match for you."

She sighed and looked away from him. "I don't play well with others. I've tried a few times, but it never really works out for me. People always end up letting me down even when they're highly motivated initially and stand to gain a lot from working with me. So, I've resigned myself to working alone, and I've come to realize that it's what I should've been doing all along."

Callum wanted to scoff at her "poor me" speech, but instead he concentrated on keeping his expression neutral. "Yeah, well, like I said, what have you got to lose? You've had some bad experiences. We've all had those. It doesn't mean you'll never have any good ones. And in my experience, those usually come along when you least expect them to." He looked away and sighed for effect but kept her face in his peripheral vision. "But suit yourself. What do I care. I don't have anything to lose anyway."

Her eyes snapped to his face and widened with surprise. "Don't you care about your life? You are all so proud of your long lifespans. Why would you just give up and throw that away? You're still young, aren't you? It's not easy to tell with your kind."

He swung his gaze back to hers. "Do you know how shifters treat those of their kind with a disability?"

She shrugged. "They're killed at birth as far as I know. Weakness is not tolerated among shifters."

"Well, congratulations." He made sure to fill his voice with bitterness. "I'm Callum. You've now officially been introduced to a shifter with a physical disability. And you can check for yourself if you want. I'm sure even with my injuries, you would be able to notice that the muscles in one of my legs are less pronounced than in the other."

Ambrosia just stared at him and didn't make any move to check that what he claimed was true. So he continued. "If you knew what I've gone through in my life, and what I'll most certainly go through for the rest of my life, you wouldn't be so quick to assume that my life is worth living. You, Ambrosia, might be the very person who can help me get the revenge I crave. The revenge I'm due. For all the hell other shifters have put me through ever since I was a kid unable to defend myself."

She continued to stare at him, but her expression was unreadable. "I don't think so. I don't think I can work with you." But her words were slow and a bit drawn out like she was still considering his proposition.

Then her eyes narrowed in suspicion. "How exactly is it that you can give me these powerful people you're bragging about?"

He gave her a deliberate small smile that didn't reach his eyes. "There are those who pretend to be my friends because of what I can do for them. I've got skills that are valuable to some powerful people."

She raised one eyebrow and crossed her arms over her chest like she didn't believe him. "Like what?"

"Hacking." He said the word like it should have been obvious. "I can hack into practically any system anywhere without leaving a trace, and retrieve or change information. I think you realize how valuable that is for people who live three hundred years and are trying to appear human."

She nodded slowly while studying his face. Her eyes were narrow with distrust, but she hadn't dismissed what he had told her.

Callum wasn't sure whether Ambrosia was good at detecting lies like some shifters were, so he had stuck to the truth, or at least a version of the truth, as much as possible. She didn't trust him, but he hadn't expected her to. As long as he could convince her to keep him around for a little longer, he might get the chance to kill her, and that was all he wanted. He would only get one chance, if he was lucky, but he would make it count.

Ambrosia pulled in a deep breath while staring at him. "I don't know. What you're saying might be the truth, but I still don't trust you."

He looked away from her and sighed. "Fine. I don't care. It's probably for the best. You're no better than them anyway. All you do is hurt people, and not just shifters. Why should I help you? It's probably better if you kill me."

"Perhaps." But she didn't move, and there was a note of uncertainty in her voice that told him she was still not ready to make a final decision.

"Fuck!"

Her swearing brought his eyes back to her face. She was looking at the wall on the opposite side of the shed where the door was probably located, like she was listening for a noise she thought she had heard. His neck wouldn't allow him to turn his head to look in that direction.

Without a last glance at him, she suddenly rounded the table he was lying on and headed toward the door. "Well, that concludes our conversation. Too bad really, it might've been interesting."

Callum wasn't prepared when something hit the

side of his face. It burned like his face was on fire, and the last thing he heard was himself screaming in agony.

CHAPTER 13

Vamika's head snapped up, and fear sent her heart racing when she heard a scream of agony from somewhere straight ahead. She had never heard Callum scream in pain before. But it was him; she was sure of it.

Before she even realized what she was doing, her legs increased their pace until she was racing through the trees. She had to get to him before Ambrosia killed him, because that was what it sounded like she was doing.

The scream abruptly cut off, and Vamika almost stumbled, her heart lurching in her chest. *Don't die! Don't die!* She was chanting the words inside her head while she pushed her legs to go faster. She had to get to him to stop Ambrosia from hurting him, and hopefully in time to save his life. He wasn't screaming anymore, and with any luck that meant he had blacked out and couldn't feel the pain anymore. Because Vamika could still feel that he was alive, but for how long would that continue to be true?

What looked like a small barn or shed became visible through the trees, and she raced toward it. But just as she was about to leave the safety of the trees to approach the structure, she was yanked back by someone grabbing ahold of her upper arm.

Her head snapped around as she snarled at Duncan. "Let me go! I need to get to him before she kills him."

He growled at her with his eyes narrowed in anger. "Running directly into Ambrosia's clutches won't help him."

Trevor and Michael caught up with them, and Trevor turned to Duncan. "Was that Callum screaming?"

"Yes, I think so." Duncan nodded and indicated the shed. "He's most likely in there with Ambrosia." Duncan shook his head with fury contorting his features.

"Well." Trevor swung his gaze to the shed and lifted an eyebrow. "There's only one way to find out. I'll go take a look through the window."

Before anyone could respond to Trevor's plan, he took off to the right for about fifty yards before he left the trees and ran soundlessly into the open. The side of the shed he was approaching didn't have any windows or doors, so there was no way for Ambrosia to spot him without leaving the shed.

Vamika yanked on her arm to try to get free from Duncan's hold on her to follow Trevor, but his grip was like a vice.

"No! It's enough that Trevor is risking his neck out there." Duncan didn't even glance at her but kept his eyes trained on Trevor as he reached the shed.

She clamped her mouth shut to stop herself from yelling at Duncan and alerting Ambrosia to their presence. Callum's life was in danger, and her whole body was screaming at her to get to him.

Trevor crept up to the corner of the shed before taking a peek around it. Obviously deciding that the coast was clear, he rounded the corner and continued silently along the wall until he reached the window. Carefully, he snuck a peek through the corner of the window before he pulled back, only to return for a second longer look. Whatever he saw made him turn and run around to the other side of the building and out of sight.

"Fuck! What does the idiot think he's doing?" Duncan let go of her arm and threw his hands in the air. "Jennie is going to kill me when I bring him back hurt."

Vamika had already started running toward the shed by the time Trevor appeared as he came back around the corner. "Ambrosia is gone," he yelled. "And Callum needs our help."

She raced past Trevor and stormed through the open door to the shed. The sight that met her almost brought her to her knees.

Callum was lying on his back on a work bench. His entire body was covered in blood, which wasn't surprising considering the state of the car. But what almost had her heart seize in her chest was the state of his face. Severe burns covered his beautiful face and the side of his head. If it hadn't been for the feeling that was telling her he was still alive, she would have thought him dead.

Vamika approached him slowly like in a daze just as

Duncan came through the door behind her and swore. "Is he still alive?" Duncan's voice was filled with shock and disbelief.

Vamika nodded but didn't turn to look at him. She kept her eyes on her mate, not wanting to look away for a second in case that would be the moment he took his last breath. She had no idea whether Callum could survive this, but she would do everything in her power to make it so. Shifters could heal from just about anything, but looking at Callum she found it hard to believe that he would ever come back from this.

His visible injuries were one thing, but there was no telling what kind of internal injuries he had suffered, and those were the critical ones. Head injuries in particular. She had heard of shifters who had died from severe brain damage, although it was rare. And with what Callum had been through, it was entirely possible he had suffered massive trauma to the brain. It was impossible to know what the accident and Ambrosia had done to him, and only time would tell if he survived. But at least he was still hanging on, and she was going to take that as a positive sign until all hope was lost.

When she came closer, she noticed the burns only covered half of his face. The other half had cuts and scratches but no burns. There was no doubt as to who had inflicted the burns. From what she had been told, Ambrosia had done something similar to Freddie, and it had killed him.

Vamika fisted her hands at her sides as fury unlike anything she had ever felt before erupted inside her. She would happily kill that woman if she ever saw her again. It was time that horrible bitch died, but before Vamika could focus on killing the witch, she had to make sure Callum got the best care she could possibly give him. Because there had to be a way to help him heal his injuries. She refused to accept anything else.

The next few minutes went by without her really noticing what was going on around her. She felt frozen in the face of all that had happened, and all she could do was stand by Callum's side with her hand on his cheek that wasn't covered in burns while she waited for the guys to get the cars. Even if Callum never fully recovered from his injuries, she would stay by his side for the rest of his life. He was hers no matter what happened from this day forward.

They managed to fit Callum in the backseat of Trevor's car with her by his side. He was lying on his back with his head in her lap and his knees bent. It was a tight fit, but they needed to bring him back to Steph as fast as possible, and none of them wanted to wait for someone to bring a larger vehicle.

According to Michael, Steph might not be able to heal Callum's head injuries. But she would be able to heal at least some of the damage to the rest of his body, and anything she could do would be vastly better than nothing.

The drive back to Leith's house seemed to take forever. Vamika was constantly checking Callum's breathing and his heart rate, fearing they would weaken or stop entirely before they arrived, but Callum's vitals stayed stable as far as she could tell. *Live! Live!* She had changed the mantra in her head to something more positive. Something that presented them with a future. It might not help, but there wasn't much else she could do for him apart from being there and holding him.

As soon as they arrived back at the house, Trevor and Duncan carried Callum inside. Michael had called ahead, so Steph was ready to start healing him as soon as they showed up.

They put Callum carefully down on the kitchen floor to allow Steph plenty of room to work her magic. But like Michael had cautioned Vamika about, Steph couldn't do anything about Callum's head injuries. Even the burns to his face were too close to his brain for Steph to take a chance on healing them.

His heart was beating steadily, and his lungs seemed to be doing a fair job. What worried Steph the most, apart from possible brain damage, was the severe damage to his throat. His body had started healing him and done a good job so far, but it was clear from the remaining tissue damage that it had been a close call. Vamika shuddered at the thought of what had almost happened. There would have been no coming back from that. She would have lost him before she had taken the time to get to know him.

Steph worked methodically to heal all the injuries to Callum's body, from his damaged throat all the way down to his toes. She spent time healing every injury she could find, except a few cuts near his heart. They were superficial and would heal by themselves as soon as the most severe injuries to his head were healed. A shifter's body didn't heal all at once. Energy was prioritized to heal the most life-threatening injuries first. Small cuts and bruises were left for later.

Vamika had a hard time keeping her hands off him while Steph worked her wonder. It was both amazing to watch what the woman could do and horrible to know that it was necessary. And Vamika felt a need to touch Callum just to make sure that his body was still warm under her palm.

Most of Callum's injuries were consistent with being in a car rolling. The only injuries that were clearly inflicted by Ambrosia were the burns to his face and head. There had been no evidence of a fire in what remained of the car.

Steph eventually sat back and lifted her gaze to Vamika. Her forehead was sweaty, and she looked exhausted. Michael had begged his mate to take a break several times, but she had refused and kept going for almost an hour until she had done everything she felt was possible for her to do.

"Thank you." Vamika met the other woman's gaze with tears in her eyes. "I will never forget what you've done for Callum and me. If you ever need anything, just tell me. I'll forever be in your debt."

Steph gave her a weak smile before shaking her head. "No. There is no debt. This is what I do, and I like doing it. It feels good to finally be able to help someone when I couldn't risk using my powers for so long. Hopefully, I've been able to do enough to help his body concentrate its energy on healing his head injuries."

Vamika nodded and let her gaze drop to Callum's face. Her mate. She wanted to let her tears fall and just fall apart. Her chest felt too tight at the moment. But she wouldn't. Not yet. Not until he got better. Or... *No!* That wasn't an option.

She swallowed hard before lifting her gaze back up to Steph. "I really hope so too. And I'm praying that his head injuries are less severe than they look."

"He could use a shower." Steph indicated the severe cuts and burns to Callum's head. "Cleaning his wounds will remove bacteria his body would normally fight easily. In his condition, he needs all the help he can get to heal."

Vamika nodded her agreement. "I'll clean him up if I can get some help to carefully place him in the shower." She swung her gaze to Duncan, who nodded back at her.

They carried him downstairs to the room she was staying in and into the adjoining bathroom. Duncan helped her remove Callum's torn clothing, and he supported her mate's body while she gently cleaned his wounds and rinsed the blood off the rest of his body.

Callum was so helpless, and it tore at her heart to see him like this. He never once showed any signs of waking up or being aware of what they were doing to him.

Vamika had to swallow repeatedly to stop herself from being overcome by tears. This was ultimately her fault. She didn't deserve to cry over Callum, but she would stay with him and nurse him back to health the best she could. After that if he told her to leave and never come back, she would. And she wouldn't blame him for it.

After drying him off, they placed him on the bed, and she tucked the covers around him. At least he was out of Ambrosia's clutches. He was safe, and she would make sure he stayed that way.

Vamika still found herself wondering how Ambrosia had come to be there right after his crash. It didn't seem likely that it was a coincidence. But the only other reasonable explanation she could come up with was that Ambrosia had followed him from this house. Taking a deep breath, she shook her head to dispel the disturbing thought. There would be time to ponder that later.

"I can stay with him if you want." Duncan was staring at her with an unreadable expression on his face when she lifted her gaze to his. "I know you—"

"No." Shaking her head firmly, she narrowed her gaze at him. "I'm staying right here."

Duncan gave her a small smile and nodded. "Good." He seemed pleased, and why wouldn't he be? It was what he had wanted for his friend all along, for her to care about him.

And if she had cared about Callum and accepted him from the start, none of this would have happened. Perhaps it was her punishment for breaking his heart. But that didn't make any sense, because Callum had done nothing to deserve this, and he was the one who was suffering the consequences.

Duncan disappeared out the door and closed it behind him, and she was left standing there a little unsure what to do. Because there was nothing she could do, except for watching over him and running for help if his condition deteriorated.

After checking his breathing again, she discarded her blood-stained clothes and rushed into the bathroom. She quickly rinsed off her body before snatching a towel and running back into the bedroom to check on Callum. He was still breathing.

She was dripping water everywhere, but she didn't care. He couldn't be left alone for long. Not in his state. While keeping her eyes on him, she quickly dried off before throwing the towel on the bathroom floor.

Vamika put on a bra, panties, and a T-shirt before sitting down on the floor next to the bed. She then put her hand on Callum's chest to be able to feel it rising and falling with his breathing.

It was comforting to feel his warm skin under her palm. As long as he continued to breathe and his body stayed warm, she could relax. Well, relax was pushing it. Her mind was still spinning with fear, regret, and hope, all mixed up and keeping her heart rate constantly elevated. She wouldn't be able to rest easy until he woke up and said he was hungry. That would be her cue to take a deep breath of relief but not until then.

While resting her head against the side of the bed, she continued to monitor his breathing. There was no way she was going to allow herself to sleep before he woke up. He might suddenly need her, and she had to be there for him if he did.

Every few minutes she lifted her head and checked for signs that he was improving or getting worse, but there was no change.

Hours went by, and she was becoming increasingly aware that his burns didn't seem to improve. They were the most obvious visible injuries on his body after Steph healed most of the others, but they didn't seem to be healing like Vamika had expected them to.

She considered asking Steph for her opinion, but she already knew there was nothing the witch could do. Callum's burns were too close to his brain for Steph to want to chance healing them. It was frustrating, but all they could do was wait and see. They had to give his body time to mend at its own pace. There was a chance that his body was working on repairing his brain at the moment, and that it was taking precedence over his skin. It was entirely possible, but it was also just a theory and did nothing to calm her.

Her body sagged against the bed, and she had to constantly pull her eyes open when they fell shut. It was dark outside, but a hint of light was telling her it was nearing dawn. It had been hours since they brought Callum downstairs, and it had been hours since she had slept or eaten. But she wasn't hungry, and sleeping would have to wait.

Vamika climbed to her feet and proceeded to stretch her cramped muscles. Next, she jumped up and down a few times to get her blood flowing again. It would help her stay awake for a little longer, but she might soon have to take Duncan up on his offer to watch over Callum. But not yet. Not until the new day was well and truly underway.

She sighed and swallowed down her tears for the thousandth time as she studied her beautiful mate lying entirely too still on the bed. He hadn't moved a finger since they had placed him there. And for every hour he didn't wake up, her hope of his recovery dimmed a little.

He should be healed already. At least enough to wake up from his unconscious state. It wasn't natural for a shifter to stay unconscious for this long. She had never even heard of it happening before. At least not with a happy ending.

Tears filled her eyes and overflowed down her cheeks when she gave in to the despair that had been trying to take over for hours. She fell to the floor beside the bed, and letting her forehead rest against his upper arm, she cried as her heart broke. She couldn't keep her emotions in check anymore. This wasn't going well. Callum was most likely dying. He was just doing it slowly. Her only consolation was that he was unconscious and couldn't feel any pain. It was a blessing, if not the blessing she had hoped for.

Vamika cried until she didn't have any more tears before lifting her head to look at him. Like she had expected, there was no change. But if he was going to die, at least he wasn't going to die alone. She was going to stay with him until his breathing ceased, and he was forever lost to her.

The bed was narrow, but she climbed up next to him. After gently moving his arm to make some space for her body, she lay down on her side next to him and put her arm around his waist. Tightening her hold on him, she rested her head on his shoulder.

She pulled in a deep breath before letting it out on a painful sob. This was how they should have been sleeping for the last few nights. They should have mated the day they met and started living their happily ever after. But by rejecting him, she had turned it into a happily never after.

CHAPTER 14

It was an amazing dream. Vamika was curled up against Callum's side, holding him tightly like she reveled in being close to him. Like she cared about him. It was glorious, and he didn't want to let it go. It was exactly what he had hoped for since he'd met his true mate.

But it was just a dream, and he needed to wake up and…well, do something. He wasn't quite sure what exactly, but something was pushing him to wake up. Telling him that it was important.

His brain was foggy, and his fight to rise to consciousness was like swimming through thick syrup. Slowly, he became aware of his surroundings, but he couldn't help wondering whether his dream still had a hold on his mind. Her small warm body was plastered against his side with her arm around him, holding him tightly.

But the more his mind cleared, it became apparent that he wasn't mistaken, and her scent was telling him that it was indeed Vamika lying next to him.

Something had obviously changed while he had been unconscious, and he was sure he had been unconscious and not sleeping. He just couldn't remember what had happened to put him under. It had to be something serious, though, because shifters didn't typically become unconscious.

It took him two attempts to open his eyes or one eye to be exact. His left eye wouldn't open. It seemed to be glued shut. In fact the whole left side of his face was stiff and unyielding, like his skin had hardened into a rigid mask that would crack if he tried to smile.

After turning his head to the right, he was able to look down at Vamika. Her head was resting on his shoulder, and he couldn't get a good look at her face from that angle, but from what he could see, she looked like she had been crying. Her eyelids were red and puffy.

His heart squeezed painfully in his chest. Someone had hurt his mate, and he wanted to know who it was so he could make sure they never did it again.

It took him a few seconds to realize she might have been crying over him. Frowning with one side of his face, he stared down at her as he evaluated whether that could be true. Was it possible she suddenly cared about him that much? It might be considering she was lying next to him and holding him, even though the last thing he remembered was her telling him to leave.

What was it that had made her change her mind about him? Something had obviously happened to him, but he couldn't for the life of him remember what. But it might explain her change of heart and perhaps the stiffness to his face. And his body feeling so weak.

Callum tried to lift his left hand, and he managed to lift it about an inch off the bed before it fell back down again when his muscles gave out. Okay, so that might explain why she had been crying over him. He had really done a number on himself or possibly someone else had. He couldn't remember.

Whatever had happened, at least he was healing. He would get better soon. A couple more hours should see him right as rain.

He felt his eye widen in shock when he noticed the light outside. Based on the section of sky he could see through the window, it was morning, and that was strange considering the last he remembered it was about midday. Had he really been out cold for almost twenty-four hours? How was that even possible? It was an extremely long time for a shifter to be unconscious, which meant that his condition might be worse than he had first thought.

Callum glanced down at the beautiful woman lying next to him. It would explain why she had been crying, though. If he was injured that badly, she might have feared for his life. He definitely would have, if it had been her lying there for hours not waking up. Just the thought made him shudder.

Focusing all his energy, he lifted his right hand and curled it around Vamika's hip. She didn't move an eyelid. She was fast asleep, most likely as a result of staying up for a long time, watching over him and crying. His mate was exhausted.

But why had he felt such an urgent need to wake up? Something had been telling him it was crucial, but the reason hadn't been presented to him.

Rotating his head, he scanned the room. He recognized it, of course. It was the one he had been staying in since he first arrived at Leith's house. Until Vamika had arrived, and he had given it to her to sleep in.

Callum looked down at Vamika again, and tightening his grip on her hip, he shook her gently. He expected her to wake up, but she didn't. Her eyelids stayed firmly closed, and her breathing didn't change as far as he could tell.

"Vamika?" His rough voice made her name sound strange, and he cleared his voice before repeating her name more firmly. "Vamika?" He shook her again, a little harder this time. Her head rolled off his shoulder and tipped back, allowing him a better look at her face.

He frowned, with the half of his face that was responsive, while he studied her completely relaxed features. But his heart rate sped up when he realized how shallow her breathing was. Up until this moment, he had thought she was sleeping heavily, but perhaps he had been wrong.

Fear for his mate helped him summon the energy to turn onto his side. It allowed him to study her more thoroughly, and his breathing almost seized at what he saw. Her skin was pale and clammy, and her lips had a blue tinge to them. He needed to do something to help her wake up. She clearly wasn't well. But he had already tried shaking her and speaking to her, and it had done nothing.

After putting his arms around her, he crushed her against him and whispered into her ear in desperation. "You have to wake up, Vamika. I'm awake, see? I'm all right. You have to come back to me. Please, baby girl.

You're mine, and I can't live without you."

Callum loosened his hold on her and stared down into her unresponsive face. Was it his imagination, or did the color of her lips look more normal than before? At least that was his impression.

"Vamika?" His voice was shaky as he stared down at her, willing her to wake up. And whether it was the sound of her name or his will that made a difference he didn't know, but her lips twitched, making him breathe a sigh of relief.

After pulling her close again, Callum smiled as he put his cheek next to hers and whispered into her ear. "I'm waiting to see your beautiful brown eyes gaze up at me. How long are you going to make me wait? I don't have all day, you know. Or night for that matter. Or perhaps I do, who knows? Anything is possible if you just wake up."

Perhaps he was foolish to expect her to suddenly accept him when she woke up. She might have been crying over him when she thought he was dying, but it might be different when he was awake.

But he wasn't going to dwell on that at the moment. As long as she woke up and was fine, that was all that mattered. She had scared him there for a minute, and he hadn't liked it. He could only imagine what she had gone through while he was down for close to twenty-four hours. Even if she didn't love him, she did care enough to cry over him, and that had to mean something.

Her sudden sharp intake of breath made him loosen his hold on her and pull back so he could see her face. She blinked a couple of times before her gaze settled on him, but it took another couple of seconds before she seemed to realize that he was gazing back at her.

"Callum." Her eyes widened before her whole face crumpled, and tears fell from her eyes. A sob racked her small frame as she buried her face against his chest, and her arm came around his waist and tightened like she needed an anchor.

Concern made his heart rate speed up. "What's wrong, baby girl? Are you all right? Why are you crying?" If she had been crying before because she was worried about him, then why was she crying when he was clearly awake and okay?

Vamika pulled her head back, and as soon as their eyes met, her face broke into a brilliant wet smile. "I'm happy, Callum. These are happy tears. I thought you might never wake up. You almost scared me to death."

She suddenly shook her head and her face fell. "I'm so sorry, Callum. I've done nothing but hurt you since we met. All this is my fault. If you tell me to leave and don't want to see me again, that's fine. I'll understand. You have every right to hate me for what I've done to you."

His one working eyebrow pulled into a frown as he listened to her blaming herself. She was right that she had tried to dismiss the fact that they were true mates, but instead of hearing her words of guilt, he wanted to know why. There had to be a reason, and whatever it was, he wanted to know.

"Stop, Vamika." He shook his head at her. "I accept your apology, and if you're waiting for me to tell you to leave, I won't. I've been waiting for you to accept me since you told me we're true mates. I could never hate you. I love you. I always will. But I really want to know why you don't, or perhaps didn't"—he lifted his brow in question—"want me."

"Didn't." She nodded as more tears leaked from her eyes, but a smile stretched her lips, and she looked happy even with her tears flowing. "I want you, but you're much too good for me. I don't deserve someone like you."

He narrowed his gaze at her with the corner of his lips pulling up in a smile. "How do you know I'm good? You don't know me yet. We've hardly talked to each other since we met. Perhaps I'm bad."

Her eyes sparkled with amusement, and she burst out laughing, surprising the hell out of him. He had briefly heard her chuckle before, but it hadn't been a happy sound. This was and it sang through his chest, making it swell with love and happiness. He wanted to hear that sound every day for the rest of his life.

His gaze dipped to her plump ruby-red lips. Moving his hand up to her neck, he started to close the distance between them. He had tasted her lips before, and it had been heaven, even if he had ended up with a bloody lip.

His gaze shot to hers when she pulled her head back. Perhaps he had been jumping the gun in assuming she wanted to kiss him, but she had said she wanted him.

She shook her head and studied the left side of his face with furrowed brows. "No kissing. Your burns are—"

"Burns?" He pulled his head back. Well, that explained the stiffness to the left side of his face and why she didn't want to kiss him. But it still stung that his face put her off that much. "I understand. Not exactly tempting to kiss me when my face is a mess."

Her eyes narrowed with a small smile curving her lips. "That's not why I don't want to kiss you right now." Her hand smoothed up his chest and continued until it curved around his neck. "Your wounds will pull, and your skin will split, and it might take even longer for you to heal. Your body has had a lot to do since your accident yesterday, and I'm happy to see that your burns are finally starting to look better. Which probably means that your more serious injuries are healed."

He held her gaze and felt himself relax. She sounded sincere, and the light in her eyes was speaking of more than friendly feelings toward him. So they had to wait a few hours to kiss until his face was fully healed. He could handle that. Maybe.

Pulling his mind away from her lips, he focused on what she had just told him. "Accident. I can't remember much from yesterday after you told me to leave this room."

She flinched at his words, but he smiled at her with the side of his mouth that was working as it should. "Can you please enlighten me as to what happened yesterday that rendered me this weak and useless?"

Vamika tightened her grip around his neck and narrowed her gaze. "You're not useless. But you were gravely injured. You don't remember driving Duncan's car?"

An image flashed through his mind, but he couldn't grasp onto it before it was gone. Shaking his head slowly, he blinked a couple of times. "No. Did I crash?"

She bit her lower lip before answering him. "That's

an understatement. You flew off the road and rolled more than a hundred yards through shrubs and trees. How you managed to miss hitting one of the trees I have no idea."

He swallowed hard as he stared into her eyes, his heart rate speeding up again. "But I didn't kill anyone?"

Vamika shook her head, and he breathed a sigh of relief. "No, you didn't. There were no signs of another vehicle being involved. Or pedestrians for that matter. You must've been going extremely fast, though, when you lost control of the vehicle."

He nodded slowly. She was probably right, but he would have liked to remember what had happened. "And the car caught fire?" His gaze swung to his hand, but the skin was smooth without any signs of burns. But that didn't really mean much seeing as they might have healed already.

Vamika sighed, and concern wrinkled her brows. "No."

His brows rose in astonishment. "Then how—"

"Ambrosia."

Shock reverberated through him, and he could feel his eyes widen when he heard the name. "She was there? Did she make me lose control of the car?"

CHAPTER 15

Vamika saw his shocked expression at the mention of the bitch's name. "We don't know if she caused your accident, but she was the one who extracted you from the wreck."

He nodded slowly, his eyes still wide with shock. "Okay. Do you know what happened next? It doesn't seem plausible that she would just let me go."

"She didn't." Vamika kept her eyes on his face and saw when he narrowed his eyes in confusion. "We found you in time and managed to scare her away. Well, at least I think that's why she wasn't there with you when we arrived."

His brows pulled down as he frowned and stared at her. "How do you know she was there if you never saw her?"

"Well." She sighed before she continued. "We didn't discover you were gone until about an hour after you left, and we had no idea where you were heading. So Sabrina and Steph did their magic thing to try to find you, and they sort of did but couldn't pinpoint your location exactly. Sabrina thought that could be due to you being badly injured or that Ambrosia was with you. Or perhaps both."

Callum nodded slowly. "That makes sense."

"And of course there's the fact that someone extracted you from that wreckage, and I can tell you that not just anyone would've been able to do that. According to Duncan even an alpha would've struggled to get to you without tools to help him. And with the amount of blood in that car, you would've been in no shape to do anything to help yourself, even if you had the shifter strength to do it." She shuddered as the image of the wreck assailed her. "It was a tangled mess of metal. I don't know how you even survived that accident at all. I'm just grateful that you did."

He smiled at her with that half smile that was all he could manage at the moment, but it was a bit strained. "So, if I understand this correctly, Ambrosia pulled me out of the wreck, and then she burned my face. I'm not sure I understand why she didn't kill me. She had the chance, and I'm a shifter, so why didn't she take the opportunity to get rid of me? It sounds like she had the time before you arrived, and it wouldn't have taken her long anyway."

His words of him being killed were enough to make her heart squeeze painfully in her chest, and she gritted her teeth against the pain. Closing her eyes for a second, she quickly pushed the possibility of him dying away from her, not wanting to dwell on what could have happened. "All that matters is that you are alive and here, and she can't get to you now. Whatever happened we might never know, but let's not focus on that. You need to concentrate on getting well."

Callum winced. "Yes well, before I start focusing on that, I have another pressing issue I need to attend to, and I think I might need your help with that."

Vamika frowned up at him, wondering what he was talking about. "Of course. Whatever you need I'll help you."

He lifted an eyebrow at her with a small smile on his face. "Bathroom?"

"Ah." She chuckled. "I'll help you. No problem. We'll get you there before you make a mess."

After getting off the bed, she helped him to sit up and put his feet on the floor. Once he was sitting, she sat down on the bed next to him and put her arm around his waist. "Okay, now put your arm around my shoulders, and don't be afraid to let me take your weight. I can handle it. I know some of you shifter guys think women are small and weak but we're really not. And it's even more true for shifter women. We can hold our own."

He grinned down at her. "I never said you couldn't." His grin reduced to a small smile that almost made him look a little shy. "But I would like to stand on my own two feet, you know? Call it pride or male ego or whatever, but it would be nice to have enough strength to at least be able to stand on my own in front of my woman."

She smiled at him, feeling her heart flutter in her chest in response to his words. *His woman.* It felt so good hearing him call her that after everything she had put him through; she had to swallow hard not to start tearing up. "Then you do the best you can, pretty boy, and I'll be right here if you need me."

His eyes narrowed at her, but the corners of his lips twitched like he was trying not to smile. "Pretty boy? That doesn't sound like a compliment. How should I take that exactly?"

Laughing, Vamika shook her head at him. "Well, you are pretty. In a male way, trust me." She made a point of dipping her gaze to his groin and licking her lips for emphasis. He was still naked, since there had seemed no point dressing him after his shower the day before. "And last I checked you were definitely male."

Callum groaned. "And I'm in no shape to prove to you just how much of a man I really am at the moment."

She laughed again. "We'll get to that, but let's get you to the bathroom first. One step at a time, you know. You still have some healing to do. Although you seem to be improving by the second."

Slowly Callum pushed up from the bed until he stood, swaying a little beside her. He had used her for support but without putting a lot of his weight on her.

"That's it. You're doing well." She smiled up at him. He looked a little pale, but other than that and the burns to his face, he was starting to look like himself again, complete with the warmth in his eyes that seemed designed to pull her to him.

He drew in a deep breath before letting it out slowly. "Yeah. Now I just have to be able to take a few steps without falling on my face."

"That's what I'm here for."

Callum chuckled, and his eye crinkled with his amusement. "To make fun of me when I fall on my face?"

Laughing, she shook her head. And a bubbling happiness spread through her chest at the fact that Callum was able to smile and joke. Just a few hours ago that had seemed like an impossibility. "No, but it would be fun to see you with your ass in the air. I mean you have a magnificent ass."

He shuffled a step forward before looking down at her with his right eyebrow raised. "Have you been checking me out?"

She nodded firmly, unable to contain the wide grin on her face. "Most definitely."

Shaking his head slowly, he looked down at the floor before he moved his other foot forward. "Good to know. And ditto by the way. Your ass is perfection, and I can't wait to grab a handful of it. But if I tried to do that right now, I'd fall on my face. And although that would show off my ass, I think I still prefer not to. I need my face to heal so I can kiss you."

"Yes, you do." Vamika nodded her agreement. She could hardly wait to taste his kiss again. "I look forward to it, and this time I promise I won't bite you."

His shuffling steps had become steadier by the time they reached the door to the bathroom. She opened the door for him and was just preparing to move through it when he stopped her.

"Vamika, I think I can handle this part by myself."

She frowned up at him, taking in the determined look on his face. "Are you sure? You're already improving, but your balance is still not much better than a drunken man on an icy sidewalk."

Callum chuckled just like she had hoped he would. "Thank you for your confidence. But a man's got to be able to take a leak by himself. My pride won't allow me to have someone assist me with that, not if I can help it."

"Okay but be careful." She raised her eyebrows at him and gave him a stern look. "I don't want to have to rush in there and pick you up off the floor after you've taken a fall and broken something."

He leaned over and brushed his lips against her forehead. "You won't have to. Trust me, I'll be fine."

"Okay." She slowly ducked out from under his arm after he gripped the doorway to support himself. "I'll be right here if you need me."

Sitting down on the bed to wait, she heard her stomach make an unmistakable noise, and she suddenly realized how hungry she was. Sabrina had knocked on the door the previous evening, or at least Vamika assumed it was the evening, and asked if she wanted something to eat. But she had refused since just the idea of food had made her stomach turn. She had been too worried about Callum at the time to even think about forcing down a meal.

Which meant that it was about twenty-four hours since Vamika last ate, and she wasn't the only one who needed to eat. Callum needed food to get his strength back and finish healing.

She was suddenly impatient to go get them some food, but Callum was still in the bathroom, and she didn't want to leave until he was safely back in bed.

A few minutes went by before he opened the door, and she immediately rushed to him.

"Have you been worried about me?" He smiled down at her from where he stood, holding onto the door for support. But apart from his grip on the door, he looked steady on his feet and in no danger of falling.

Nodding, she smiled up at him as she breathed out a relieved sigh. "Yes, after seeing you just lying there for hours and hours, showing no sign of waking up or even improving, I guess it's going to take me a little while to stop worrying."

He gave her a small smile as he took a step toward her. "Yeah, I can understand that. I think I would've gone crazy if it had been you." His face turned serious. "I can't even think about it without my mind spinning with fear."

Callum took the last two steps to close the distance between them, before he wrapped his arms around her and pulled her close. "I need you, Vamika." He kissed the top of her head. "Always. I hope this means that you want me too."

"I do." She nodded against his chest. His hard chest, so smooth and warm against her face. "But." Tipping her head back to look up at him, she pushed against his hard abs. *Jeez, the man is ripped.* But there were more important matters to attend to besides letting her hands explore his amazing body.

He loosened his hold on her and met her gaze, looking a bit apprehensive.

"Food." She smiled up at him while letting her hands smooth up to his chest. "We need food. You particularly. And I will go get us some while you stay in bed."

After a couple of seconds of seemingly considering what she'd said, he nodded. "Okay. I guess trying to climb the stairs wouldn't be a wise move right now."

"No, and if you had claimed that it was, I would've

had to shackle you to the bed."

He chuckled and winked at her, which looked a little funny considering his left eye was open just a crack. "Sounds like fun but I think we'll save that for when I have recovered."

Heat rushed through her at his words, but she ignored it. There would be plenty of time for fun later, but first they needed food, and Callum needed more healing time.

After leaving him sitting on the side of the bed, she rushed up the stairs to the kitchen, trying to dispel the heat that had settled in her lower belly. He had refused to lie down, claiming that he had spent way too much time in bed already, and if he was going to spend any more time there, he would need a good reason to. And there had been no doubt as to what kind of reason he was talking about.

Most of the other temporary and permanent residents were in the kitchen when she hurried through the doors. And Duncan immediately approached her with a hopeful expression on his face. "How is he?"

Vamika nodded and smiled up at the big man just as his mate came to stand by his side. "He's awake and talking. Still weak, though, so I'm going to bring him some breakfast to eat downstairs. I don't want him trying to conquer the stairs just yet."

"Thank God." Duncan's face split in a huge grin. "We've been really worried about him, and I don't know how many times I've wanted to check on you guys. But being with his mate was the best thing for him." He gave her a pointed look.

Vamika felt a sudden need to defend herself, and

she gave him as sincere a look as she could manage. "I've been by his side the whole time, touching him and hoping it would make a difference. Whether it had an effect or not I don't know, but he's awake now and improving with every minute."

Duncan nodded and gave her a warm smile. "I think it had an effect."

"Let's go see him." Julianne put her hand on Duncan's arm. "Just for a couple of minutes while Vamika prepares his breakfast."

Narrowing her eyes, Vamika took a step toward Julianne before she could stop herself. "Duncan can. You can't."

Julianne flinched at her harsh words, and Duncan took a step toward Vamika as he narrowed his eyes. "Why?"

"Oh, for fucks sake." Vamika threw her hands in the air in exasperation. "He's naked. Do you want your mate to see Callum naked?"

"Oh." His eyes widened before he burst out laughing. "I hadn't thought of that. No, you're absolutely right." Turning to Julianne, he shook his head firmly. "You stay here." Then he spun and hurried out of the kitchen.

Vamika quickly made them a few sandwiches and poured some juice into a couple of glasses before she put it all on a tray and carried it downstairs.

"Can you open the door for me?" she yelled from outside the bedroom door, knowing that Duncan was in there with Callum.

Duncan opened the door for her with a smile and waved her inside, before he stepped out of the room and closed the door behind him.

Callum was back in bed, sitting up with a couple of pillows supporting his back. The sheets were covering him up to his hips, leaving his upper body on display. Her eyes were drawn to his lap, even though she had seen him naked just a few minutes ago. But the fact that his male parts were covered somehow made him even more sexy and enticing.

A deep chuckle had her eyes snap to his. "Oh, so you know where my eyes are." He grinned, and she noticed the left side of his face was more responsive, and his left eye was fully open. The burns to his face were finally showing signs of significant improvement.

Smiling back at him, she moved over to the bed and put the tray gently down on his thighs. "I hope you like sandwiches. It was all I could think to make on short notice."

"They look great. Thank you."

"Then give me a few more seconds and you can eat." She took a step closer to him and leaned in to study his face.

Keeping his eyes on hers, he frowned. "What? Is something wrong?"

Smiling, she met his gaze. "No. Everything is great. Your burns are starting to look more superficial, like the deeper layers of your skin are almost completely healed. How does it feel?"

"Better." His frown smoothed into a small smile. "Like the rigid mask it felt like I was wearing has softened."

"Good." After she leaned in, Vamika brushed a kiss over the corner of his mouth, unaffected by the burns, before pulling back and looking down at the food. "Now eat."

Callum didn't move, and after a few seconds, she raised her gaze back up to his. He was studying her with an unreadable expression on his face.

"What's wrong? Are you feeling worse?" Fear shot through her that his condition had somehow deteriorated again even though he looked better.

"I need more of those."

Frowning, she cocked her head. "What do you mean?" He wasn't making any sense. If he was hungry, there was food on the tray right in front of him, and she could always bring him more food.

"Kisses." A small smile curved his lips. "I need more of your kisses."

Vamika burst out laughing. "After you've eaten, pretty boy. Food first, then kissing."

Callum's smile widened. "Is that a promise?"

Grinning wide, she nodded. "It is."

"Good. I'll hold you to that." He winked at her before looking down at the tray in his lap.

Vamika felt her insides flutter in anticipation. She was falling for this man. Hard. And it wasn't just the mating bond talking; it was him. His easy humor, his caring nature, and everything else that was part of making this man so amazing. There was no one like him anywhere, and she was incredibly happy that she hadn't actually taken the step to find a human man to mate. She hadn't felt ready for a mate yet, so she'd waited, even though she knew if she mated someone, there would be no chance of her past catching up to her.

CHAPTER 16

They ate in silence for a while. Callum had been hungrier than he had realized until he took the first bite. For some reason the taste of food made his body wake up to the fact that he required sustenance after healing for almost twenty-four hours.

Vamika had gone quiet, and her eyes had lost focus like she was deep in her thoughts. And he let her stay in her head since his own mind was a bit of a tangle as well at the moment.

Callum still had trouble believing that he'd been out for so long, and the fact that Ambrosia had been there was disturbing. He didn't believe for a second that it was a coincidence her coming to his rescue right after his accident. But how she had come to be there when he himself had never planned to leave Leith's house was a question he'd have to contemplate more later. That witch was much stronger and more resourceful than he'd thought, and he would have to up his game to find her.

After polishing off two sandwiches in quick succession, he lifted his gaze to his beautiful mate and sighed in contentment. She gave him a small smile while chewing, and he let his gaze really take in her appearance.

Her eyes looked tired, and there were dark circles under her eyes that were clearly visible against her rich sepia skin. Her black hair was gathered in the usual braid, but it was a bit messy like it had been braided in a hurry before she went to sleep.

Callum didn't know for how long she had been sleeping beside him before he woke up, but from how she looked, it wasn't enough. She needed rest, and he would make sure she got it. Even if he had to pretend to need a nap and would like her to join him.

Because if he'd learned anything about his mate, it was that she was stubborn, and just telling her to rest for a few hours wasn't likely to be received well. His woman had a mind of her own, and even though it would probably lead to more disagreements between them, he wouldn't have it any other way. Nothing was sexier than a woman with a backbone.

"Thank you, Vamika. I think that's the best sandwich I've ever had."

Chuckling, she shook her head slowly. "I don't believe that for a second. But you must've been hungry. I believe the Germans have a proverb about that."

He lifted an eyebrow at her. German sayings weren't his specialty.

"Hunger ist der beste Koch, which translates to hunger is the best chef or everything tastes better when you're hungry."

He smiled. "Well, I guess that's true. So, you speak German then?"

She picked up the tray and deposited it on the floor before sitting back down on the side of the bed. "Not really, but I guess I've picked up a few things along the way."

"I think it's time you told me a little more about yourself." He kept his eyes on her face to catch her reaction to his words, and he wasn't surprised when she flinched before looking away. "Why does that scare you, Vamika? I don't care about your past. Everyone has one. But you're my mate, and I want to know everything about you. Nothing you tell me will change the fact that you're mine. We'll still be perfect for each other."

Her gaze slowly moved back to his. She might have been trying for a blank expression, but there was a hint of pain in her eyes that he didn't like. "I don't have a past that's particularly interesting or sordid. But there are people and events that I'd rather forget."

Callum nodded slowly. He wasn't surprised, but it still filled him with a burning anger. Whatever those people had done to her was the reason she had rejected him without taking the time to get to know him. They had hurt his mate, and he needed to know who they were so he could prevent them from ever hurting her again. If they even so much as thought about approaching her, he'd kill them. And he might even take his time doing it, to make sure they knew real fear before they died. He had never really wanted to kill anyone before, except for Ambrosia, but that was before realizing that someone had hurt his mate.

Unclenching his jaw, he gave her what he hoped

was a gentle smile. "You don't have to tell me anything you don't want to. Start with something you feel comfortable telling me." He wanted to know who had hurt her right this second. But he had to bide his time. Having her clam up because he forced the issue wasn't the way to go. He'd probably find out sooner by coaxing her gently into telling him about herself.

"Okay." The word was drawn out like she was reluctant to give in.

Moving a little to the side, he patted the bed beside him and widened his smile. "Better yet, why don't you lie down beside me and keep me company. I think I might need a little lie-down after breakfast." He winked at her. It was only a single bed, but he was more than willing to share it with her. Snuggling sounded like a perfect after-breakfast activity.

His suggestion produced the reaction he had hoped for. Smiling, she eyed his hand that was still patting the bed. "Of course, you do." She lifted her gaze to his. "And this wouldn't be an attempt to seduce me, by any chance?"

"Of course not." He widened his eyes, like he was horrified at the notion, before giving her a wicked smile. "Would I do such a thing?"

She laughed. "I wouldn't put it past you."

"Well, all the more for you to look forward to then."

Vamika shook her head at him, but there was a smile on her face. After rising to her feet, she turned and put her knee on the bed.

"But there's one rule." Callum lifted one eyebrow at her and crossed his arms over his chest.

She froze and narrowed her eyes at him. "And what

is that?"

Grinning, he lowered his gaze to her chest. "You have to remove your T-shirt and pants."

Amusement lit her eyes, and she shook her head at him again. "So what you're telling me is that it would be more difficult to seduce me with my clothes on."

"Exactly." He gave her a nod. "Now get on with it. I'm waiting."

"And not very patiently." Grinning, she resolutely gripped the bottom of her shirt and pulled it over her head.

Callum's jaw slackened as he took in the sight of her. She wasn't completely bared to him since she was still wearing a bra, but it was a lacy number, showing the outline of her darker areolas against her flawless rich sepia skin.

His shaft chose that moment to wake up and decide that his energy was restored to the point that he could engage in some fun and games with his mate. And he had absolutely no objections to that. It was high time they mated, but before that he wanted to pleasure his mate until she was begging him for his cock. That was, if he could handle waiting. He'd already been desperate for her for days, and with his body finally waking up, he would soon be struggling for control.

Next, she grabbed the elastic of her yoga-style pants and pushed them down her legs before kicking them off her feet.

The sight of her in just her bra and panties did nothing to help him control his desire. The cream bra and panty set she was wearing was sexy and complemented her dark skin beautifully. But he still couldn't wait to remove the scraps of fabric to get a proper look at what lay beneath.

"You look hungry." The happiness in her voice drew his gaze up to hers. She was biting her bottom lip while giving him a small smile.

He nodded. "I am." His voice was so rough it sounded more like a growl. "Famished actually. But I think you might be able to help with that. In fact I'm sure you have something I'll enjoy eating."

Her eyes widened, and she sucked in a breath at his words. And it didn't escape his notice how she squeezed her thighs together.

"Now come her." He licked his lips and patted the bed beside him. "You promised to tell me a little about yourself while I feast my eyes and perhaps other parts of my face on your body."

Vamika complied without saying a word, but she was moving like she had an itch between her legs, and her lips were parted. Whether she would be able to tell him anything while being this turned on he didn't know, but he would have fun pushing her to do so.

He turned onto his side as she lay down beside him, careful not to touch him with any part of her body, which was a feat with the bed being so narrow.

But this no touching thing wasn't going to cut it. He needed to feel her skin.

Pulling the sheets that were still covering him to the front of his body, he exposed his side and his upper leg while still hiding his erection.

Vamika's eyes followed his movements until settling on his still-hidden cock with a frown. "That's not fair." Her gaze found his. "I have undressed and am almost naked."

He chuckled. "Almost, yes. I think this makes us

about even. But don't worry, we'll be naked eventually. Before that, though, you'll need to tell me something about yourself."

"Um." She rolled her lips together. "What would you like to know?"

Callum held her gaze while he put his hand on her thigh and let it glide along her soft skin up to her ass. "What's your favorite color?"

"It's...oh." Her eyes widened when he grabbed a handful of her ass, making sure his pinky grazed her folds, which were still covered by her panties.

He let his hand stay there without moving while staring into her eyes. "You were saying?"

"Um." She swallowed and blinked a couple of times. "Deep cerise."

Grinning, he nodded slowly. "Perfect. Do you have lingerie in that color?" After loosening his grip on her ass, he slid his hand slowly down her thigh while letting his pinky glide over her folds and clit.

Her hand grabbed his shoulder like she needed something to hold onto. "No." The word was little more than a breath.

Callum put his hand on her waist before moving it around her back to the fastening of her bra. "Then we have to get you some." After unsnapping her bra with one hand, he let his thumb slide just beneath the bottom edge of her bra and follow it until he brushed against the underside of her breast.

As predicted, she sucked in a breath at his touch. She was so responsive, and he loved it, his cock already throbbing between his legs in anticipation of plunging into her tight and wet sheath. But he was doing his best to stay in control while teasing her.

***

Vamika was captured by Callum's heated gaze while she tried to breath normally. She had a feeling his teasing had only just started, and she was already about to spontaneously combust. She wanted to rip her panties off and sink down onto his hard shaft. Because there was no doubt that his cock was hard under the sheet he was clutching to his stomach.

She would let him tease her for a while longer, but if he made no move to fuck her within a reasonable amount of time, she would have to take matters into her own hands and make it happen.

His hand moved to her shoulder. "I can't wait to see you in deep cerise lingerie. The color will make your skin glow."

His words made her smile. He was so sweet. But she needed more than sweet at the moment. "Callum."

He flashed her a wicked smile. "Yes, baby girl." There was no doubt he knew exactly what he was doing to her.

She was about to tell him off for teasing her when he put a finger under her chin and tipped her head back a little. He then slowly closed the distance between them until his lips slid gently against hers.

Vamika moaned and pushed her mouth more firmly against his. And apparently that was all that was needed to break some of his admirable control.

Callum groaned, and his hand cupped the back of her head when he crushed his lips to hers in a desperate kiss.

She opened her mouth and welcomed his tongue into her mouth before sliding her own against his and moaning at the sensation.

The kiss quickly grew more frantic, igniting her whole body with a need like she had never felt before. There was an ache deep inside her that only Callum could satisfy and only by mating her.

He suddenly broke their kiss and pulled back to look at her. His eyes were shining with the golden yellow of his wolf, evidence that his need to mate was riding him hard as well.

"Fuck, you're stunning." He stared into her eyes, making her realize he was probably talking about the color of her eyes. No doubt her eyes had changed to those of her wolf as well.

"I could say the same about you." Her voice was huskier than normal.

Callum grinned, and she shivered at the sight of his longer-than-usual canines. It had nothing to do with fear, and everything to do with desire racing through her in anticipation of them mating. This was the man she was going to spend the rest of her life with, and they were about to make that an irreversible fact.

Someone hammered on the door, and Vamika felt her eyes widen in disbelief. Who the fuck would even think to bother them at this time?

It was no surprise that Callum felt the same. "Who the fuck is it?" His voice was a furious snarl that should have warned whoever it was out there to clear off immediately.

"I'm so fucking sorry to bother you." Duncan's voice sounded through the door. "But we know where Ambrosia is, and we need to leave. Now."

Callum's growl was ferocious, and she felt him fist his hand behind her head. "Fuck." He spoke the word on a defeated sigh while staring into her eyes. "This was supposed to be our time."

Vamika nodded, just as deflated as he sounded. "It was." Her whole body was burning with the need to come and the need to become one with this man. But that would have to wait because of a bitch who was on a mission to kill their kind.

"You'll have to give us a few minutes." Callum yelled while staring into her eyes like he had a plan.

"Okay but make it quick," Duncan answered.

Before she realized what Callum intended, she was on her back with her legs in the air and her panties already halfway down her legs.

"I'll have to make this quicker than I intended." He pulled her panties all the way off and threw them on the floor before separating her legs and staring down at her drenched pussy from where he was sitting on his knees by her ass. "But I want you to come before we leave, and I want to taste you again."

Vamika's channel clenched, and she moaned in response to having his gaze down there. Her body was begging her for release, but she wanted him to come as well. "What about you?"

He glanced at her face and shook his head. "I'll wait until we can get time alone to mate. I want to have time to worship you and satisfy you properly when we mate. It's a life-changing event, and I won't rush through it. I want it to be memorable."

Vamika swallowed back the emotions that were threating to clog her throat. This man was the sweetest mate a woman could possibly dream up. He had the most amazing tongue, for talking, kissing, and licking her. Which he proved when he buried his face between her legs.

She couldn't help the shriek that escaped her as he went at her like he meant to devour her. He had said that he would have to make this quick, and he was proving it the way he attacked her from all angles at once.

His tongue was lapping at her clit with rapid movements like she was a lollipop, and he was intending to win a lollipop-licking competition. Two fingers suddenly drove into her weeping channel, and she gasped as her internal muscles clenched around his digits, desperate to keep them inside her.

The way he was lapping at her swollen nub and pumping his fingers inside her was already driving her crazy when his hand covered her breast and pinched her nipple. It brought her right to the edge, and she sucked in a breath and held it in anticipation of what was to come.

And Callum didn't disappoint. He sucked hard on her clit and pumped his fingers harder inside her, but what sent her soaring was his thumb brushing over the nipple he had just pinched, sending a zing of sweet pain through her body.

Her back came off the bed when ecstasy made the muscles in her whole body tighten. Screaming his name, she bucked her hips against him, the pleasure he was creating threatening to take her mind, but he didn't let up until she was shaking from fatigue.

She heard him chuckle as she sucked huge gulps of air into her lungs, trying to get her brain to come back online. There was still a deep ache inside her that wasn't going to be satisfied until they mated, but the recent mind-boggling orgasm would hopefully do well to tide her over until then.

Callum got off the bed, then stood beside it. He gripped her hands and pulled her up to a sitting position. Which put her almost face to face, so to speak, with his rigid shaft. It was deep red and throbbing, evidence of the need that was clearly running rampant in his body.

She pulled her hand out of his and wrapped it around his engorged member before he realized what she intended.

He froze, and his eyes widened as he stared down at her. "Vamika, we don't have time." His voice came out strangled, and a shudder ran through his body.

She let her hand slide up his thick shaft and over the stretched, shiny skin of the head. Staring up at him, she nodded. "Yes, we do. Now back up and get on your knees."

Swallowing hard, he did what he was told, and she followed him down to the floor while slowly sliding her hand up and down his cock.

What she wouldn't give to take him inside her. He would feel amazing settled deep in her channel, and she would be able to watch him lose control and wield that weapon inside her like he was meant to.

But that would have to wait. At the moment her mate needed her to pleasure him to help him hang in there until they had time to mate.

Vamika gave him a quick smile before bending and wrapping her lips around him. She swirled her tongue around the rim before taking as much of him as she could into her mouth.

Callum groaned, and a shudder ran through his body. As she lifted her head, she felt his hand wrap around her braid.

She started bobbing her head up and down faster while she stroked the base of his length with her hand. His hold on her braid tightened, like he was holding onto it for support, and she made sure to tug on her braid a little when she tightened her lips around him and sucked him deep into her mouth.

He roared, and his hot cum filled her throat as his cock jerked in her mouth. Swallowing down everything he gave her, she was struggling not to smile with happiness at giving him this much pleasure. Knowing she was able to make him vibrate with the power of it would never get old, and she couldn't wait to do it again when given the chance.

CHAPTER 17

Callum looked down at his mate curled up beside him. They were in the backseat of Michael's rental on their way to Bryson's clan. It was located not far from Culloden Moor to the east of Inverness. A female acquaintance of Bryson's had noticed a witch visiting a house just a few miles from the clan village, and based on the description the woman was able to give, there was no doubt that the visiting witch was Ambrosia.

The woman had thought to take note of the license plate number of the car Ambrosia was driving, and Callum had been able to find the name of the person who rented the car from the rental company. Another fake name, of course, which was to be expected, but at least this time Callum had thought to check the rental company's records for a copy of the driver's license Ambrosia had presented to them. And it had a photo on it.

He was kicking himself for not thinking to do that with her other fake identity. But he was going to plead insanity on that one, even though it had happened before he met Vamika, and his mind got scrambled from her rejecting him.

Finally, they had a photo of the woman they could send to every clan and pack in Scotland and perhaps even England if necessary. Someone had to know Ambrosia's true identity, since she was or had been mated to a shifter. Perhaps they could even locate her mate, but whether that would help them at all Callum wasn't sure.

He quickly sent the photo of Ambrosia to everyone in their group and told them to forward it to all the alphas they knew for them to distribute within their packs and clans.

Callum glanced down at his mate again. Vamika was sleeping soundly with her hand on his thigh. He'd encouraged it as soon as they had settled in the car. It was obvious she hadn't slept much while he was unconscious, and she needed some rest before they arrived at Bryson's place.

They didn't have an exact location of Ambrosia's whereabouts at the moment, but they knew where she had been a couple of hours ago. And they had a new name to go with the woman even though it was a fake one. Jane Brown this time as opposed to the previous Jane Smith. It seemed the evil bitch had a preference for the name Jane.

What was worrying him was how quickly she had been able to start using the new name. It was an indication that she'd had both names set up from the start. Which was an extraordinary amount of preparation on her part. And it made it clear she had been prepared, and perhaps even expected, to have people following her.

The logical next question was of course how many other fake names she had lined up just in case. It made tracking her a nightmare because she might be using different identities for dealing with different people or establishments.

Callum sighed. He didn't like bringing Vamika along, knowing how dangerous this witch was. Every instinct in him was telling him to keep his mate somewhere safe. But she would never have agreed to that. Particularly after his recent encounter with Ambrosia.

But then he imagined all his friends were thinking the same way about their mates. And none of the mates were having it. There were no pushovers among these women. They were all strong and capable and would need convincing reasons to let their mates face a dangerous situation without them. Even Sabrina nearly dying hadn't changed that fact. The women wanted to be right there next to their mates no matter what happened.

Callum sucked in a sharp breath when he suddenly remembered Ambrosia standing by his side in a shed, asking whether Leith was dead yet after suffering the loss of his mate. He immediately recognized that it was a flash of memory from when he had been taken by Ambrosia after his car accident, but he couldn't remember what happened before or after. The scene was kind of hazy. But two things were clear. One, he hadn't been unconscious continuously from when the accident happened until he woke up next to Vamika. And two, Ambrosia still thought Sabrina was dead.

He quickly found Leith's name on his phone. Leith

answered after a couple of rings. "Callum. Have you been able to discover something useful?"

"Yes, but that's not why I'm calling. I just remembered something. I had a sort of flashback from when Ambrosia took me to the shed after my accident yesterday. She doesn't know that Sabrina survived. Ambrosia believes she's dead, and I think it would be a good idea for us to keep Sabrina out of the spotlight as much as possible not to alert the bitch to the fact that she is still alive. If Ambrosia is counting on Sabrina being dead and you, Leith, being incapacitated because of her death, we have an advantage."

Leith was quiet for so long that Callum thought he might have lost him. "Leith, are you still there?"

"Yes." Leith sighed. "It is just hard every time I am reminded of what happened. I am trying my best to forget what happened that day to retain my sanity and not get too protective. But if that is what Ambrosia believes, I completely agree that we should make sure she keeps believing it. It is to our advantage if she underestimates us."

Callum nodded even though Leith couldn't see him. "Exactly. Which means you and Sabrina shouldn't join us when we go to check the house Ambrosia was visiting."

"Agreed. We will all go to Bryson's first. We can discuss how to proceed once we get there. I believe the woman who warned Bryson about Ambrosia is still at his house, and we will get to talk to her. According to Bryson she is a witch, although not a powerful one."

"Another witch." Callum couldn't help chuckling. "They're suddenly everywhere."

Leith chuckled as well. "True. Just a word of caution, though, Callum." The other man's voice was back to being serious. "Bryson and his clan adhere to the old ways of shifters. I think it might be to your advantage to enter Bryson's house at my side, just to make sure there are no misunderstandings as to your status. And make sure to tell Vamika about this, too, although I think she may already have met the panther alpha."

Callum felt his spine tense at Leith's words. "What exactly do you mean by that?"

"I mean that Vamika already knows the ways of these panthers and Bryson's rather forward pursuit of women, but I do not believe she is at risk even though you two have not yet mated. He has a preference for blond women, and even if he was to try something with your mate, Vamika would shut him down quite forcefully, I believe."

A chuckle reached Callum through the phone, and he recognized it as coming from Sabrina. "So, it's only me you didn't think would have the spine to say no, then?" There was a challenge in her voice, even though she sounded amused, and Callum suddenly felt like he was intruding in a personal discussion.

Leith sighed. "My angel, that is not—"

"Yes, it is." Sabrina laughed. "But I'm sure I'll be able to think of ways you can make it up to me."

Leith chuckled. "I'm sure you will, and I look forward to it."

"Um." Callum didn't want to hear where this conversation was going. "I guess we'll talk when we get to Bryson's then."

"Yes." There was a smile in Leith's voice like he

knew they had made Callum uncomfortable. "And thank you. We will see you there."

As soon as he ended the call, Steph turned around in the passenger seat and stared at him. "Ambrosia thinks Sabrina is dead?"

He nodded. "She does, and we have to make sure to act into that."

"Absolutely." She grinned. "We have to come up with a good plan to use that for all it's worth. Have you been able to find out where Ambrosia is now?"

Callum shook his head. "No. But I've found a photo of Ambrosia that I've distributed to all of you. Hopefully, we'll soon know who she really is. But I'm not sure whether it will help us or not. She might not be using her real identity anymore."

"Have you been able to find out who's living in the house she visited this morning?" Michael glanced at him in the rearview mirror.

"I'm just going to dive into that now." Callum met Michael's gaze in the mirror for a second. "I should have something by the time we arrive at Bryson's."

Callum glanced down at Vamika before focusing on his laptop. He still couldn't get over the fact that they were going to meet another witch soon. It had only been a few days since he became aware that there was such a thing as real live witches, and since then they had been popping up left, right, and center. This latest one wasn't powerful, but still. How come most shifters had been unaware of this whole group of supernaturals? Most witches must be incredibly good at concealing their power to stay hidden for so long.

Just by using the power of the internet and the information that was publicly available, he was able to find some interesting facts about the house that Ambrosia had visited. Or rather, the facts were remarkably uninteresting.

The owner of the house was a woman in her sixties, and she also seemed to be the only resident. She was recently retired, and had until five months ago worked in healthcare, more specifically in a mental institution. There was nothing to suggest she was anything other than a regular person with a regular life. Unless she was a witch, as well, and was supporting Ambrosia in her quest to eradicate shifters. But if she was, there was nothing to suggest that from her mundane life. But then there was always a chance the woman was concealing something.

Taking it a step further, he checked her banking history going back about a year. At first glance there was nothing out of the ordinary. Regular payments for utilities and other expenses were going out. Up until five months ago, her salary had been going in, which at that point was replaced by her pension. Except that when she retired, she stopped spending money on food and other normal necessities. There were no charges to her account from the use of a bankcard and no withdrawals of cash. Which suggested that this woman was receiving cash from someone that she was using to cover a lot of her living expenses.

Callum kept at it for a while longer, trying to find something to indicate where the woman was getting her money. He had his suspicions, but he wanted to make sure he didn't overlook something obvious.

Vamika pulled in a deep breath, and he looked down at his mate. Her eyes blinked open, and she turned her head to look up at him, before her eyes swung to his open laptop. "Hard at work I see." Her gaze returned to his, and she smiled.

"Well." He grinned down at her. "I didn't have a mate to occupy me, so I thought I might as well do something useful."

"Oh really." She sat up before moving over to press herself against his side. "You need me to occupy you?"

Chuckling, he looked down into her warm dark-brown eyes. "Absolutely. I would go so far as to suggest that you should make that your new occupation."

She laughed. "I'll consider it, but you know there are so many things I could do with my life." Her eyes sparkled as she teased him.

"True." Averting his eyes, he nodded slowly and did his best to look serious and pensive. "I'm sure there's a market for short and cute somewhere. Although they would probably want gentle to go with it and—"

"Callum!" Her eyes narrowed, and he sucked in a breath when her hand was suddenly underneath his T-shirt, exploring his abs.

"Vamika." He tried for a warning tone, but it came out a bit shaky. His heart rate was already speeding up from her gentle touch.

She gave him a wide-eyed innocent look. "I can be gentle." Her hand moved to his chest. "Or not." She pinched his nipple.

Callum's whole body jerked, and he let out a low groan, as the enticing mixture of pleasure and pain shot directly to his cock. His already semihard shaft swelled to rock-hard within seconds, and he fisted his hands to stop himself from grabbing Vamika and placing her on his lap.

"What are you kids up to back there?" Steph's amused voice sounded from the passenger seat, but she didn't turn to check what they were actually doing. Which was probably a good thing. Callum had no doubt that his eyes would betray how turned on he was from Vamika's teasing touch. His body was so ready to claim his mate that it didn't need a lot of encouragement to prepare for that event.

His mate bit her bottom lip as she grinned up at him. "I'm sorry," she whispered. But she didn't look sorry. Not even a little bit. She looked like she was going to burst out laughing any second.

Callum lifted an eyebrow at her and shook his head slowly. He then leaned down and whispered in her ear. "I will punish you for this behavior. Perhaps I'll tie you up and take my time teasing you before I'll eventually let you come. I can suck on that cute little pleasure button between your legs until you're so close you can practically taste your release, but then I might need a little break to play with myself."

She gasped and pulled her head back to stare at him. "That's cruel." But her eyes were shining with need, and she squirmed on the seat beside him.

He nodded, but he couldn't hold back his grin at her reaction to his words.

Michael cleared his throat. "According to the GPS, we're there in about five minutes."

"Thanks, Michael." Callum frowned as he remembered Leith's description of Bryson. The panther alpha sounded like a real asshole.

"What is it?" Vamika cocked her head as she studied his face. "You look like you just ate something that didn't agree with you."

"Have you met Bryson before?" Callum kept his gaze on her face to see her reaction.

She nodded without reacting to the mention of the panther alpha's name. "Yes, I went there with Euna to get her settled with his clan. Do you know who Euna is?"

"I've never met her, but I've heard of her. She's the woman from your pack that Freddie was planning to mate right?"

Vamika nodded with her eyes narrowed in anger. "Yes, Freddie was an asshole. But thankfully, he was an arrogant asshole who loved to brag about everything he had done and was going to do. I overheard him boasting to his idiot friends that he was going to mate Euna when she turned eighteen. I immediately went to Euna and asked whether she had agreed to mate Freddie, and she said that she had. But from the look on her face, there was no doubt she was scared, and with a little coaxing, she admitted to having turned him down, but he hadn't taken her no for an answer. He had told her they would mate the day after her birthday, and if she refused or told anyone about their planned mating, he was going to hurt her parents."

Callum had heard about Euna, but not all the details of how Freddie had treated her. Sabrina had said that the young woman had seemed scared and uncertain, and Freddie's horrible treatment of her was likely one of the reasons for that.

But Euna wasn't the reason Callum had asked Vamika whether she'd met Bryson. "Leith said that I should walk beside him when we enter Bryson's house to avoid any misunderstandings about my status. And that was after he told me that Bryson's clan are following the old rules of etiquette. I got the feeling Leith is worried that they won't accept me because of my leg, and he wants to protect me. And it's a nice gesture, but I'm used to standing up for myself when necessary. Accepting someone's protection like that doesn't feel right. It's like admitting that I'm weak and not good enough."

Vamika's eyes hardened, and her jaw tensed as she listened to him, but she waited until he paused to say anything. "If they so much as hint that you're not welcome or treat you like you're second rate, I'll make sure they regret it."

He couldn't help smiling at his mate's protective instinct toward him, and the flash of fury in her eyes just made her more beautiful. "Thank you, Vamika. I love that you would stand up for me, but I need to do that for myself, or I'll never get the respect I deserve. Having someone protect me only makes me seem weaker in other people's eyes."

Vamika frowned. "But I can't stand by and let them hurt you. I won't be able to. You're my mate."

"Do you think they would go so far as to hurt me, though? I've never met anyone from this clan before, but you have. What do you think?"

The car stopped, and they were suddenly out of time. Michael and Steph opened their doors and started getting out, and Callum was about to do the same when Vamika spoke.

"Wait." She stared into his eyes. "This clan might behave old-fashioned in many ways, but I don't think they will hurt you. Bryson can come across as arrogant and a bully at times, but he usually reserves that kind of behavior for those he knows are at least as powerful as he is. He likes to challenge people who are on his own level or stronger, but he doesn't step on people who are weaker than him."

"Okay." Callum nodded, not sure what else to say. Bryson sounded like an unusual alpha. Old-fashioned, a bully toward his superiors, and a protector of the weak. At least that was how it sounded like to Callum, and he was suddenly curious to meet the guy.

They got out of the car, and Callum grasped Vamika's hand in his. Leith might not think Bryson wanted Vamika, but Callum wanted to make sure there was no doubt as to whom she belonged. And he was prepared to fight for her if necessary, even a man like Bryson, who was much stronger than himself. But it would be unusual for a man to try to take another man's true mate. True mates were revered and protected among shifters. But then Bryson didn't know they were true mates yet, and from Leith and Sabrina's conversation, it sounded like the panther alpha had tried something with Sabrina. Although from what Vamika had just said, that might have had something to do with Leith being an exceptionally strong shifter.

He lifted his gaze to the porch and felt himself frown when his eyes landed on the alpha. Vamika had said Bryson could come across as arrogant, and she was right. The man was imposing to say the least. Dressed like he was about to go to war in all black combat attire, with a powerful body to match. Tall, wide, and covered in tattoos, Bryson looked like a mean one-man war machine, and he was playing into that image the way he stood with his feet a foot apart and his arms crossed over his puffed-up chest.

Callum had a feeling there weren't many stupid enough to pick a fight with this guy. Perhaps that was why Bryson liked to challenge more powerful shifters, because they were the only ones who would stand up to him.

Trevor pulled in and parked beside them, and Trevor, Jennie, Duncan, and Julianne stepped out of the vehicle. Leith and Sabrina were already standing outside their car, obviously waiting for their whole group to arrive before approaching Bryson and his welcome party of five standing behind him on the porch.

As if on cue, Leith and Trevor nodded at each other before walking toward the porch with Sabrina and Jennie following right behind them. Duncan and Michael followed next with their mates right behind. It was a show that clearly identified who was mated and to whom.

But since Callum and Vamika weren't mated yet, they couldn't follow the same procedure. Instead, they fell in behind the others and walked toward the porch hand in hand.

Bryson and Leith greeted one another by gripping each other's forearms, before Bryson gave Sabrina a small bow, which she acknowledged by nodding back at him. The same procedure followed for Trevor and Duncan, the other two alphas among them, and their mates.

Michael wasn't an alpha, which meant he only received a small bow like Steph did. And then it was Callum's and Vamika's turn to approach the alpha.

Callum wasn't quite sure what he had expected from Bryson, but it wasn't the small bow he received like he was just another wolf. The man didn't so much as glance at Callum's leg, even though he hadn't made any effort to hide his limp while approaching the porch. Bryson then turned to Vamika and greeted her the same way.

"Please follow me." Bryson turned and headed into the house, and Leith took a step forward to follow him before turning to Callum with an eyebrow raised in question.

Callum shook his head at Leith to indicate that he wasn't intending to walk beside him into Bryson's house. Leith wanted to ensure that everyone knew Callum was under his alpha protection, which was an honor, according to the old ways, but Callum wanted it to be clear that he could stand on his own two feet both literally and figuratively speaking.

Leith gave him a small nod with one corner of his mouth pulled up in a small smile, and Callum took that to mean that Leith understood.

They followed Bryson into the house in the same order they had approached the porch. And the members of Bryson's clan who had been standing on the porch followed behind Callum and Vamika.

CHAPTER 18

They entered the large living room Bryson used to receive guests. It looked the same as Vamika remembered, except that several tables had been pushed together to form one long one, and the couches had been moved to accommodate them all.

Bryson took his usual seat in the large armchair at the head of the table before indicating that they should all find a seat.

The alpha was just as intimidating as always, but there was something in his eyes that was different. A haunted look like he was struggling with something that pushed him outside his comfort zone. It was a strange look for him and completely at odds with his brawny heavily tattooed persona. She wasn't sure everyone else noticed it since most of them hadn't met him before, but she certainly did.

His black hair was still short, like the last time she had met him, but he had recently trimmed his beard back to allow the skin of his jaw to be visible through the black stubble. It was a recent change evidenced by the fact that the skin of his jaw was a lighter shade of amber than the rest of his face. Bryson's grandfather and grandmother on his father's side had been from Morocco, giving him an exotic appearance like herself.

Bryson's clan members all took seats on the couches on the right side of the table from their alpha. And the rest of them filled up most of the remaining seats with Leith and Sabrina closest to Bryson on his left.

She sat down next to Callum close to the other end of the table from the clan alpha. Callum put an arm around her shoulder and pulled her close, making her turn her head to smile up at him. The action was a sign that he needed her close, but it was also a show of ownership in a setting like this, both of which warmed her heart and made her happy he would soon be officially hers. He returned her smile, but there was a tenseness in his jaw and in the rest of his body that spoke of his unease of being surrounded by so many unknown shifters when they weren't mated yet.

To alleviate some of his tension, she leaned into his side and put her hand on his thigh. He wasn't the only one who would feel better once they were mated and nothing could ever separate them again. But they would get to that as soon as they had a chance to be alone for more than fifteen minutes.

"Welcome." Bryson's deep voice broke the silence in the room, and Vamika turned her head to look at him. "And thank you for coming at such short notice and in such numbers. Fia will join us shortly. She had to step out for a few minutes." A shadow passed over Bryson's face when he mentioned Fia's name.

Vamika frowned. Bryson was usually cool as could be. Presumably Fia was the witch who had noticed Ambrosia visiting a house not far from the clan village. The alpha's reaction when mentioning the woman's name had her intrigued, though.

"In the meantime, please help yourselves to some coffee and tea." Bryson nodded at the steaming pots of tea and coffee on the table before he swung his gaze around the table to look at each and every one of them. "I would like to thank you all for your efforts to try to capture and destroy Ambrosia. And at a considerable risk to your own safety." His gaze stopped on Leith and Sabrina. "I'm happy to see that you are both alive and well. I'm sure everyone here will agree with me when I say that your deaths would've been a terrible loss to the Scottish shifter community as well as beyond."

"Thank you, Bryson. I do not think I need to tell you that I am happy about that as well." Leith reached over and took Sabrina's hand in his like he needed the reminder that she was still there with him.

"And in relation to that, there has been a development that you all need to know about." Leith turned his head to look directly at Callum. "Callum, a young wolf from Fearolc, was captured by Ambrosia after a serious car accident yesterday. He was gravely injured and does not remember much from the time after the incident, but he recalled something the evil witch said before Vamika, Trevor, Duncan, and Michael were able to scare her away. Please tell them what you remember, Callum."

Callum nodded. "Unfortunately, I don't remember a lot of what happened, but I do remember Ambrosia asking me how Leith was doing after the loss of his mate."

Vamika felt her jaw drop in shock. Several other people looked stunned as well, including Duncan and Julianne, so at least she wasn't the only one Callum hadn't told about what he had recalled. But since Leith and Sabrina already knew, he must have called them while Vamika was asleep in the car.

"Why didn't you tell me as soon as I woke up?" she hissed in a low voice as she narrowed her gaze on him.

His lips twitched before his gaze lowered to hers. "Because you were too busy teasing me, baby girl. My mind has a tendency to stall whenever you do that."

A few people around the table chuckled quietly, but the reality of what had happened to Sabrina at the hands of Ambrosia soon quelled their amusement.

Callum lifted his gaze to Bryson. "We can use Ambrosia's ignorance to our advantage, but it requires Leith and Sabrina to stay out of the public eye as much as possible and everyone else to act like the two of them are gone."

Bryson nodded. "Absolutely. I'll make sure—" His words suddenly cut off when his eyes snapped to the entrance.

A tall, beautiful redhead had just entered the room, and as they watched, the woman sashayed across the floor toward Bryson like she was the queen of the manor. And by the way Bryson was staring at her with his mouth slightly open and his eyes filled with admiration, he wasn't averse to that idea.

"Bryson." The woman's low yet firm tone, and the way she lifted her eyebrows at him, gave the impression that she meant it as a gentle reprimand for forgetting himself as a host, which was confirmed when she continued. "Aren't you going to introduce me to your friends?"

Vamika's eyes snapped to Bryson to see his reaction, expecting him to act with authority to save face as an alpha. But to her surprise he didn't.

He simply nodded at the woman, like her words were law, before turning to look at Leith and Sabrina with a neutral expression on his face. "This is Fia. She lives not far from here with her mother."

Bryson turned his gaze back to Fia where she had stopped a few steps away from him. But this time there was none of the naked awe that had been in his eyes just seconds earlier. "Please have a seat." He indicated the unoccupied seat at the opposite end of the long table from himself.

Fia nodded and moved over to the smaller armchair that was close to where Vamika and Callum were sitting. Vamika tightened her grip on Callum's thigh to stop a shiver from racing through her body. There was something unnerving about Fia, but Vamika wasn't sure exactly what made her think so.

"Fia." Bryson's gaze was on the woman as he spoke. "Why don't you tell everyone in your own words what happened earlier today?"

Fia nodded with a small gentle smile curving her lips. "I'd be happy to. Thank you, Bryson."

The woman swung her gaze around at everybody sitting around the table before she started. "I was walking past a house this morning on my way to a small shop I was going to visit, when a woman exiting the house caught my attention. I'm sure Bryson has already informed you that I am what most people would call a witch, with some gentle powers that help me encourage the growth of vegetables and herbs in my garden. My mother has the same abilities I do, and together we are making a living growing high-quality produce for local restaurants and shops."

Fia cleared her throat gently before continuing, her gaze seeming to find Sabrina's and holding it. "The woman exiting the house caught my attention for a specific reason. She was exuding a lot of power, a lot more than I've ever felt from any other person before, including the people I know to be shifters. But then shifters are usually quite good at concealing how powerful they really are, and the older and more powerful the better they are at concealing it, in my experience."

The woman's gaze moved to Bryson, whose power could be felt like a low hum in the room. It was common for the alpha's power to be the most prominent in his domain, even with visiting alphas in the room. None of the visitors were there to challenge Bryson, so they automatically tamped down their power as a sign of respect.

"I watched the woman get into her car and drive away without approaching her." Fia's gaze moved back to Sabrina. "Her power didn't feel friendly to me. There was something malicious about it that made me keep my distance. But I made a note of her license plate number just in case it would turn out to be useful, and I came directly here to tell Bryson about my experience."

Bryson nodded. "And I'm grateful that you did. Based on your description of her, we have reason to believe this woman was Ambrosia, the witch I told you about who's made it her mission to kill shifters."

Fia nodded back at Bryson. "And I can believe that. With a power that malicious, her intent isn't a good one."

Sabrina's voice sounded from the other end of the table. "It's interesting what you say about feeling her intent in her power. Is that usual for how you feel people's power, or was that a specific case? The reason I'm asking is that I can pick up a person's power level, but there's not usually a temperature to it if you see what I mean."

"I do." Fia smiled, but there was a tenseness in her body when she met Sabrina's gaze this time. "I usually sense a color with the power. And the darker the color the more likely the owner of the power is to act in a destructive way. Ambrosia's color was a really dark red, as dark as I've ever seen anyone's power before. Most people have a tone of color somewhere close to the middle of the scale when it comes to light versus dark, indicating that most people are not all good or all bad. We have the potential for both, depending on what happens in our lives and our strength of character."

Sabrina nodded. "I agree and thank you for elaborating on your ability. It's very interesting."

CHAPTER 19

Bryson followed the exchange between Fia and Sabrina with interest. He'd known about Fia being a witch for a couple of years after feeling her power in passing and confronting her about it. As the alpha in the area, he kept a sharp eye on any other supernaturals entering what he considered his territory. They might be allowed to stay if they didn't oppose his sovereignty, otherwise he sent them on their way, and if necessary by force.

But Fia had turned out to be something other than a shifter or vampire or any other kind of supernatural he had ever heard of. She was a witch, a creature he believed only belonged in fairy tales. But once again the fairy tales and myths proved to have more truth to them than he'd expected.

Fia wasn't a threat, though. Her power was no match for him or any of his shifters. So, he'd let her stay within his territory along with her mother. They were no danger to his clan or his rule. And of course, there was the fact that she was a remarkably stunning woman that he'd expected to have warming his bed within a few days of meeting her.

That hadn't turned out quite the way he had anticipated, though. His charm, his body, his status and his money, he'd tried to use them all in imaginative ways to entice her to come to him, but so far nothing had worked. And after two years of trying, he was getting a bit concerned as to why he was still so obsessed with her. But for some reason, he couldn't get her out of his head, and it was affecting him more than he had thought possible.

Fia's eyes on him pulled Bryson out of his mind. He'd been listening but with less attention than he should.

Her gentle smile locked his gaze on her face even though her gaze moved to Leith and Sabrina sitting on the couch next to his chair. "Bryson told me that you might be able to find out more about the person or people living in the house Ambrosia visited. Have you had a chance to look into that yet?"

"I have." Callum answered from the opposite end of the table, and he went on to tell them what he'd found out about the names Ambrosia was using to hide her real identity and the details he'd been able to gather about the female owner of the house Ambrosia had been seen visiting that morning. The young wolf was obviously good at retrieving information, but more impressive was the amount of relevant information he'd been able to find in such a short time.

Bryson's gaze slid back to Fia, and he barely held back a sigh of hopelessness as his gaze took in her beautiful almond-shaped hazel eyes and her full lips. What he wouldn't give just to get the chance to kiss her. Just once to be able to assess whether his fantasy of kissing her was anywhere near the real experience.

Bryson mentally shook his head at his own thoughts. He needed to move on and find another woman to fuck. It would clear his unhealthy obsession right up and help him return to his old self.

He had always had plenty of women wanting to be his plaything for a few nights, and the ones who hadn't immediately seemed interested he'd pursued until they couldn't resist his advances any longer. It had been fun until it started to get repetitive.

And that was when he'd started going after other shifter male's dates or girlfriends. Never shifters from his own clan and never mated women. The panthers in his clan were his to protect, and fucking a mated woman was a hard pass even for him. And even if he'd been open to the possibility, it was rare that a mated woman would be interested, anyway. Unless she wanted to use him as a revenge fuck to get back at her mate for something. But he didn't want to be used. And some people would no doubt see the irony in that.

Pursuing other men's women had been fun, though, and he figured it probably saved the men some heartache in the long run. If a woman could be lured away from the man she was supposed to care about that easily, then she would eventually leave anyway and probably hurt the man in the process.

Fucking those women was a thrill, but even more thrilling was goading their men into a fight, and the more powerful their men were the better. He had ended up in some great fights that way, and so far he had only lost twice. And both times the other shifter had cheated by either bringing a weapon to the fight or hitting below the belt—literally. The second of those he should have seen coming since the woman had proclaimed to everyone that the man was useless in bed and that Bryson was a sex god. If it hadn't been for Bryson's trusted clan members stopping the fight when the other man crushed his balls, the man would surely have taken the opportunity while Bryson was incapacitated to kill him.

There was only one problem with his plan to move on and find another woman. He had already tried it many times over the past two years, but no other woman could hold his interest long enough for him to bother pursuing her. And the ones who had pursued him—and there had been plenty of those—he'd turned down flat because the lack of challenge turned him off.

If it hadn't been for the fact that thoughts of Fia made his shaft solid as granite in seconds, he'd probably conclude that his skirt-chasing had left him impotent. Which was a condition unheard of among shifters. But his right arm could attest to the fact that he had no such problem. The number of times he'd jerked off in the last couple of years with a fantasy of Fia running in his head, it was a wonder his right arm wasn't thicker muscled than his left.

Bryson had wondered a few times whether Fia might be his true mate, and he'd been tempted to believe it if his feelings and need had been constant or increasing over time. But they weren't, and that was what confused and frustrated him the most. His need was like the ocean tides, ebbing and flowing with time. As soon as it started to get to a level that was making him think she might be his mate after all, it would suddenly die down and lie almost dormant for a while until it gradually increased again. Only lately it had seemed to increase faster than before.

"That's interesting. What do you think, Bryson?"

Fia's question snapped him out of his troubled thoughts, and he had to do a quick recap of what had been said in the last couple of minutes while he had partially tuned out what was going on around him. It was one of his skills, though, that came in handy during long meetings with people who liked to hear themselves talk. He could think about other things while still absorbing what was being said and looking like he was paying attention.

Callum had been explaining his conclusions from checking the banking history for the female owner of the house. The owner was receiving cash from someone that covered a lot of her living expenses, and it was a good chance that someone was Ambrosia.

Bryson nodded and looked at Callum. "I think you've done an outstanding job, Callum, and you're more than likely correct. However, in order to find conclusive evidence, we need to visit the woman in question and talk to her. Preferably without her realizing why we are there and what we are after. It would be safer for everyone, not the least for this woman, if Ambrosia never hears of our inquiries. Unless of course this woman is a witch as well and supports Ambrosia in her quest to end shifters. But even if that is the case, I doubt she's very powerful. I think we would've picked up on a powerful witch living in the area."

Most of the people seated around the table nodded their agreement, including Fia, but the beautiful redhead had a strange expression on her face. Her eyes were a little wide, and her jaw tense like she was taken aback by his words.

"I agree." Leith nodded. "Which leads us to the question of who should visit the owner of the house. And I have a recommendation."

Bryson nodded to the man seated on the couch with his mate. "Please go ahead, Leith."

Leith was probably the most powerful shifter he had ever met, and yet Bryson had made a pass at Leith's woman the last time they visited. Sabrina was a beautiful woman, and before he met Fia, Bryson would have actively pursued her. But lately he only acted like that to play into the expectations of his panthers. He had no more interest in Sabrina than any other woman who wasn't Fia. Thankfully, Sabrina only had eyes for the tall long-haired man who was her mate, and Bryson didn't end up having to fight Leith. Which was a good thing considering that if there was one shifter he was sure he'd never beat in a fair fight, it was Leith.

"Thank you." Leith leaned forward in his seat. "It is important not to scare this woman, which means that the people paying her a visit should appear as nonthreatening as possible. I propose three people who I think will handle this task perfectly: Callum, Vamika, and Fia."

Bryson felt his eyebrows rise in surprise. He had automatically assumed he would be one of the people visiting this woman, seeing as he was the alpha in the area. But if he disregarded his own wish to talk to her and his ego, he had no trouble seeing Leith's logic.

Nodding slowly, he let his gaze settle on Fia. "I concur. Fia will be able to sense if the woman has any power and determine her intent if she does."

Fia's eyes widened a little at his words, like she was surprised at his faith in her, before she smiled and nodded. "I'll do my best."

"Thank you." Bryson gave her a small smile before moving his gaze to Callum.

The wolf was frowning and looking down at Vamika while holding her tightly pressed against his side. There was no doubt that these two would mate soon based on the way they were constantly touching and looking at each other. And Bryson had to admit that he was surprised. The last time he met Vamika, she had been downright unfriendly toward the men in his clan, including himself. But she had obviously met a man she could tolerate and even love in Callum.

"What do you think, Callum and Vamika? Do you feel comfortable approaching the owner of the house?" Bryson kept his eyes on the pair. "Some of my panthers will be stationed at strategic places in the vicinity to make sure you have back-up if necessary."

They both turned to look at him before Callum spoke. "We'll do it. I'd prefer it if Vamika stayed here, but she'd never accept that."

"Damn right, I wouldn't." Vamika's eyes narrowed as she turned her head back to look up at Callum.

Callum grinned down at her. "I'm learning, see?"

Bryson smiled at that. No wonder Vamika liked the young wolf. He let her make all the decisions for him. That was one thing Bryson would never accept from a woman. He was the alpha, and he would always be the one in charge. Anything else would be unacceptable.

After discussing various ways to approach the owner of the house Ambrosia had been visiting, Fia, Callum, and Vamika left in Michael's rental car. The car would be possible to trace to Michael, but seeing as he was an American tourist with no permanent residence in Scotland, it seemed like the best option.

Four of Bryson's panthers left in another car to keep watch over the house and the nearby area while Fia, Callum, and Vamika did what they could to discover the reason for Ambrosia's visit and her connection to the owner of the house.

Bryson walked back into the living room where a couple of his clan members were still chatting with their guests. He was just about to sit down in his armchair when Sabrina spoke.

"Bryson, can we speak to you privately, please?" Her hand was on Leith's arm, but the man's gaze snapped to his mate's face at her request like this was as much of a surprise to him as it was to Bryson.

"Of course." Bryson straightened and beckoned them to follow him. "We can speak in my office."

He felt himself frowning in wonder as he led the way down the hall and into his office. The room was located at the back of the house with large sliding doors leading out to a patio overlooking the manicured garden. It was a serene place to work or just kick back for a few minutes in peace and quiet. He cared about his clan and enjoyed the energy of his people surrounding him, but his busy clan life also made him appreciate the occasional moments he was able to spend by himself.

Turning toward Leith and Sabrina, he swept out his arm toward the couch facing the patio. "Please have a seat." Sabrina's expression was an unreadable mask, and he felt his apprehension rise as he wondered why she wanted to speak to him without other people listening.

Bryson sat down in a large armchair situated to one side of the couch before looking at Sabrina and giving her a nod as a sign to go ahead.

She narrowed her gaze at him. "How well do you know Fia?"

His heart lurched in his chest at her question, but he tried to keep his expression from betraying his surprise. Studying her face for a few seconds, he wondered where she was going with this. "I met her about two years ago. She and her mother live a couple of miles away. They keep to themselves a lot. Why?"

Sabrina pursed her lips and studied him right back for a few seconds before continuing. "You mentioned the last time we were here that she's not powerful. Would you say the same about her mother?"

Bryson nodded, still unsure where Sabrina was going with this. "I've only really met her mother once when I went to talk to Fia at their house. Her mother invited me in for coffee." Which Fia had made clear was against her wishes, but he didn't say that. "I'd say none of them have anywhere near the power Ambrosia or you have, or Michael's mate for that matter. I'd like to know why you are asking me these questions, though. Do you want them to join in a possible showdown with Ambrosia?" The thought didn't sit well with him. He didn't want Fia anywhere near that malicious psycho.

Sabrina glanced at her mate, and he lifted an eyebrow at her in question. Sighing, the blonde swung her gaze back to Bryson. "I've got the ability to sense people's power signatures and levels, even when they try to hide it. Not like Fia, who can feel people's propensity toward good or evil. I can tell if people are a shifter or a witch, which became clear to me when I learned about shifters and started to get familiar with their power signatures. And I can tell if people are hiding their true power level, like I knew that Leith was far more powerful than he made it seem when I met him."

Bryson frowned and crossed his arms over his chest. "You still haven't told me where you're going with this."

Sabrina pinned him with her gaze. "Fia is more powerful than she's letting on, but she's extremely good at hiding it. I can tell, but I don't think anyone else can. Her control is solid as steel, and I believe it would take a lot to make her lose it."

Bryson shook his head slowly. She couldn't be implying what it sounded like. "What do you mean by more powerful? I mean she can't be in your league; I would've picked up on it."

Chuckling, she rolled her eyes at him. "Fia's an extremely powerful witch, Bryson. Of the witches I know, her power level is second only to Ambrosia's. And she's been hiding that from you for two years."

Staring at Sabrina, Bryson felt his jaw drop. That couldn't be right. Why would Fia lie to him like that? And how was she even able to? Sabrina had to have it wrong. He winced and rubbed at his chest as a burning sensation flared for a second.

Shaking his head, he narrowed his eyes on the blonde. "I can't believe that. It's been two years. If what you say is true and Fia's that powerful, she would've slipped up at some point. No one can hide their power for two years without a single lapse in control."

Sabrina looked at Leith. "How difficult is it for you to keep your real power level from being detected? Does it take a lot of conscious effort, or is it mostly automatic for you by now?"

Leith shrugged. "I do not usually have to think about it anymore. But then I have centuries of experience. It took me quite a few years to reach that level of effortless control. Fia, I believe, is still in her late twenties. But based on what you have taught me, the control witches have over their power can vary significantly between individuals, so perhaps it is possible for a witch. For a shifter I think it would be unusual to attain that level of control in such a short time."

Bryson nodded and let his irritation show. "Exactly. I can't believe Fia would be able to hide her power like that. And why would she? I appreciate you wanting to warn me about what you believe is the case, Sabrina, but you're wrong about her."

Leith's brows pulled together, and his power suddenly ramped up and slammed into Bryson, making him jerk in his seat. He'd felt Leith's power before, but not like this. It was clear that the man didn't take kindly to Bryson being so dismissive of his mate's words.

"That is not what I said. Are you calling my mate a liar, or her ability to sense power a fraud?" Leith leaned toward Bryson with his eyes glowing emerald green with rage.

Bryson steeled himself against Leith's power, not wanting to back down but not wanting to escalate the situation either. "No, I—"

"Leith!" Sabrina put a hand on her mate's arm. "There's no need for that. Bryson is entitled to believe whatever he wants. I came here to tell him what I know, but it's up to him whether he wants to trust my word or not. It doesn't matter." Her gaze swung to him, and her blue eyes cooled considerably. "He's free to think he's infallible and all-knowing. Now let's go back to the others while we wait to hear from Callum and Vamika." Sabrina rose from the couch.

"Wait. Please." Bryson shot to his feet. He was struggling to believe he was wrong in his assessment of Fia, but he couldn't let this opportunity to hear Sabrina's assessment of the beautiful redhead pass him by. "I'm sorry, Sabrina. I must admit that I find this hard to believe, but I would like to know what else you can sense about her. She's a bit of a…mystery to me." Fia was more of a frustration than a mystery to him really, but he would never admit to that out loud.

Sabrina's sudden laughter made him jerk back like she had slapped him, and he clamped his mouth shut to stop himself from telling her to shut up. He couldn't remember the last time someone had laughed at him outright. It had to be years ago. A wolf alpha had tried that, but he soon quit laughing when his mouth filled with blood and broken teeth.

"Mystery. I suppose that's one way of putting it." Sabrina's eyes were filled with mirth at his expense. "You mean she hasn't let you fuck her yet despite your persistent efforts?"

His spine tensed. How did Sabrina know about that? Nobody knew about that. Or did they? Had he been less cautious than he'd thought?

Sabrina shook her head with eyes still filled with amusement. "Don't worry, Bryson. I'm not going to tell anyone. It was obvious to me, but it might not have been so obvious to everyone else. I've got a tendency to notice things about people."

He gave her a stiff nod, not sure what to say to that. There was no point denying it. It would only make her more certain that her assessment was correct. And she'd already said that she wasn't going to tell anyone, so he'd just have to take her word for it.

Clearing her throat, Sabrina let her face become serious. "It might interest you to know that she's not as unaffected by you as you might think. But she seems determined to keep her distance to you. I'm not going to speculate as to why, though. Perhaps you should try to have an actual conversation with her that doesn't revolve around your need to impress her or lure her to your bed. I'm sure you've already tried both plenty of times, and if it hasn't worked in the last two years, then why would it start working now? My advice is to treat her with respect and show genuine interest in getting to know her as a person. Who knows? It might work."

Bryson swallowed, needing a second to come up with a suitable response. "Thank you for your advice, Sabrina." Nodding stiffly, he tried to smile, but it felt more like a grimace. "I'll think about it."

"Please do." Sabrina turned and headed toward the door to the hallway, and Leith followed her after giving him a short nod.

Bryson took a deep breath before letting it out slowly. His mind was spinning, and his heart was racing, and he didn't know how to feel about Sabrina's criticism and advice. He knew he wasn't particularly good at receiving any of those things, preferring to find his own way and stand behind his decisions no matter the outcome. And since he could hardly remember an outcome that had been less than satisfactory, he was clearly good at it. Except in his dealings with Fia.

He liked what Sabrina had said about Fia not being as unaffected by him as she seemed to be, but it was troubling as well. Because what did that mean exactly? Did it mean that she might actually let him fuck her a few times if he played his cards right? Or did it mean that she had feelings for him, and that if she gave in, it was because she expected more than sex?

The second alternative should scare him since he had no plans to find a mate and settle down anytime soon, but for some reason it didn't scare him as much as he thought it would. Did that mean that he was actually getting ready to settle down? Surely not. He wasn't ready for that kind of commitment or that kind of monotony.

CHAPTER 20

Callum drove as they headed toward the house Ambrosia had been visiting that morning. Hours had passed since the evil bitch had been there, and it was impossible to know where she was at the moment. Hopefully, she was far away from the house and had no reason to visit a second time in one day.

He had checked her phone number registered with the car rental company, but it had been disconnected the day before. And he hadn't had time to set up any searches based on facial recognition or license plate number. The uncertainty was making him antsy. He hated the fact that he was bringing Vamika into a potentially dangerous situation.

But they had Fia. And she had assured him she could sense Ambrosia's power if she was close by and had promised to warn them if she felt the evil bitch or any other person with power inside or close to the house. If that happened, they would simply continue past the house like they were headed somewhere else.

He parked a couple of hundred yards down the street from the house and turned off the engine before looking at Fia in the rearview mirror. "Will you give us a minute?"

She nodded with a small smile on her lips. "Sure. I'll be right outside."

With his brows furrowing, he turned to look at Vamika, where she was sitting in the passenger seat looking at him with one eyebrow raised and her head cocked to one side. "I'd feel better if you chose to stay in the car." Her eyes narrowed and her lips parted, but he continued before she could voice her protest. "Not because I don't believe you're strong or capable. Just simply because I love you and don't want to see you hurt."

Her face softened into a smile. "I could say the same about you, Callum. I love you, too, and there's only been a few hours since you woke from being unconscious. The sight of you lying there hurt and not knowing whether you were going to wake up will haunt me for the rest of my life. I don't want to ever experience that again."

His chest expanded with warmth and happiness. "You love me?"

She laughed. "Don't look so surprised. Of course I love you. How can I not? You're an amazing man, Callum."

"I... Thank you. I didn't think you had feelings like that for me yet. But I was hoping that with time—" A finger pressed against his lips silencing him.

"Kiss me." Vamika fisted his shirt and pulled him toward her, and he wasn't about to refuse her.

Their lips met and slid against each other, and he

groaned at the feel of her. He put his arms around her and pulled her against him as tightly as he could while sitting in the front seats of the car. Deepening the kiss, he swiped his tongue inside her mouth, savoring her taste, and she moaned into his mouth.

She was his. Callum still couldn't quite believe it. Hopefully, in just a few hours, she would be his for real. Forever. A word that had a new meaning with a true mate by his side.

A knock on the passenger side window made him growl low in his throat in annoyance. But there was no denying the fact that they needed the reminder of where they were and why, or they'd probably continue kissing until one of them gave in to the mating bond's insistent pull and jumped the other right there in the car.

Callum pulled back and stared down into Vamika's eyes. They were lighter than usual. A clear sign they needed to stop before they both sported wolf eyes in the middle of a village. Most people would probably shrug and assume they were wearing contact lenses, but it wasn't something they should count on.

Cupping her cheek, he smiled at his mate's slight pout. "I know. I don't want to stop either. But in just a few hours, we will mate and spend the rest of our lives together."

Vamika sighed and nodded. "I know, but I'm getting impatient. I'm not going to be able to wait much longer. I'm already drenched just from kissing you for a couple of minutes."

After pulling in a deep breath, he groaned at her scent of arousal. She smelled like mate and sex, *and holy hell*, he was getting desperate. He wanted her like he'd never wanted anything before. His cock was throbbing, his balls were pulled up tight, and his whole body was tense with the need to make her his.

Leaning back in his seat, he closed his eyes. "It feels like I've got a steel bar in my shorts. There's a reason I'm wearing loose clothes but damn."

Vamika chuckled, and he turned his head and scowled at her. But he wasn't able to prevent his lips from twitching with amusement.

She put her hand on his thigh and squeezed. "Let's go, pretty boy. We have work to do. And the sooner we get it done, the sooner we get to go back and barricade ourselves in our room."

Smiling at her, he nodded. "You're right. Let's do this."

They exited the car and were greeted by an amused Fia. "I'm sorry, but you're very cute. Acting like teenagers when you're clearly not. I think it's about time you mate. There can be little doubt that you're made for each other."

Vamika laughed. "We will as soon as we can get some time to ourselves."

Callum smiled, but he was a bit confused by the witch's words. How did she know they weren't already mated? Nobody had said anything to her about that as far as he had heard, and she hadn't been there when they'd first arrived at the panther's house. Could she somehow sense that they weren't mated?

Fia nodded. "Hopefully this won't take long, and we'll find out why Ambrosia was visiting the house without too much trouble."

Callum nodded and put his arm around Vamika before pulling her close to his side. The owner of the house had seemed innocent enough based on the information he had been able to find on her. There was nothing to suggest that she was an evil or even unusual person, but that didn't prove anything. A lot of supernaturals were camera and social media shy. They stayed out of the public eye as much as possible and those who could afford it had people on their payroll who regularly searched for and removed unwanted information that had somehow ended up on the internet.

There was no reason to believe the owner of the house was a supernatural, though, apart from the fact that Ambrosia had paid her a visit. And there might be a good explanation for the evil bitch visiting that had nothing to do with Ambrosia being a witch. Hopefully, they would have that explanation in a few minutes.

Fia walked in front of them as they strolled along the sidewalk on their way to the house. They were on the opposite side of the street from the house, giving them a good view of the place from a distance and a possibility to walk on past without getting too close if something felt off.

They had discussed various plausible excuses for knocking on the woman's door before they left Bryson's house, but ultimately, the success of their mission would depend on the woman's personality. Either she was open to talking to them or she wasn't.

Fia rang the doorbell with Callum and Vamika standing a few steps behind to seem as unthreatening as possible. Standing as a collected front outside her door wouldn't serve their purpose. They weren't there to scare the woman.

Twenty seconds went by without a sound from

inside, and Callum was just about to suggest that Fia ring the bell again when the sound of hurried footsteps approaching the door reached them.

The door was yanked open, and a woman was standing there, looking like she had just been doing some vigorous exercise. Her face was red, and some of her graying hair had escaped her ponytail.

"Yes, can I help you?" She looked at Fia like she didn't really see her, the woman's mind still on whatever had occupied her a minute ago.

"Good afternoon, we were just—" Fia's opening line was cut off when a sound of something crashing to the floor reached them from inside the house.

"Oh no, not again." The woman's eyes closed for a second, and her shoulders sagged, before she abruptly turned, leaving the door wide open, and ran back inside the house, disappearing through an open door to the right and down the hallway. A few seconds later, they heard soft voices, but they were too low to make out the words.

Fia turned to them. "I'll go inside and ask if she needs help. This might be our golden opportunity."

Callum nodded. "We'll stay here for now until you've had a chance to see what's going on. Three people barging into her house uninvited might be a bit much, even if she left the door open."

Nodding, Fia turned and crossed the threshold. "I'll be back soon."

But she didn't get more than a few steps inside the house before a young woman came rushing out from the room the older woman had entered just seconds earlier. Her eyes were wild as she headed directly for the entrance, bumping into Fia in her hurry to get to the door.

A gasp sounded from Vamika beside him.

Callum followed his instinct and caught the woman in his arms to stop her from running outside and into the street. The young woman didn't seem like she was all there, and the information he had read about the female owner of the house came back to him. She had been working in a mental institution, and judging by the confused look in the young woman's eyes, he had a feeling she might belong in one.

"Just relax. Don't worry. I've got you." He spoke softly while she struggled to get away from him.

The owner of the house came rushing back into the hallway, looking more distressed and disheveled than before. "Oh, Mary. What is the matter with you today?" She raised her gaze to Callum. "I'm so sorry. She's not been herself these past few days. I don't know what's going on with her. She was doing so much better before that. Ever since…she got here she has been improving. Except these last few days. I just don't understand what happened to make her so agitated. We have followed the exact same routines. But she can't sleep. She hardly eats anything. And I was telling her mother just this morning that I don't know what to do anymore. She may need more help than I can give her."

Callum had just opened his mouth to give a comforting reply when he froze. Her mother had been there that morning, and the young woman's name was Mary.

His jaw dropped as realization sent his mind spinning. Mary clearly wasn't dead. She hadn't died like Freddie had told Henry and Vamika. Mary had survived.

Callum closed his mouth and pasted what he hoped was a pleasant smile on his face. "I'm so sorry to hear that. You're taking care of her for her mother?"

"Yes." The woman nodded. "But it's turning out to be more difficult than I expected. I'm just one person, and I can't stay awake twenty-four hours a day to take care of her and make sure she doesn't hurt herself or others." She shook her head with a sad smile on her face before seeming to realize something. "I'm Barbara. Thank you so much for stopping her. Will you please help me bring her back inside? I think I might have to give her something to calm her down. It seems the only way to calm her these last few days, when it's only supposed to be administered as a last resort."

"Of course." Callum nodded. "I'll bring her inside. Just lead the way to where you want her settled. You mentioned she was getting better. When did she take a turn for the worse?"

Barbara threw her hands in the air. "Just a few days ago. I can't even remember which day it was. The last few days have been a blur. I don't think I've slept more than a couple of hours."

Callum gently guided Mary inside and followed Barbara down the hallway. The young woman was still struggling in his arms while making incoherent noises. With his strength she couldn't get away from him, but he had to be careful not to hurt her.

They entered a living room toward the back of the house, and Barbara pointed at the couch. "Please, if you can get her to sit there with you for just a minute. I'll be right back."

The woman disappeared through a door to the right into what looked like a kitchen.

Callum maneuvered Mary carefully around the coffee table before sitting down with her next to him on the couch. She was still struggling to get free, but her efforts were waning. Perhaps she was starting to realize he wasn't going to let her go, or she was simply too tired to fight anymore.

He glanced at Fia and Vamika, who had entered the room behind him. Fia had a blank expression on her face, whereas Vamika looked shocked. And the way Vamika was staring at Mary, there was no doubt she recognized the woman. Which was conclusive evidence that Mary was indeed Ambrosia's daughter.

Barbara came back into the room with a syringe in her hand. "Just a couple of minutes, poor dear, and you'll feel better," she cooed at the young woman before jabbing the syringe into the flesh of Mary's upper arm. "There now. I'm so sorry to have to do this to you again." The woman's eyes were sad when she studied Mary's face, but the young woman didn't seem to understand what was going on around her.

"What happened to her?" Callum took in Barbara's tired eyes and sallow face. She'd mentioned not getting much sleep lately, and the evidence of it was all there in her face. "I'm assuming that she has not always been like this."

Barbara's gaze met his, and she gave him a weak smile. "Your assumption is correct. Her condition stems from her trying to take her own life. Her body survived, but her mind did not. There is a possibility that it's due to a lack of oxygen to the brain for an extended period of time, but the doctors haven't been able to find any evidence of that, leading them to believe that it's a mental condition. It's even possible that the mental break happened before, and perhaps even was the cause of, her attempted suicide, but according to her mother, that's not the case. But the poor woman is distraught, of course, and she may not want to acknowledge the facts staring her in the face. They're simply too painful to consider."

Callum nodded his understanding. "I'm sorry to hear that. It can't be easy for a mother to see her daughter like this." Barbara didn't seem to have any qualms about talking to strangers about Mary's condition and history, making him think that Ambrosia had never shown the woman her evil side. If she knew what Ambrosia was capable of, she wouldn't have been so quick to divulge information.

Barbara shook her head slowly, her gaze once again resting on Mary's face. "No, it isn't. And I think she's prepared to do just about anything to get her daughter back, but I'm not so sure that's possible. I don't know what caused her mental break, whether it was a specific event or if it's a hereditary condition, but with her deterioration these last few days I don't think there's any other option but to get her settled in a suitable mental institution. She needs more help than I can give her."

Nodding, Callum slowly eased his hold on Mary. Her body was sagging against his, the medication clearly taking effect. "Will you be all right by yourself for now, or do you want us to stay until you can get someone to help you? I don't think you should be taking care of her alone anymore."

Barbara's tired eyes lifted to his. "I'll be fine, but

thank you for asking. Her mother will be back sometime late this afternoon or early evening. The sedative should keep the poor dear calm until then."

"If you're sure." Callum made sure Mary rested against the back of the couch before letting go of her.

"Yes. Thank you."

"No trouble at all. I hope you find a good solution for her." Giving Barbara a small smile, Callum rose from the couch.

She gave him a small nod in return, and he took that as a sign that it was okay to leave. Barbara had never asked why they rang the doorbell in the first place, but it was understandable with how tired she was.

Callum, Vamika, and Fia exited the house and crossed the street before any of them said anything. Vamika's eyes were still wide with shock, and Callum wasn't surprised seeing as she had just seen someone she'd thought to be dead. He had also believed Mary to be dead, but he'd never met the woman before, so the impact from realizing that they'd been misinformed wasn't as great for him.

Vamika shook her head before looking up at him. "So, Mary is alive. I didn't see that one coming. I'd mentally prepared myself for meeting another evil witch, but not for seeing a ghost."

Callum smiled, but before he could respond Fia spoke.

"I take it that was Ambrosia's daughter. Bryson told me about her, but I'm not sure he mentioned her name."

"Definitely Ambrosia's daughter." Vamika frowned. "Just a broken version of her, and Freddie's death apparently made her worse."

"Just what I was thinking." Callum nodded slowly. "Barbara has her hands full, and she doesn't even know what she's dealing with. Ambrosia clearly hasn't told her the whole story of what happened, and why would she if the woman doesn't even know about shifters and witches? Barbara would most likely conclude that the mental issues run in the family."

"Freddie was Mary's mate then?" Fia looked at Vamika before lifting her gaze to Callum. "The wolf who mated her without making sure she knew what it meant?"

"That's being kind." Vamika narrowed her gaze. "Freddie knew exactly what he was doing. I wouldn't be surprised if he did it out of spite to punish Henry for ruining his plan to mate Euna."

They reached the car and got in, but before Callum started the engine, he looked at Fia in the rearview mirror. "Fia, can you call Bryson and tell him what we've just discovered? I think his panthers should stay in the area and keep an eye out for Ambrosia. We can't approach her here in the middle of the village, but if we tail her to somewhere more remote…" He intentionally left the sentence hanging. They would have to come up with a plan for that scenario, but first they had to have people stationed close to Barbara's house who would be able to see Ambrosia when she arrived and would follow her when she left.

Fia nodded with an unreadable expression on her face. "I will." There was something strange about Fia. He just couldn't quite put his finger on what it was. It was just a feeling that she was hiding something.

Callum started the engine and pulled out into the

street before glancing over at Vamika to see her staring straight ahead with her brows wrinkled. "Are you all right?" He reached over and let his hand skim her thigh.

She turned her head toward him, and her expression smoothed into a weak smile. But her eyes were still troubled. "Yes, I just can't get over the fact that Mary is still alive. Why on earth would Ambrosia kill Freddie when she knew her daughter was still alive? She'd have to know that it would hurt her. Or did she think that it wouldn't for some reason? It makes no sense to me. Ambrosia clearly cares about her daughter and still she does something that is known to destroy a mate."

Callum nodded. "I agree, and I don't think we'll know the answer to those questions unless Ambrosia explains them to us. And, well, she's not likely to do that, is she? But there has to be a reason why she thought she could kill Freddie without killing or hurting Mary. And now she's probably realizing that she fucked up. I just hope it won't set her off on a more extreme shifter killing spree."

CHAPTER 21

They arrived back at Bryson's house, and the alpha, a couple of other panthers, and most of their own party were on the porch waiting for them. Fia had relayed what they had discovered over the phone to Bryson, and he'd probably had time to give the others the highlights before their arrival.

Vamika exited the car and walked around the back of the vehicle to meet Callum before they approached the house together. The feeling of his arm coming around her sent a thrill through her body. In just a few days he'd gone from being a stranger, to a threat, to becoming her anchor, her lifeline, and her companion. She could no longer envision a future without him. It was strange how fast her life had changed but it had certainly changed for the better.

They hadn't yet reached the porch when another car pulled up, and she felt the hairs on the back of her neck stand up. She knew that car. It was her father's. Apparently, he was still driving the same car he had been when she'd last seen him. When she'd still been living at home.

But that wasn't home for her anymore. Home was no longer a place. It was wherever Callum was.

Vamika pressed herself tighter against Callum's side. The arrival of her father wasn't just unexpected; it was what she had dreaded ever since she left his house.

Callum must have understood that something was wrong because he turned his head to look down at her. "What's wrong? Do you know the people in that car?"

The car doors swung open, and her father stepped out. And that was when she realized he wasn't the only occupant of the car. Another man stepped out as well, and the sight of him made her shudder with distaste. He hadn't changed much since she last saw him. Andrew, the asshole her father had promised her to, had the same arrogant expression on his face that he'd had back then.

There was no doubt as to why they were there. What she had trouble understanding was that the asshole still wanted to mate her. Why hadn't he found someone else? It wasn't like her father was well off or anything. But the pack she grew up in was quite wealthy so that might have something to do with it. At least she knew it wasn't her personality Andrew was enamored by. Vamika was just a puzzle piece in something bigger. She just didn't know what it was. But it had to be something that would be beneficial to her father and perhaps the pack.

"Vamika!" Her father made her name sound like a curse and a command rolled into one.

She was just opening her mouth to respond to him when Callum pushed her behind him. "You don't get to address my mate like that. Either you speak to her with respect, or you don't speak to her at all."

"Your mate?" Her father's face contorted in rage. "You mated someone without my consent, Vamika? That was not your decision to make, you little slut, and I require compensation from your mate."

Callum's power flared, but he didn't lash out. Instead, he took a few measured steps toward her father.

Vamika wasn't going to let him do this alone, though, and she hurried to his side. "He's my true mate. Dad." She put extra emphasis on the last word as she made a grimace of loathing. He'd never acted like a real dad should. Something she had realized after witnessing how other dads typically behaved toward their daughters. Or sons for that matter. He'd never acted like anything other than a military commander toward her. "And we haven't had a chance to mate yet, but we will by the end of the day." There was no point trying to convince her father they were already mated. He'd smell that they weren't if he got close enough. And being caught in a lie would only make them look weaker.

Her father's gaze dropped to Callum's legs, and his lips wrinkled in disgust. "You're not mating a cripple. Not on my life. Whether you're true mates or not doesn't make any difference. I have a signed contract, and it includes you mating this exceptional wolf." He indicated Andrew, who was standing a couple of steps behind him to the right.

Callum's laughter took her by surprise, and her gaze snapped to his face. This didn't seem like the right time to burst out laughing.

"Contract. Are you for real?" Callum snorted and shook his head. "Do you even know which century we're living in? Vamika can do whatever she wants. It's her choice, not yours. And I'm her choice and she's mine. Being true mates seals the deal the way I see it. But if you want to fight me for her, I'll be happy to oblige you. She's worth it."

Her father narrowed his gaze at Callum, and his hands fisted at his sides. Being laughed at wasn't something he was used to, but she was betting it had taken him by surprise. And perhaps even impressed him a little. Not a lot of people had dared to laugh at him before. At least not to his face.

"I won't fight a cripple. It would be an unfair fight. And it would be pointless since the outcome wouldn't matter anyway. I have the law on my side. She's my daughter, and I decide who she mates. That's how it's been in our pack for centuries, and that's how it's going to stay."

Callum shook his head and chuckled. "If you don't have the balls to fight me, why didn't you just say so? But Vamika's mine. It's as simple as that. Your pack rules don't apply here. And even if they did, I would fight you and kill you if necessary to keep her at my side."

Her father sighed and rolled his eyes, like Callum was being a difficult child. "So how much do you want then? Because I assume that's what this is about. Money. I'm sure we can come to a comfortable arrangement that will suit us both."

"Money." Callum spat the word. "No amount of money would be enough for me to give up Vamika. No amount of money is worth the loss of your true mate. But you wouldn't know anything about that, would you? Because you have no integrity or honor. We have nothing more to discuss." At this Callum spun and grabbed her hand before starting toward the porch.

The sound of crunching gravel had her glancing back toward her father, and she gasped when she saw him only six feet behind them ready to attack. Vamika had never witnessed her father actually attack or fight someone before. He just wasn't the type. Threats and commands were everyday occurrences, but fighting wasn't his style. So seeing him ready to pounce was completely unexpected, and fear sank its icy claws into her spine as she realized he was going to hurt her mate.

But before she could do anything to warn Callum about her father attacking or push him out of the way and step in to let her father attack her instead, her mate let go of her hand, crouched low, spun, and landed a punch to her father's abdomen all in one fluid motion. The impact made a sound almost like a gunshot it was that hard.

Her father hunched in response to the hit before staggering forward a step, and Callum used the opportunity to kick his legs out from under him, making him land face first on the ground at Callum's feet.

Too busy watching Callum dealing with her father, she didn't pay attention to Andrew. Until his arms suddenly snaked around her waist from behind, and she was pulled tightly against the front of his body as he walked her backward.

Callum spun toward them, and his jaw tensed in

fury. Stalking toward them, his gait was a little stilted like it always was, but the way he moved was nothing less than predatory. He was magnificent, the wolf in him so close to the surface that his eyes changed, and his muscles were straining as he prepared to fight Andrew for her.

But it wasn't just the sight of Callum that had her undivided attention but his power. It surrounded him like a forcefield, making her channel slick and achy with need.

This wasn't the time to drool over her mate, however. Vamika had an annoying asshole to deal with, and she had a few tricks up her sleeve that would work perfectly for that. After joining Henry's pack, she had made sure to hone her fighting skills, and she had specialized in fighting larger opponents. Which was a necessity since every male shifter was bigger than her.

She threw her head back, catching his chin with the back of her skull. The surprise of her attack made Andrew loosen his hold on her, and she used the opportunity to turn in his arms until she could reach between his legs and get a solid grip on his balls, which she proceeded to squeeze hard.

Andrew's reaction was immediate. Howling in pain, he dropped to his knees and bent over with his hands protectively cupping his groin. She had fought dirty, but this way he might get the message that she would never be a good mate to him. Knowing the pain she could cause, he would most likely rethink his intention to mate her. At least that was what she hoped. And he would be stupid not to.

Callum's laughter behind her had her turning around. "I doubt he'll want to mate you after that. If I was him, I'd make sure to stay out of your reach at all times."

Vamika chuckled as she let her gaze take in the magnificent shifter who was her mate. "That's what I was going for."

Callum was still chuckling when he grabbed her hand and pulled her toward the porch. Glancing back, she admired their handiwork. Her father was just getting up from his faceplant in the gravel, and Andrew was still on his knees cupping his bruised balls and making small, choked whining sounds. She wasn't going to stay to see them off. Vamika had nothing more to say to her father, and she'd be happy if she never saw him again. He wasn't worth even one more second of her life.

Someone started clapping on the porch, and as she turned to look, more people joined in and cheered. Apparently their show was appreciated by the audience. And knowing how these people revered their mates, she wasn't surprised. Even Bryson and his panthers, who prided themselves on following old shifter etiquette, practiced free will when it came to choosing their mate.

Grinning, she turned her head to look up at Callum. "Well, now that you've met my sorry excuse for a father, I guess there's nothing or no one to prevent us from going ahead with our mating."

He smiled down at her before turning serious. "I think you're right, but unfortunately there's this issue with an evil witch that we have to attend to first."

They all walked into the house except for a couple of panthers that Bryson instructed to stay outside to make sure her father and her wannabe mate left without making any more trouble. It was really for their own benefit, preventing them from making bigger fools of themselves than they already had.

After sitting down in the living room, Vamika snuggled against Callum's side. It had already been a long day even though it wasn't yet dinnertime. And all she wanted to do was crawl into bed with her mate and stay there for a very long time.

Bryson's voice had her turning to look at the alpha. "So Mary is alive, and Ambrosia will be back later this afternoon." There was a tick in his jaw and a wrinkle between his brows as he stared at Fia, and Vamika got the feeling he didn't quite trust the witch for some reason. "We need a plan to take the bitch down without her daughter or the owner of the house ending up being collateral damage."

"Yes." Leith nodded his agreement. "We will not be able to take her down in the village without gaining a lot of unwanted attention from witnesses. Not to speak of the damage her magic can do to humans and shifters alike. We need to lure her away to a safe place. The question is how we will be able to do that without her attacking us. We have to come up with a good excuse for her to agree to accompany us somewhere else. But even then, she already knows that we are trying to stop her, so, why would she accompany us anywhere?"

"Or..." Callum spoke up. "We'll follow her when she leaves the house this evening and hope she'll go somewhere we can approach her safely. At least safely with respect to the general public. I don't think anyone is safe around her after seeing what she did to Sabrina."

"I agree." Bryson nodded at Callum. "That sounds like the best solution unless she takes her daughter with her when she leaves. But even if she does, we might have to seize the opportunity to take her down if it presents itself. We don't know how many other chances we'll get before she kills again, and sacrificing Mary while horrible might be our only option. But let's hope it doesn't come to that. Ending up with an innocent person dead is not something any of us wants."

Vamika felt her stomach twist at the thought of Mary being killed in the crossfire so to speak. It wasn't fair to the woman. Her only mistake had been to agree to have sex with Freddie. Talk about ending up the victim again and again. "I don't feel good about Mary being hurt. I didn't like the woman, but none of this is her fault. And she's already been through hell. Whether she'll survive now after Freddie's death is anyone's guess, but we have to make a plan that includes measures to prevent her death by our hand. Hopefully Ambrosia won't take Mary with her when she leaves the house tonight. I mean what is Ambrosia supposed to do with her daughter in her current condition? Mary's mind seems to be gone. She needs proper care, and I don't believe her mother is capable of giving her that."

Most of the people seated around the large table nodded their agreement, but nobody said anything for several seconds. The fact that their actions to destroy Ambrosia were necessary at all was something none of them relished, but the possible death of an innocent woman just made it that much worse.

Fia was the first one to speak. "Ambrosia is a witch,

which makes this first and foremost a job for witches."

There were several protests from the people in the room, but Fia held up her hand to indicate that she wasn't finished. "I know some of you don't agree but hear me out first please. We are three witches here, and together we need to come up with a way to render Ambrosia unable to attack us before we can kill her. Either we must ambush her, so she literally doesn't have time to retaliate before she's dead, or we have to find a way to freeze her mind until we can take her down. She has already proven that she will kill without hesitation, and as long as she has the time and mind to attack, she'll do it."

"Do you think you can come up with a way to freeze her mind as you call it?" Bryson's brows wrinkled with doubt. "It sounds similar to Ambrosia's ability to stop or stun people. Do any of you possess a comparable ability?"

"Why don't you let us discuss this between ourselves, and we'll see what we can come up with." Fia held Bryson's gaze with a neutral expression on her face. "Would you mind if we use your library for a while? Having all of you comment on our discussions will only distract us and make our planning inefficient."

Vamika noticed that Fia didn't really answer Bryson's question. Whether that was a deliberate evasion was impossible to say, but it was likely. The witch seemed somewhat secretive even though she had been forthcoming with some information about her abilities. Or perhaps Vamika was just being overly suspicious.

"Of course." Bryson nodded, but his expression

was rigid, and his nostrils flared like he was trying to conceal his irritation. "You know where it is."

The three witches got up and left the room, but not without some grumbling from Sabrina's and Steph's mates. They clearly weren't happy to let their women out of their sight when Ambrosia might still be in the area.

Leith sighed. "I do not like the fact that this confrontation is going to rely on our mates. I would much prefer it if I was at the front when we approach Ambrosia, and Sabrina could stay at a safe distance and perform whatever magic they can come up with to stop that nasty creature. However, irrespective of how the witches want to play this, we need a backup plan or two in the event things does not go as planned."

"I think a surprise attack is our safest bet, but we have to be prepared to kill her while she is attacking us. That means our attack cannot fall apart even if some of us are hit by her magic and rendered seriously hurt or dead. The people still standing will have to continue fighting until Ambrosia is destroyed or this will never end. Unless there is a means for us to protect ourselves against her magic. But I believe Sabrina and Steph would have mentioned it if that was at all possible."

There were several nods and murmurs of agreement around the room, but nobody had any immediate comments to Leith's serious message. As far as Vamika knew, they were up against a far more powerful enemy than any of them had ever confronted before, and as attested to by the grave faces around the table, it was starting to sink in that not everyone might come away from this alive.

Shifters had traditionally had some internal skirmishes, but when fighting other shifters, they knew what they were up against. There were no secret powers or abilities that they had to allow for. And fights between shifters groups were few and far between these days, so most shifters didn't have a lot of practice fighting an enemy who wanted them dead.

"If you'll excuse me, I need to get my laptop." Callum rose, and Vamika immediately followed suit. Just the thought of being separated from him for more than a second made her heart speed up and goosebumps break out all over her body. "Do you have somewhere I can work for a little while, Bryson? I'd like to see what I can do with the new information I've got on Ambrosia. It might help us find her if we lose her again."

The alpha nodded. "You can use my office. It's down the hall on the right."

"Perfect. Thank you." Callum grabbed her hand as he turned toward the door.

As soon as they entered the hallway, he looked down at her and smiled. "I was hoping you'd join me." Squeezing her hand, he sighed. It sounded like a sigh of happiness, making her smile as her heart fluttered in her chest.

After picking up his laptop from the car, they headed back inside and down the hall to Bryson's office. It was a tastefully decorated room, with access to a patio overlooking the beautiful garden surrounding the house.

Callum pulled her toward the couch, and she frowned as she looked up at him. "Don't you want to sit at the desk? It's more comfortable than the couch when working."

"It is." He grinned as she sat down beside him. "But there won't be any room for you in that office chair, and I can't stand the thought of not having you close. I need to feel you next to me. An inch between us is too much right now." As if to emphasize his words, he put his arm around her shoulder and pulled her close as he held her gaze. "I wish I could work one-handed, or better yet not have to work at all."

Vamika laughed and reached up to bury her fingers in his silky hair. "Give me one kiss, and I promise I'll try not to distract you while you work."

He didn't hesitate to comply with her request, but her intention of a short kiss was soon forgotten when their lips locked. His hot mouth sent tingles throughout her body, and she found herself caught in the need to be as close to him as physically possible.

And he seemed to be similarly affected. Without any warning, he gripped her hips and swiftly moved her to straddle his lap, before his hands slid to her ass and pulled her closer until her clit was pressed firmly against his erection. Wolf eyes were staring into hers, his jaw tense with pent-up desire.

"Callum," she moaned as he started grinding his hard length against her pussy. "I need you to fuck me. Hard."

"Oh, I will." He gave her a grin that was all teeth, like he wanted to devour her in the literal sense.

There was no doubt that they were both getting so desperate that it was only a question of time before they would rip each other's clothes off and fuck without a care for where they were or who was watching. Mating was quickly becoming more important than anything else, dignity be damned.

CHAPTER 22

Callum had just grabbed ahold of Vamika's shirt and was about to pull it over her head when the door to the office burst open, and Duncan entered the room. "Ambrosia has just arrived at the house, and there's shouting coming from inside. It's attracting onlookers. We have to get over there as soon as possible to try to diffuse the situation. Our witches are leaving now. Are you coming?"

"We're coming." Callum's voice was low and growly, and he inwardly swore when he abruptly lifted Vamika off his lap. There was no excuse good enough not to join the others in what sounded like a messy and dangerous situation, even though his cock was hating him and throbbing uncomfortably to show its dismay.

Vamika's lips were compressed into a tight line as she grabbed his hand and helped him to his feet. Her body was probably giving her hell as well for ignoring the desire that was no doubt running rampant inside her.

His gait was more stilted than it usually was when they hurried out of the office to follow Duncan as he disappeared down the hallway toward the entrance. But as they walked out the door and saw the concern on everyone's faces while they crowded into the cars, the gravity of the situation finally started to penetrate his lust-addled mind.

They ended up in a car with three of Bryson's panthers. All the others from their party had already left, leaving him to worry that something would happen to them before Vamika and him could even get there.

Not that Callum wanted to bring his mate into this at all. He hated the fact that it was necessary. But the truth was that it was vital that they were there to support the others. It was exactly like Leith had said earlier. If something happened to one or more of them, the rest of them still had to fight to take the evil bitch down. They didn't know when or if they would get another chance, particularly considering Ambrosia was getting stronger.

Callum put his arm around Vamika and pulled her close as the car sped toward the house. The image of Sabrina flying through the air after being hit by Ambrosia's magic was still vivid in his mind, and he was going to make sure nothing like that happened to his mate. They would stay in the background until they could get an overview of the situation and assess how they could best support the others. The witches would be front and center along with their mates and the other alphas. They hadn't discussed the fighting set-up in detail, at least not while Callum and Vamika had been present, but it was the commonly accepted strategy to have the strongest members of a group lead the attack.

Vamika's hand was gripping his thigh, her fingers digging into his flesh. And he could feel the tension in her body steadily increase as they got closer to the house.

And he was feeling it as well. This day might change his life and everyone else's life around him. They might even lose someone. And not just someone but a friend or a mate.

He shuddered at the thought and quickly pushed it to the back of his mind. Instead, he let his anger take over. His anger and resentment toward Ambrosia, who was trying to destroy everything they held dear, everyone they loved. They had to get rid of her. This couldn't go on any longer. It would wear them down, while she would spend the time getting stronger.

The street was littered with people when they arrived. Innocent people who could easily get hurt. But curiosity was pulling them in like flies to shit, and they had no idea the danger they were in. If they knew they would probably run as fast as they could away from that house. Or not. Humans had a tendency not to avoid threats to their lives if it meant missing a good show.

With all the people gathered, they had to park a couple of hundred yards away. Trevor and Duncan were just passing the gate to the front yard of the house, their heads seen above the crowd of people. Presumably the witches had already entered the house and were doing whatever they could to defuse the situation and stop Ambrosia.

They exited the car and hurried toward the house. The noise from the crowd outside was masking any sounds that might have been coming from inside. And it was impossible to know what was going on in there, since there was nothing to see from the outside of the house.

A few of Bryson's panthers were standing guard outside the gate, obviously trying to prevent people from going inside and ending up getting hurt. The police had yet to arrive on the scene, and in this case, it was a good thing. They would only end up getting hurt as well since they had no idea what they were up against and how to handle this situation. But the police would surely arrive any minute, meaning that they didn't have much time to incapacitate the witch. The cleanup would be a mess, but that was a worry for later.

Callum gripped Vamika's hand as they entered the front yard, but as they neared the porch, he pulled her back to slow their progress. "Careful! We have no idea what's going on inside. Let's take this nice and easy. No rushing. I want to have a chance to see what's coming at us before it's upon us. If we run inside, we'll only end up hurt or we'll cause someone else to get hurt."

Vamika glanced at him and nodded as they ascended the porch together. "Perhaps we should go around the back. We don't know where people are. There are no sounds coming from inside, and that doesn't bode well, if you ask me."

Nodding, he stopped right before they reached the front door. It was open but not enough to give them a clear view inside. "I agree. Let's go around the back."

He turned and headed toward the corner of the house with Vamika in tow. There was a narrow passageway between the house and the fence separating the property from the one next-door.

They had just rounded the corner into the passageway when there was a sound like a pop. Callum acted on instinct and pressed Vamika against the wall, before curving his larger body around her smaller one to protect her. Less than a second later, there was a loud boom, and all the windows in the house blew out, raining glass all around them.

A couple of seconds went by while Callum tried to swallow down the shock of what had just happened. He had friends inside that fucking house, and he wanted to race in there to check on them immediately. But leading Vamika into an unknown situation was unacceptable.

Callum pulled back and quickly scanned Vamika's face and body. His heart was racing, and he had to specifically focus on his hands to get them to release their tight grip on her shoulders. She looked fine apart from her wide eyes and the death grip she had on his shirt. "Are you all right, Vamika?" Putting his hands on each side of her head, he stared into her eyes, trying to detect any sign that she was unwell or hurt.

She nodded vigorously before clearing her throat. "I'm fine. What about you? Did you get hit?"

Frowning, he tried to check for any pain. But the adrenaline coursing through his body was camouflaging any pain he might have otherwise felt. "I don't think so."

"Turn around." She let go of his shirt before grabbing his forearm and pulling to make him turn and show her his back.

He obliged and turned the other way to let her have a look at his back. She didn't immediately say anything, but she didn't gasp either, so he quickly concluded that he was fine.

Just as he was about to turn back to her, there was a slight burning sensation in his shoulder when she picked at something there. It was probably a glass splinter that had embedded itself in his skin.

"That's it I think," she said from behind him, followed by her pulling in a deep, shaky breath before letting it out on a sigh. "Only a small cut as far as I can tell. You can turn back around now. I think we were lucky that we had just rounded the corner." Vamika turned her head and studied the side of the house. "There are hardly any windows on this side of the house, and none of them are close to us."

A wail sounded from the back of the house, and Callum's whole body tightened in trepidation at the sound. They both hurried down the passageway in that direction, until he put a hand on Vamika's arm to stop her just before they reached the back corner of the house.

Carefully, they snuck a peek around the corner. His heart lurched in his chest when he saw someone lying on the back lawn just a couple of yards from the house. But it was impossible to tell who it was, since all he could see was the person's legs. The rest of their body was hidden behind a bush.

"Fuck!" He kept his voice low. "Someone's down, but I don't know who. We have to go check on them, but not until we know it's safe. Stay behind me while we approach slowly. If I tell you to run, run back the way we came, and I'll be right behind you." His whole body tightened in apprehension and anger before he uttered his next words. "If Ambrosia is the only one left standing, we're no match for her. But hopefully, that's not the case."

Vamika nodded and reached out to grip his hand tightly. Her eyes were still too wide, and her breathing was faster than normal.

Callum pulled in a deep breath before crouching low and creeping slowly along the wall of the house toward the back entrance, his hand still in Vamika's.

They were only three feet from the door when someone spoke inside. "Is everyone all right?" It was Fia's voice, and it was followed by several people answering in the affirmative. And Callum recognized at least three of those voices as belonging to his friends.

The relief made him sag against the wall for a second before he rose to his full height and turned to Vamika. She was smiling up at him, having obviously heard them as well.

Together they hurried to the back entrance, and the sight that greeted them was one of the best Callum had ever seen. His friends were all there in the living room, either already standing or getting to their feet, and nobody looked hurt. Unless you counted the shocked expression on several faces. Whatever had happened had obviously put some of them on the floor, but it hadn't killed them.

"Oh, thank God." Vamika's voice was a bit shaky. "What happened? I mean all the windows exploded, but you all seem okay. How is that even possible?"

Those were the exact questions he had wanted to

ask, but he had been too stunned to find his voice. Stunned in a good way, from realizing that his friends were alive and well.

Fia sighed. "I had to put up a protective barrier between us and Ambrosia, and when she attacked, it created a shock wave. I'm afraid she managed to get away, though, using our confusion and shock to flee."

Suddenly remembering the person lying just behind them, Callum turned around to see Barbara on the ground. After quickly closing the distance to her, he crouched by her side and tried to find her pulse. She had a small cut on her forehead but apart from that, she had no visible wounds.

Barbara suddenly coughed, and a few seconds later, her eyes blinked open to stare at the sky. She slowly turned her head until her eyes found his face and settled there. A frown creased her forehead for a moment before her face smoothed into a weak smile. "You." Her voice was weak, but at least she recognized him. It was a good sign.

"How are you feeling, Barbara?" He smiled down at her. "Are you in pain?"

"My leg. I think I've done something to my leg."

Callum nodded. "We'll get you a doctor. Does it hurt anywhere else?"

A few seconds went by before she slowly shook her head. "No, I don't think so. But I feel a bit dizzy."

Callum smiled. "That's no surprise. I think you hit your head when you fell."

"But..." She blinked a couple of times. "But what happened? Are Mary and her mother okay?"

"There was some kind of explosion, I think." He couldn't tell her what had actually happened, but he wanted to stick to the truth as much as possible. "I was in the area when I heard it, but I'm not sure what caused the blast. I'm sure the police will be able to find out what happened, though. They'll probably be here any minute."

"The ambulance is on its way." Vamika's voice sounded from right next to him, and he turned his head to look at her. "I'm sure you'll be up and about in no time."

"Mary?" Barbara frowned as he turned back to her. "Is she all right?"

Callum glanced over his shoulder. He didn't have an answer to that. According to Fia, Ambrosia had fled, but he didn't know whether she had taken her daughter or if Mary was still in the house somewhere.

His eyes found Fia where she was standing just inside the back entrance. "Fia."

The redhead turned in his direction. "Yes?"

"Do you know where Mary is?"

Fia nodded. "She left with her mother."

Callum gave her a small nod before turning back to Barbara. "Mary left with her mother, so I'm sure she's fine."

"Okay." Barbara nodded slowly as her eyes seemed to lose focus. "That's good." Her head rolled to the side when she lost consciousness, but her breathing stayed calm and even. Hopefully, the paramedics would be there soon and take her away to treat any injuries she'd sustained when she was knocked to the ground by the shockwave. At least that was what he assumed had happened to her.

Sirens could be heard in the distance. They were out of time, and they still had to come up with a credible story to tell the police. A gas explosion wasn't plausible since there was no sign of a fire.

"Go." Bryson's commanding voice came from behind him, and Callum turned to look at the alpha panther, who had come outside. "I'll talk to the police and sort out this fucking mess. This is my territory, and I know some of them from before. Leave through the back gate and get out of here. There will be a lot of questions to answer, but the more people the more questions."

Callum had his doubts that they would be able to walk away without someone noticing them. They were a crowd of about fifteen people who left the property through the back gate to wander down the parallel street to the one where they had parked the cars. Strangely, there weren't a lot of people in the street, but their group was still noticeable to the few who were present.

They had only walked about fifty yards when a man approached them and wanted to know what was going on. Turning to the man, Callum plastered what he hoped was an open and honest expression on his face before telling the man that they weren't sure what had happened, but that the woman living there was okay, save for a broken leg and a possible concussion. The answer seemed to appease the man's curiosity and concern, and they were able to continue down the sidewalk without anyone else approaching them.

After following the street for a few minutes, they took a left and were soon back in the street where they had parked their cars. There were still a lot of people outside Barbara's house up the street, but the emergency services had arrived, and the police were currently working on setting up a perimeter around the house to keep the crowd at a safe distance. The emergency services had no way of knowing what had actually happened, and Callum found himself wondering if they would manage to come up with a plausible explanation for what had caused the windows to blow out.

CHAPTER 23

It didn't take their group a long time to get back to Bryson's house, and they all gathered in the living room like before. Everybody who had been staying at Leith's house was present as well as Fia and three of Bryson's most trusted panthers.

Sabrina was the first one to speak. Her eyes were narrow when she stared at Fia. "That was quite a show you put on there. I think you might have some explaining to do. I believe the term you used to describe your powers earlier was gentle, but your performance back there was anything but gentle. And trust me it's not a complaint. You saved us all back there, but I must admit that I feel a bit betrayed. I don't know why you felt the need to hide the strength of your power, but you have deceived everyone here."

Fia sighed and looked down at her hands, which were folded in her lap. "I know and I had my reasons, but I can't tell you those. They're private and need to stay that way for a while longer."

Giving a humorless chuckle, Sabrina shook her head slowly. "I don't need your reasons, Fia, but there is one who will. And I don't believe he'll back down until you explain them to him. I hope for your sake they're good."

"Bryson." Fia nodded and visibly swallowed. "I know." The woman fisted her hands in her lap, and her shoulders sagged. It was obvious she didn't look forward to that talk. Or talk was probably putting it mildly. It would be more like an interrogation from Bryson's side.

Nobody said anything for ten seconds. The shock of what had happened still wasn't out of their systems. At least that was how it was for Callum. They needed time to process what had occurred and the fact that they were all still alive.

And then they needed to come up with a plan for what to do next. Ambrosia and Mary were both gone, and Callum hadn't been able to set up any system to track them. He would have to go through the information he had gathered and see if he had overlooked something that could be used to locate them.

But that would have to wait until he was able to think clearly again. At the moment his mind was a mess from the shock they had just had, and more notably from the desire running rampant in his body. His need had taken a break in the midst of the threat to Vamika's life and thinking his friends were dead, but it was back with a vengeance, and the hard evidence of that was barely hidden by his loose clothes.

Leith cleared his throat before speaking. "Ambrosia left with her daughter, Mary. We need to find her, but

I think this day has been eventful enough. And it would be good to have Bryson join us when we try to come up with a new plan to find and catch her. I suggest we find some available rooms in Inverness tonight, to be back here bright and early tomorrow morning. Please give our best to Bryson when he gets back from dealing with the police. Hopefully, it will not take him all night to answer all their questions."

Callum felt a jolt of anticipation shoot through his body at Leith's words, and he looked down at Vamika sitting next to him. She bit her bottom lip when she met his gaze with heat shining in her eyes. There was no doubt she was thinking what he was thinking. Inverness. They were going to stay the night in Inverness, and it wouldn't take them a long time to get there. Which was infinitely better than driving all the way back to Leith's house before they could mate.

Ready to leave immediately, Callum glanced around the table at the other couples in their group. Judging from the smiles on their faces, they were eager to leave as well. Having just survived a life-threatening situation probably had something to do with it. They needed to spend time with their significant other to celebrate that they were still alive and together.

A couple of minutes later, they were in their cars and on their way to Inverness. Leith had promised to call ahead to make sure there were rooms waiting for them when they arrived.

Callum would finally be able to spend a whole night with Vamika, and just the thought had his blood flow heading south at such a high rate that he was feeling lightheaded, which was crazy seeing as his dick was already hard as granite. To say that he was horny would be the understatement of the century. His body was a ticking timebomb of desire, and anybody delaying their mating would be running the risk of receiving his wrath.

There was only one thing they needed to do before they could go to bed. They needed food to sustain their energy through the night, because sleeping wasn't something he was planning to do a lot of at the hotel.

"What do you want to eat?" Callum whispered against the top of Vamika's head. She was sitting tucked tightly against his side in the back of Michael's car. Her hand was on his thigh, gently caressing his bare skin beneath his shorts, and although it was driving him wild feeling her hand that close to where he desperately wanted it, he didn't want her to stop.

"Eat?" She tipped her head back and looked up at him with an expression like he had just told her the car was about to change into a plane.

Callum chuckled. "Yes, eat. We need food if we're going to last through the night, baby girl. Or are you planning to sleep?" He lifted an eyebrow at her.

She shook her head as she burst out laughing. "No, definitely not. Sleep is the furthest thing from my mind. So, I guess that means we need food. Although, how I'm going to be able to focus on eating right now, I'm not sure."

He laughed. "I know, but something is better than nothing. What would you like?"

Her lips pursed in thought before she spoke. "Whatever takes the least amount of time to prepare and can be devoured quickly."

Callum threw his head back and laughed. "That's my girl, practical and with an eye for the important stuff. I like that."

She chuckled as she met his gaze. "What did you think I was going to choose? A five-course meal?"

"Oh, I wasn't worried about that." He shook his head as he grinned down at her before continuing in a whisper, "If you had chosen something like that, I would just have had to fuck you while you ate. Women are supposed to be excellent at multitasking, aren't they? At least that's what I've heard."

Vamika shook her head as she laughed. "Well, that's a combination I haven't tried before. Might be fun, but I think we'll save that for another day."

"Whatever you say ma'am. I'm up for it if you are."

They arrived at the hotel—the same one the group had stayed at the last time they were in Inverness. Thankfully, Leith had managed to secure rooms for all of them. And it didn't take them long to check in and order room service.

They entered their suite, and Callum closed the door behind them. The woman at the check-in counter had assured him their food would arrive within fifteen minutes, and Callum hoped it would. Their mating was long overdue, and he was getting desperate. His body was practically vibrating with need, and even the thought of waiting another fifteen minutes before he could take Vamika to bed was pure torture.

She turned to him, and they stared at each other from three feet apart. He wanted to rip her clothes off and carry her to bed immediately, but he held himself back. If he touched her, he didn't think he'd be able to stop when the food arrived, and he wanted to make sure she was fed for what he had planned for her. But his hands were itching to touch her skin, and every second felt like an hour.

"Callum." Vamika's voice was husky, and her expression was pained. She took a tentative step toward him, like she knew it was dangerous to get too close, but she just couldn't help herself.

But it was enough to break his resolve to stay away from her until they had eaten. He closed the distance between them in one long stride before grasping her hips and lifting her until her wide eyes were level with his own.

Her legs wrapped tightly around his waist, and he groaned as her hot center pressed against his achingly hard shaft. "Oh fuck," he rasped and stared into her heat-filled eyes, his own no doubt burning just as hot. "I want to watch you come all over my cock, and I can't wait much longer. If the food's not here within the next five minutes, it will just have to wait until after we've mated."

"Agreed." The word had barely left her mouth before she pressed her lips to his, and he took full advantage of the situation. Their tongues met as he slowly walked the few steps to the nearest wall. As soon as her back hit the flat surface, he pressed his shaft harder against her, making her moan into his mouth in response.

Shuddering, Vamika broke the kiss. "I need you. Now!" Her eyes were pleading, and she squirmed, his determination to wait wavering as he felt her hard nipples against his chest through both their shirts.

After moving one hand under her ass, he inched the other under her shirt while staring into her eyes. They were almost black with her need. Her lids fluttered shut, and she sucked in a breath as he brushed his fingers over the silky skin of her stomach on his way north.

Cupping one breast through her bra, Callum tested its weight in his hand. The soft globe filled his hand exactly the way he liked it, like her breasts had been created with him in mind. And perhaps they had. They were true mates after all. It shouldn't be a surprise that everything about her seemed so perfect to him.

She gasped when he pinched her hard nipple through the lacy fabric. "Callum." His name was spoken on a moan, and he groaned as the sound alone was enough to make his balls pull up tighter. He'd never been this turned on in his life. A part of it was the mating bond pulling them together, but the main reason for his desire was the amazing woman in his arms. He couldn't have picked a better mate if he'd tried. She was strong and stubborn, yet caring and vulnerable, all wrapped in the most irresistibly beautiful package.

And the contrast to his own looks might be some of the reason he found her beauty so enticing. Black hair to his blond, rich sepia skin to his fair complexion, short to his tall stature and perhaps most importantly, her softness and curves to his hard muscles.

Kneading her breast in his hand, he bent his head and nuzzled into the side of her throat before extending his jaw over the muscle there and biting down gently. Her reaction was immediate.

CHAPTER 24

Vamika gasped, and her whole body convulsed when Callum's teeth sank into her shoulder. The bite was nowhere near hard enough to break her skin, but with how needy she already was, it was all that was required to send her spiraling into an orgasm that shook her body.

She ground her pussy against his hard length as pleasure pulsed through her body, making Callum growl against her shoulder and rock his hips against her.

The pleasure died away, and she sagged in his arms, her forehead resting against his shoulder. But the usual feeling of being sated wasn't there. Her channel was still aching to be filled, and her clit was throbbing with the need for more attention.

There was a knock on the door. "Room service," a pleasant female voice called from outside the door.

Callum took a step back from the wall, and Vamika lifted her head from his shoulder before meeting his gaze. Heat simmered in his eyes as he gave her a tight smile, no doubt a result of his need threatening to drive him crazy.

She unwrapped her legs from around his waist, and he let her slide down his body until she stood on the floor.

"I'll get it." He turned before she had a chance to respond and went to open the door.

She took a quick look down her body to make sure her shirt was covering her breasts before heading over to the table. Food was the last thing on her mind at the moment. But for Callum's sake she'd force down a few bites of the salad and fruit she'd ordered. The salad had been the lightest meal on the menu and the only thing she could even contemplate eating.

After thanking the woman delivering the food, Callum closed the door and rolled the cart with their food and drinks over to the table. There was a wicked smile on his face when he rounded the table to where she was standing, and she tipped her head back to keep her eyes on his while he closed the distance between them.

Her breath hitched when she let herself take him in. Callum was male beauty personified, and she was a damn lucky woman because his beauty wasn't his only perfect characteristic. He happened to be a really caring person, a trait she wasn't used to in a shifter male except for Henry. But she had never had any sexual interest in her alpha. Henry had always felt more like an older brother to her than a potential mate.

"I have a proposition for you." Callum lifted an eyebrow at her in challenge, with the wicked grin still intact on his face. "The food will stay warm for a while under those covers. Well, mine will anyway. Yours is already cold. We can mate before celebrating the start of our mated life with having dinner together."

She frowned up at him. It sounded like a perfect plan, but it didn't explain his wicked grin.

Without warning she reached out and palmed his thick length through the fabric of his shorts, making him suck in a startled breath. "What aren't you telling me?"

He chuckled, his eyes becoming hooded as she stroked him, and his voice was rough when he answered her. "I expect you to sit on my cock while you eat."

Her eyes went wide until she remembered their conversation in the car and a smile curved her lips. "Multitasking."

"Yes." He chuckled, but it ended on a groan when, instead of stopping her upward stroke when she reached the waistband of his shorts, she let her fingers curve over the edge and caress the head of his one-eyed monster just peeking out from the garment.

"Vamika." He choked on the last syllable of her name when her finger gently caressed down his frenulum.

She was just opening her mouth to say something when he suddenly moved, and before she knew what was happening, she was in his arms being carried toward the bedroom.

"I need to claim you, and if you have any objections, you have to state them now." His voice was rough, and his jaw was tense like he was barely holding it together.

The desperation he displayed to make her his sent a jolt of need directly to her hot core, and she moaned and squeezed her thighs together. "No objections. I want you to claim me. And I want to claim you."

The heat in his gaze was intense when he lowered her down onto the mattress. "Your wish is my command, Vamika. It always will be."

He stood and gripped the bottom of his shirt before pulling it over his head and revealing his muscular upper body. The sight drew a moan from her, and her hands itched to explore every inch of his sculpted form.

Next, he gripped the waistband of his shorts and pushed them down his thighs, and his cock sprang free from its confinement to stand proud between his legs. It almost looked bigger than before, but it must be the angle from which she was seeing it while lying down on the bed. He was bigger than anyone she'd ever had sex with before, but she had no doubt that he would feel good inside her.

As soon as he had stepped out of his shorts, he put a knee on the bed and grabbed the bottom of her shirt. "If we're going to mate, we'll have to get you out of these clothes."

Nodding, she sat up and helped him remove her shirt. The sight of his magnificent body and the significance of what they were about to do had robbed her of her words. Her mind was a mess of need and awe and joy, making her heart race and her channel leak. She was going to spend the rest of her life with a shifter, something she had been adamant that she would never do. But Callum wasn't just any shifter, he was the one. The perfect man for her.

"Vamika?" His right hand cupped her cheek, and his thumb skimmed the sensitive skin under her eye. "What's wrong? Do you...need some more time?" The mixture of fear and sadness in his voice brought her gaze to his.

She hadn't even realized she was crying. The enormity of the situation must have had a bigger effect on her than she'd thought, but her tears had nothing to do with sadness and everything to do with how much her life had changed for the better. And all because she had met Callum. But the beautiful man didn't know that. He believed she was having second thoughts.

Smiling at him through her tears, she put her hand on his that was still cupping her cheek. "No, Callum. I don't need more time. I know what I want and it's you. Only you. You're the best thing that's ever happened to me. Henry told me I would thank him one day when he ordered me to go to Leith's to spend time with you. He said that I'd thank him when I got to know you and realized that you were perfect for me. And he was right. I owe him a thank you, a big one. Because you are exactly what he said you would be—perfect."

Callum's face split into a huge smile. "Perfect. Sounds like I have a lot to live up to. You really know how to make a man work for it, don't you?" His eyes sparkled with amusement.

Chuckling, she shook her head. "You don't have to live up to anything. All I want is for you to stay the way you are. You're already perfect." Letting go of his hand, she climbed to her knees. "Now help me get out of these clothes. I want to finally feel you inside me."

He was quick to comply and got to work on taking off her jeans while she unclasped her bra, which soon joined his clothes on the floor, but Callum was taking his time unzipping her jeans. It was like he wanted to savor the unveiling of her pussy to him, even though he had seen it and touched it before. He'd even sucked on her clit, and just the thought of his mouth on her again was enough to push her desire to an almost unbearable level. She moaned and squirmed as her channel clenched and more of her wetness soaked into her panties.

Callum groaned, and his tongue shot out and licked his lips. "You smell so fucking delicious. I hope I won't embarrass myself and come before you do." He pushed her jeans and panties down just enough to reveal her to him but instead of continuing to push them down her thighs, he put his hand between her legs and cupped her soaking wet lady parts.

Vamika sucked in a startled breath at his touch, before moaning when a finger pushed slowly inside her. "Callum, that's—" Her voice choked off when his thumb suddenly pressed down on her clit, making the swollen nub throb against the pad of his thumb and shoot sparks of pleasure through her body.

"Stand!" His command took her by surprise.

"Wh...what?" Blinking a few times, she tried to focus on his face. She was already getting desperate for her climax, and he had barely touched her yet.

Callum pumped his finger slowly in and out of her. "You heard me. Get on your feet on the bed. I'll help you." His words were laced with power that licked at all her sensitive areas, and she gasped and squirmed against his hand.

"I'm not...sure I can...if you keep...touching me...like that. And your power..." She rocked her hips against his hand, unable to even think about anything other than the glorious pleasure he was giving her.

Chuckling, he snatched his hand away before grasping her hips and lifting her to her feet.

She couldn't help the whine that escaped her at the loss of his fingers. He hadn't touched her for long, but it had been enough to make her body burn for him and narrow her focus down to one thought—to have his cock inside her. It was long overdue, and she might spontaneously combust if it didn't happen soon.

"Don't worry, baby girl. I won't leave you alone for long." Callum grinned at her before letting go of her hips.

Vamika gripped his shoulders to keep from toppling over while he pushed her jeans and panties down her legs. Her knees were like jelly, but she managed to step out of her clothes with his help.

As soon as her clothes disappeared, his hand was back between her legs, a finger pushing inside her aching channel while his thumb slid over her clit. But she needed more than his fingers. They were great, and she loved what he could do with them, but there was only one appendage that was going to satisfy the desperate hunger inside her, and it was larger than all of his fingers together.

Wrapping a hand around his thick shaft, she put the other hand on his hip to steady herself before dropping to her knees on the bed in front of him. A strangled gasp escaped him when she tightened her grip and bent to lick the precum leaking down the side of his cockhead.

"Vamika, I..." Whatever he was about to say was lost in a groan when she sucked as much of his length into her mouth as she could without choking. Pulling back slowly, she vibrated her tongue against his frenulum, and his whole body seemed to tense. "Stop...please. Or I'll come." His hand fastened around her braid and pulled gently.

She released his shaft with a small pop before sitting back on her heels and looking up at him. "Then come here and lie down on your back. I want to claim you as my mate."

His eyes darkened as he nodded. "Yes, ma'am."

He crawled onto the large bed next to her before turning over onto his back with his upper body supported on his elbows and a small smile curving his lips.

Vamika didn't waste time in straddling his hips. His cock felt like it could have been made of steel when she wrapped her hand around it and brushed the tip against her wet folds until it was aligned with her entrance.

A low growl made her look at Callum's face. He was staring at where his shaft was meeting her sheath with his eyes wide and his jaw slack, like it was the most captivating sight he had ever seen.

His expression spurred her on, and she sat down a bit faster than she had intended, forcing his thick length more than halfway inside her before she stopped with a gasp at the burning sensation. His large rod was stretching her channel wider than it had ever been stretched before.

"Fuck!" He shuddered beneath her, and his eyes

seemed to lose focus for a few seconds as his upper body dropped back on the bed. "You're so tight. Please slow down. I want to last longer than ten seconds."

Unable to speak, she nodded and put her hands on his chest, before lifting her hips until just the head of his cock was still inside her. Taking a deep breath, she slowly lowered herself back down. There was still a slight burn, but the pleasure as he filled her far surpassed the discomfort. Another slow up and down motion and she let out a long moan as his shaft settled fully inside her. The pressure on her sensitive internal walls from his girth was enough that any small movement would tip her over the edge. And she wanted that, but at the same time she wanted to draw it out and torture herself with the feeling of being so close.

"Vamika, look at me." Callum's voice was deep and rough, and his hands gripped her hips.

His words made her realize she had closed her eyes, all her focus on the amazing feeling of having him buried deep inside her.

She opened her eyes and tried to focus on his face while trying to stabilize her breathing. "I didn't realize how big you are until now. I knew you were big but not that it would feel like this."

His expression tightened into a frown as she spoke, and she hurriedly added, "Good. I mean you feel so good inside me. Like I'm going to orgasm if you so much as lift your pinky."

His lips curved into a grin. "Does that mean you want me to lift my pinky, or do you want me to wait?"

Vamika stared at him for a few seconds. She knew

he was as desperate for release as she was, his straining muscles practically vibrating under her hands. And still he offered to wait to allow her to savor the tension until she couldn't take it anymore. Amazing was too weak a description for this man.

Her internal muscles suddenly tightened around his shaft, and her eyes went wide when she felt her orgasm start to unfurl like a hot blaze from deep inside her belly.

"Callum." She gasped his name just as he growled. The next thing she knew she was on her back with him pounding into her, driving her orgasm to a crescendo as she screamed in ecstasy.

Sharp teeth sank into her shoulder, and her instinct made her lift her head and clamp her jaw over his shoulder close to his neck, nicking his clavicle with one sharp canine.

At the first taste of his blood, pleasure more powerful than anything she had ever felt exploded through her and shook her body with the force of it as Callum's cock jerked inside her with his release.

CHAPTER 25

Callum didn't know how long he had been lying there, trying to gather his mind and focus on pulling air into his starved lungs. He might even have blacked out for a little while from sheer pleasure.

But for the first time in days, his need wasn't front and center in his mind, and his balls weren't feeling full to bursting.

He lifted his head and took in the sight of the beautiful woman he had just mated. Vamika, his true mate. The love of his life and the woman he was going to spend the rest of his living days with. And she was a wolf.

Him, a cripple, deemed by many shifters a weak and inadequate being who shouldn't even be allowed to live, was mated to a beautiful female wolf who cared about him and considered him perfect. What more could he possibly want after this? His life was already complete.

Vamika's eyes blinked open, and she gave him a

weak but happy smile. "Hasn't anyone told you that it's impolite to stare?"

He chuckled. "Maybe, but when it comes to you, I consider it my privilege to stare. You're my true mate and the most beautiful woman in the world. You can't expect me not to rest my eyes on you as often as I can. It goes against all my instincts."

"Really." She laughed. "Why don't you take a break from staring at me and kiss me instead?"

Callum chuckled. "Sure." He brushed his lips against hers lightly before deepening the kiss. But instead of the heated frenzy that had characterized their kissing prior to mating, this kiss was slow and filled with love and happiness. His chest felt like it was about to burst with the intensity of his feelings, and he poured them all into the kiss, trying to convey what she meant to him without using his words.

But it didn't take long for their kissing to change, growing more heated and demanding as their bodies remembered the pleasure they had given each other and wanted more.

Callum broke the kiss and lifted his head to grin down at Vamika, his shaft already hard and ready for action. "I believe we agreed to celebrate our mating with dinner. Are you hungry?" He lifted one brow in question while rocking his hips, his cock rubbing against her thigh.

She laughed. "I might be, but not for food."

He chuckled. "But you need some food as well. Satisfying two hungers at once is an amazing deal. You should take it before I change my mind." He winked at her.

Shaking her head slowly, she grinned at him. "Oh,

I'm not worried that you'll change your mind. All I need to do is touch myself and you won't be able to stay away."

Her words kicked his desire up a notch as he was reminded of her coming to him while he was sleeping on the couch two nights ago. Believing him asleep, she had played with herself right in front of him, and even though her panties had been in the way he'd loved watching her.

"Right. That's it." He was up and moving toward the living room with Vamika in his arms before she realized what he intended, as evidenced by her wide eyes and her gasp. "I hope you're prepared to be speared by your new mate. I'm eager to bury myself inside your tight sheath again, you know."

"No shit." Her surprise had changed into amusement, her eyes sparkling as she looked up at him. "You're not exactly trying very hard to hide that fact."

Laughing, he used his leg to pull a chair out from the table before sitting down with Vamika straddling his lap, her back resting against his chest. After grasping her hips, he lifted her until his erection nudged at her entrance before lowering her slowly onto his straining shaft, forcing a drawn-out moan from her.

Her body was hot and wet, and he shuddered as he sank into the tight confinement of her welcoming pussy. It wasn't long since he had come so hard his balls had felt like they had been running on empty. But even so they were already pulled up tight in preparation for another release. They would have to wait, though, because he wanted to take his time playing with his mate until she was desperate to come.

"There are rules." He pulled the cart closer and grabbed the plate with her salad to put on the table in front of her.

"Which are?" She rocked her pelvis, pulling a groan from him.

Callum took a deep breath to try to control his need before answering her. "You're not allowed to touch yourself. And you have to eat." Sliding the chair closer to the table, he parted her thighs until her knees were locked against the side of the table with her thighs spread wide. His knees fit under the table but hers didn't while she was sitting on his lap. "But I can touch you everywhere."

Her channel clenched around his shaft, and he growled at the glorious sensation before he could stop himself. He had to take control of the situation, or she'd have him coming inside her in no time. And that wasn't part of his plan. Not yet anyway.

He reached between her legs and found her clit, her thigh muscles tensing when he started circling the swollen nub with his middle finger.

"Callum," she gasped, and rocked her hips in response to what he was doing. "It's—"

"Sweet torture. I know. Now eat." He ground his teeth together in an effort to focus on something other than the way her tight, slick channel felt sliding against his aching cock. This wasn't supposed to be about him; it was supposed to be about her. At least mostly about her. But suppressing his own pleasure while teasing her was proving more difficult than he had thought.

One of her hands brushed against the one he had

between her legs, and he growled low next to her ear. "I told you the rules. No touching yourself."

Her chuckle held a note of glee. "I'm not going to. But you said nothing about touching you."

He frowned. "I'm inside you. You're not going to be able to—" His words choked off when her hand slid between his parted legs and closed around his testicles.

She laughed. "You were saying?" Her hand caressed and kneaded his balls gently.

The pleasure that had been building steadily since he lowered her onto his cock, started growing at an alarming rate. But he wasn't going to tell her to leave his balls alone. He loved what she was doing to him. The only problem was that he was going to come before his mate, and he'd much rather have her come with him.

Using two fingers, he rubbed her clit between them, gradually increasing the pace of his fingers' movement. The rate of her breathing soon increased until she was panting as she squirmed on his lap, her thigh muscles tense, like she was trying to close her legs.

"It's too good." The words were forced out through her panting. "I'm going to come."

"Then come, baby girl." He spoke through his teeth, holding on for dear life as she danced on his cock, her hips moving at an amazing speed.

Her finger suddenly found the sensitive spot right behind his testicles, and he felt his eyes widen as the orgasm he had been trying to hold off surged through him. He roared and his hips jerked as his cock jumped inside Vamika. When she screamed and her sheath started pulsing with her orgasm, milking him of every last drop, his vision blurred with the intense pleasure. It was unlike anything he had ever felt before, like her orgasm was amplifying his own.

When the powerful pleasure finally died away, he sagged against Vamika's back, unable to think clearly. He'd heard that true mates were able to sense each other's feelings, but he'd never envisioned anything like this. Their mating had been powerful and amazing, but even that couldn't quite compare with what had just happened. Nothing could.

Several minutes went by before Callum managed to mobilize enough strength and willpower to move. Raising his head from where it had been resting against Vamika's shoulder, he smiled at her limp form. At least she had pushed her food out of the way before collapsing over the table.

From what he could see, she hadn't eaten much, and he wasn't surprised. Eating while teasing her had been a bad idea. The slow build he had planned just hadn't been feasible with how responsive she was, and the way she had moved had driven him to completion much faster than he had anticipated.

"Are you awake, baby girl?" He smoothed his hands up her back to her shoulders, before leaning forward to investigate the mating bite he'd given her. The wounds had closed, but the scabs still looked fresh. They would be gone in less than an hour, though, leaving the pink scars that would adorn her shoulder for the rest of her life as visual proof of their mating. Sighing in contentment, he let him himself revel in his happiness.

"Mhm." Vamika pulled in a deep breath, before letting it out on a sigh as she peeled herself off the tabletop to lean back against his body. "But I think I need some sleep soon. Your way of making me eat didn't work very well, but you succeeded in wearing me out."

He laughed. "At least I succeeded in something."

After sliding the chair back, he rose with her in his arms, his soft cock slipping from her warm body. A mix of their fluids ran down his thighs and instead of taking his mate straight to bed as he had planned, he headed for the bathroom.

Smiling, he put her down on shaky legs. "Sit down and show me that pink pussy." He grabbed a hand towel and went to the sink.

She snorted as she sat down on the edge of the bathtub, but she did as she was told. "What are you planning now? I'm not sure I can handle another of your crazy ideas just yet. Not after the amazing orgasm you just gave me. It was almost like your pleasure combined with mine, turning it into something completely mind-blowing."

Crouching before her, he gently cleaned her pussy and her inner thighs with the wet towel. "It's a true mate thing, I think. I felt it, too, and I can definitely get used to that."

Vamika didn't respond, and he lifted his gaze to hers to find her staring at him with her head cocked to one side.

"Is something wrong?" He frowned as he studied her face, but he couldn't decipher her expression.

"No." Her face lit up in a smile. "Everything is perfect. It's just…your care amazes me. I've never met anyone like you."

Callum shook his head slowly. "I should've cleaned

you after we mated. I'm sorry I didn't, but in my defense, I think my mind was blown. Mating the woman I love. You've made me the happiest man alive."

Her eyes were shiny when she rose to her feet, and he stood as well. Throwing her arms around his neck, she rested the side of her face against his chest. "I love you, too, Callum." She then lifted her head and looked up at him. "Now let's go have dinner to celebrate before we go back to bed. I want this to be a night we'll remember for the rest of our lives."

His chest felt like it was filled with butterflies, and he wasn't sure his feet touched the floor when she grabbed his hand and pulled him out of the bathroom. He'd found his happily ever after, and he couldn't wait to embark on the rest of their lives together.

EPILOGUE

Bryson was wide awake and furious. It had taken him hours to answer all the questions the police had for him, but he wasn't surprised after what had happened at the house. If he hadn't known that magic was involved, he would have been just as confused as to what had happened. So, there was no surprise that they were stumped as to what had trashed the interior of the living room and blown out all the windows in the house.

They had finally accepted his statement that he had just walked inside the house when it happened, and he didn't know the cause. But it had taken a long time to convince them, and it was after midnight by the time he got back to his house.

Bryson should be tired, but there was no way he could relax after everything that had happened that day. He had already been pacing in his office for the better part of two hours, but his mind was still spinning. It had been no revelation that Ambrosia's power was substantial, but he hadn't expected Fia's power to be just as formidable. She had hidden that fact from him deliberately, and he, the fool, had believed her and never suspected her of deceiving him.

Stopping in front of the large windows, he stared into the garden without seeing what was right in front of him. And it was due to the fact that it was still dark outside. Why had Fia lied to him? Why hadn't she just been honest about her power and what she could do? It was a sign that she didn't trust him obviously. But why didn't she? He couldn't remember doing anything to her that would give her a reason not to trust him.

Pain stabbed through his chest again, and he rubbed it like that would make it go away. The pain had been coming regularly since this afternoon. It was strange. Random pain like that wasn't something he was used to, and it had started right after the events at the house. Perhaps it had something to do with the magic he had been subjected to. But he was a shifter, so why should that affect him for hours afterward? Whatever it had done to him, it should have been healed hours ago.

Bryson spun and started pacing again. He should be in bed sleeping, but there was no way he was going to be able to rest after what Fia had done to him. The anger and disappointment kept his mind spinning. But more worrisome was the hurt he felt for being deceived by her and the fact that she felt she couldn't trust him. He shouldn't be affected like this by her actions, and the fact that he was, was unsettling to say the least.

Bryson was aware that he was obsessed with her, but he had assumed it was an infatuation born from the fact that she refused him. Perhaps he had been wrong all along? The thought that she might be his mate had crossed his mind from time to time, but it hadn't made sense, considering his interest had been fluctuating with time. If she really was his mate, his need for her should have increased rapidly with time until it became unbearable. But two years had gone by without that happening, and that should be conclusive evidence that she wasn't his true mate.

"Fucking bitch! You will tell me why, and if you refuse, I will make you." His whole body was tense with rage, hurt, and need. A need he didn't want to acknowledge at the moment, but his anger and hurt wasn't enough to quell it. His thick shaft was testing the strength of his pants, trying to get his attention. But he wasn't going to give in. He wasn't going to jerk off to the image of Fia again until he'd had it out with her. His balls weren't going to like that with how they were currently insisting that they were going to explode if he didn't empty them soon. But his nuts would just have to fucking take it, because he wasn't going to surrender to his need.

∞∞∞∞

Fia was sitting at her kitchen table with her head in her hands. The one thing she had been trying to avoid for two years had happened. She'd had to use her full power in front of Bryson, and there was no doubt he would confront her about it. Lying to him for two years wasn't going to go unpunished. She had deceived him, but worse she had hurt his pride.

When she talked to him for the first time, she had

been charmed that he had taken an interest in her. She had already known whom he was by then, since his power was easy to detect from a distance. But it had taken him almost a month to discover her and her mother after they moved to the area, and it was only due to him almost crashing into her when she exited a small shop.

Fia had happily shared that she was a witch when he had asked what she was, but as was her habit, she hadn't disclosed the extent of her power. People tended to feel threatened by powerful people and particularly those who were far more powerful than themselves. Thus, hiding that fact about herself was second nature to her, and she didn't make an exception for Bryson.

And it was just as well because it hadn't taken her long to realize he was a man she needed to stay away from. Extremely attractive, he was the perfect mix of his Moroccan and Scottish heritage. Exotically dark and mysterious mixed with the height and muscle of a Scottish rugby player. And beneath it all was an intelligent mind. Bryson was more perceptive than was good for him. And her.

To say that Fia had been attracted to him was an understatement, and he had made no secret of the fact that he was attracted to her. She'd had no intention of acting on her attraction, though, and that should have been the end of it. But that was until she realized the true nature of their attraction.

Lying to him about her power level was an offense to the alpha panther, but that wasn't her biggest problem. The magic she'd had to use to protect everyone against Ambrosia had also burned away the spell she had put on Bryson two years ago. And the spell once burned away completely, wouldn't work as well a second time. Which meant she would soon have to face her destiny.

It had been inevitable that it would happen at some stage, but she had hoped to have a bit more time before giving up her fight. The spell had weakened over the years, and she'd had to reinforce it several times already, but she had counted on having at least one more year before it faded too much to be effective anymore.

But from one second to the next, that had all changed. Her fight was over. In just a matter of days, her need and his would pull them together, and she wouldn't be able to thwart the mating bond any longer.

Fia let out a choked sigh that sounded more like a sob, and tears pricked her eyes. True mates. It was supposed to be a rare and amazing bond between two people, a connection deeper than any other. But to her it sounded more like a curse than a blessing. How could it be anything else when her true mate was the biggest fuck boy in all of Scotland?

∞∞∞

Vamika moaned as delicious heat gathered in her lower belly in response to the tongue laving at her clit and two fingers pumping into her channel. She had lost count of the number of times they'd had sex since the night before, but it must be in double digits. But she wasn't complaining even though her mind and body were both telling her she needed sleep. There would always be time for sleep later, and if she happened to fall asleep while walking or in the middle of a conversation, so be it. As a newly mated woman she had a good excuse.

Burying her hands in Callum's hair, she rocked her hips against his talented mouth. This would never get old. Not in a million years. But she was starting to wonder if they would be able to stay out of bed long enough to do anything other than fuck each other's brains out.

She gasped and tried to squirm away from him when he vibrated his tongue against her sensitive clit, the sensations so intense that her internal muscles clamped down on his fingers. "Callum, I—" Her words were cut off by a scream when pleasure ripped through her, the heat in her belly erupting without warning and engulfing her in pulsing pleasure.

Callum's thick cock rammed into her, taking her breath away and cutting off her scream as the feel of his mounting pleasure pushed her higher. Her whole body was shaking with pounding pleasure, and her lungs were burning from her inability to breath by the time he roared and pumped his seed inside her in powerful jets.

It took a while for her breathing to settle after Callum collapsed on top of her. His blond hair was tickling her ear, and she couldn't help smiling when she remembered him calling her his dark goddess sometime during the night. It was fitting seeing as he was her fair god.

Pulling in a deep breath, he lifted his head to give her a brilliant smile. "Good morning, my beautiful mate. Are you ready for breakfast with the others?"

She chuckled. "Your enthusiasm is amazing. Aren't you tired?"

He nodded, his eyes warm. "Yes, but since spending the night making love to you is the reason why I'm tired, I don't mind. I'm sure we'll catch up on sleep eventually." His lips curved in a wicked grin. "But I'm warning you, it might take years for that to happen."

Laughing, she let her eyes fill with the love she felt for him. "I think I can live with that."

"Good." His expression sobered. "I should've asked you after what happened yesterday, but with all the people surrounding us and my mind preoccupied with the need to mate you, it got pushed to the back of my mind. Is your father the reason why you rejected me? The reason you didn't want to be owned as you called it?"

Vamika nodded as she stared up into his concerned eyes. "Yes. The pack I grew up in has a vastly different view of a woman's place than you and your male friends obviously have. All my childhood and youth, I thought it was normal for the man to own his mate. He would make all the decisions, and her opinion wasn't taken into account in any of them. I realized a long time ago that I didn't want a life like that, but the real awakening came when I discovered that my father had sold me to Andrew without even telling me, in exchange for some kind of beneficial connection.

"Andrew pretended to want me because he liked me for a while, but when I turned him away, it became apparent that I didn't have a choice. I was going to be his mate whether I wanted to or not. That's when I ran away and joined Henry's pack. I had met Henry a few times in my youth, and he had always treated everyone with respect, even women. I didn't trust anybody, but he was the most honorable man I had ever met. And I swore to myself that I would never mate a shifter."

Callum sighed and stared into her eyes. "I'm sorry you had to go through that, and I promise you that if you never want to see your dad again, I will make sure he doesn't get near you. But I hope you understand that I consider you mine. Not my property, but mine to love, mine to take care of and mine to pleasure. It's an honor as well as an obligation. And it works both ways. I am yours like you are mine."

Vamika felt her eyes fill with tears at his words. She had no objections to be Callum's. Even being his property would have been okay because she knew he would always treat her with love and respect. But being equals was the best foundation for a good relationship.

She threw her arms around him and held him tightly. "I love you, Callum. I always will."

"I love you, too, baby girl." She heard the smile in his voice. "Which reminds me. I have to thank Henry for ordering you to spend time with me, and for being there for you when you needed a new family."

"I know what he wants the most." She loosened her tight hold on her mate.

Callum lifted his head to smile at her. "And what's that?"

She returned his smile. "To find his own true mate. So, if there's anything we can do to help him with that, I know he'll be eternally grateful."

---THE END---

BOOKS BY CAROLINE S. HILLIARD

Highland Shifters

A Wolf's Unlikely Mate, Book 1
Taken by the Cat, Book 2
Wolf Mate Surprise, Book 3
Seduced by the Monster, Book 4
Tempted by the Wolf, Book 5
Pursued by the Panther, Book 6
True to the Wolf, Book 7 – May 2023
Book 8 – TBA

Troll Guardians

Captured by the Troll, Book 1
Saving the Troll, Book 2
Book 3 – TBA

ABOUT THE AUTHOR

Thank you for reading my book. I hope the story gave you a nice little break from normality.

I have always loved reading and immersing myself in different worlds. Recently I have discovered that I also love writing. Stories have been playing in my head for as long as I can remember, and now I'm taking the time to develop some of these stories and write them down. Spending time in a world of my own creation has been a surprising enjoyment, and I hope to spend as much time as possible writing in the years to come.

I'm an independent author, meaning that I can write what I want and when I want. I primarily write for myself, but hopefully my stories can brighten someone else's day as well. The characters I develop tend to take on a life of their own and push the story in the direction they want, which means that the stories do not follow a set structure or specific literary style. However, I'm a huge fan of happily ever after, so that is a guarantee.

I'm married and the mother of two teenagers. Life is busy with a fulltime job in addition to family life. Writing is something I enjoy in my spare time.

You can find me here:
caroline.s.hilliard@gmail.com
www.carolineshilliard.com
www.facebook.com/Author.CarolineS.Hilliard/
www.amazon.com/author/carolineshilliard/
www.goodreads.com/author/show/22044909.Caroline_S_Hilliard

Printed in Great Britain
by Amazon